Praise for David Lida's *One Life*

"David Lida's *One Life* is full of suspense and beautifully described moments that often conjure Juan Rulfo's *Pedro Paramo*. Like his courageous protagonist Richard, who often journeys to the most dismal and violent places in rural Mexico in search of an elusive history, Lida fearlessly explores the stark places that often shape the human spirit."

— Maria Venegas, author of
Bulletproof Vest: the Ballad of an Outlaw and his Daughter

"Lida, himself a mitigation specialist and writer with deep ties to Mexico (where he lives), pours personal emotion into his story. In the process, he brings an elusive sense of dignity to a world where it is seemingly lost."

— *Kirkus Reviews*

"David Lida's daring novel *One Life* will take you on a journey to darkest Mexico, where daily life is rich with irony and pathos, violence and humor, destitution and the homeliest of comforts. Richard, your travel guide, is on a mythic quest; he must descend to the underworld and come out with a story that will move the stone hearts of a Louisiana jury to mercy. His goal is to save the life of a condemned woman whose name, Esperanza, means hope. One life, his for hers. Gripping, suspenseful, worldly, and wise, this thought-provoking novel never lets up and the serious moral questions it raises resound long after the final page is turned."

— Valerie Martin, author of *The Ghost of the Mary Celeste*

"As I followed Richard, the unraveling narrator of David Lida's *One Life*, I kept seeing, peeking around the corner, the whiskey priest from Graham Greene's *The Power and the Glory*. They both minister to a population so forsaken it has lost faith in mercy. For the Mexicans of Lida's novel, there are only labor and fate, the former measured by dollars, the latter doled out by the country that issues them. Which only makes Lida's achievement more remarkable: To follow Richard is to relinquish Anglo time, Anglo logic, Anglo law — to say nothing about the assumptions that obtain about here and 'down there.'"

— Boris Fishman, author of *A Replacement Life*

Praise for David Lida's *Travel Advisory*

"Forget your romantic notions about south-of-the-border idylls. Writer David Lida gets at the contradictory, elusive reality of Mexico in this disturbing and powerful debut collection...elegantly conceived and executed...a powerful and original writer, one to follow, wherever he takes us next."   — *New Orleans Times-Picayune*

"David Lida's powerful, sympathetic, and critical imagination renders Mexico and Mexicans from seemingly every angle — it is like being let in on a secret, one detail at a time."
                   — Luc Sante, author of *Low Life* and *The Factory of Facts*

"Disturbing, provocative and often darkly funny, the stories in *Travel Advisory* go a long way toward explaining the duality many of us feel toward Mexico."   — *San Antonio Express News*

"Gritty and unforgiving...paints a convincing, unvarnished picture of a struggling country."   — *Publishers Weekly*

"Gets under your skin...the power of Lida's stories lies in their tawdry, unraveling characters and the uncompromising, even disastrous situations in which they find themselves in this land of sorcery, squalor and seduction."   — *Time Out New York*

"Observant, engrossing, horrifying, warmly humane and cooly yet devastatingly satiric stories. An intimate and convincing fictional portrait of contemporary life in Mexico."
                   — Francisco Goldman, author of *The Ordinary Seaman*

"Simultaneously perverse and purifying, *Travel Advisory* ushers in a talented writer with a mordant eye."   — Rita Mae Brown

"These short stories ... capture Mexico at its essence, in intimate glimpses rather than generalities... an easy, narrative style that flows freely from devastating satire to equally insightful compassion."   — *Paper*

The Unnamed Press
P.O. Box 411272
Los Angeles, CA 90041

Published in North America by The Unnamed Press.

1 3 5 7 9 10 8 6 4 2

Copyright © 2016 by David Lida

ISBN: 978-1-939419-95-8

Library of Congress Control Number: 2016952136

This book is distributed by Publishers Group West

Cover design & typeset by Jaya Nicely

david lida

ONE LIFE

a novel

The Unnamed Press
Los Angeles, CA

For my dead

Whosoever destroys the life of a single human being, it is as if he had destroyed an entire world; and whosoever preserves the life of a single human being, it is as if he had preserved an entire world.

— The Talmud (Mishnah Sanhedrin 4:5)

Whosoever kills an innocent person, it is as if he has killed all of humanity, and whosoever saves the life of one, it is as if he has saved the life of all humanity.

— The Qur'an 5:32

Oh, Mexico, I never really been but I'd sure like to go.

—James Taylor, "Mexico"

CONTENTS

ONE
LIFE

OPENING STATEMENT

I thought of death constantly, but rarely imagined how I would die. Pressed to conjure a vision, an optimistic picture emerged: I'd be one of those lucky slender guys who quietly sneaks into old age in a T-shirt, with thinning silver hair and respectable muscle tone. Not as vigorous as in youth, but without any serious debilitating conditions. You know the type. The guy you see in Starbucks wearing half-frame glasses doing the crossword puzzle, or enjoying the spring sun on a park bench—one of those guys younger men admire, and about whom women remark, "He looks great for his age." A man who whistles past the boneyard until checkout time, which comes instantly and unexpectedly of a heart attack or a stroke. If it happened from seventy onward, I would have been more than satisfied. Who needs to live any longer than that?

It never entered my mind that at forty-two I would die suddenly and unexpectedly while passing through a dicey no-man's-land between where I'd been born and the home I'd made. It's true that dying that way was congruent to the life I had been leading. Some people thought I was reckless because I had never been afraid of Mexico City, and never frightened of the two-donkey towns to which I traveled, where the previous day they had kidnapped the police chief, or a week earlier six people died in a score-settling shootout on the dusty outskirts, or a dozen headless bodies were found in a mass grave. Where at any moment convoys of skinny soldiers swimming in their uniforms, their faces covered with ski masks, balancing Kalashnikovs against their shoulders, patrolled the unpaved streets. All of that was a problem, but none of it was *my* problem. I thought I lived in a protected bubble because of the work I'd taken on, trying to help save people's lives.

Not that I was some kind of devil-may-care macho who purported to be fearless. Travels through *México profundo* came under the realm of acceptable risks. Other things petrified me. I was dreadfully afraid of contracting a hideous illness, like the ones that had killed both my parents. If I got sick, who would take care of me? After my divorce, I had no wife, no children, no mother or father, brothers or sisters. The thought of dying alone unsettled me, but I was scared shitless when I imagined an extended period of sickness and pain with no one around to alleviate my suffering.

It happened in a karaoke bar in a strip mall in Ciudad Juárez. I had been listening to a poor devil—a stocky guy with a Fu Manchu moustache—warble "A Mi Manera," the Spanish-language version of the song "My Way," off-key. (What a way to go, right?) Contrary to the cliché, before I died, my life didn't flash before my eyes. Not precisely. A few Polaroids and postcards crossed my mind. The first snapshots were pornographic; I won't bore you with the details. Let's just say that while alive I thought of sex constantly, so it wasn't strange that it occurred to me as the life left my body. Occasionally I had imagined a happy death while making love. That I didn't come close to dying that way was just one of life's malicious curveballs.

I remembered a middle-aged woman with dyed red hair, singing a song called "Gema" as she prepared her stall in a Mexican market early one morning. An old man in a white straw cap, snoozing in a pew in a seventeenth-century church. Sneaking a can of Coca-Cola into a jail in my backpack. A rangy woman with Mardi Gras beads strung around the brim of her hat, pulling up one of the legs of her cargo pants to reveal a .38 Special inside a concealed-carry holster.

My father on his deathbed at Saint Vincent's. He wouldn't let go, despite the pain, the grief, the agony, all those chemicals coursing through his ruined, diminished body. He clutched my hand and opened his mouth wide to scream, yet no sound came out. A silent shriek: my last image of Dad. My mother in a housecoat, slowly killing herself by lighting up one cigarette after another. Feeding the olives from my Martini to Carla, our little secret that she was two months pregnant. After we lost the baby, her absence emanating from a gunmetal-gray cell phone that refused to ring.

The lavender carpet of jacaranda leaves on the sidewalks of Mexico City in springtime. Oranges, freshly cut in half and glistening, in a stall outside the market. An aging black man who sat with me patiently after I burst into tears. The ramshackle church in the middle of the middle of nowhere, the choir singing "I'll Fly Away."

Once I realized I was dying, there was wonder: I was oddly content, even relieved. I had liked my life. It had been short but often sweet. I smiled inwardly. Was this what they meant when they said you should beware of what you wish for? I was given a death so quick that there was no time to suffer. Sure, I would have liked to have lived longer. If I had actually made it to seventy years, I probably would have wanted to keep going. *When I die, hallelujah, by and by, I'll fly away.* Why couldn't that have been the last song I heard? "My Way"?

Regrets? I had a few. But most of them were so trifling they didn't even merit consideration. Still, I cannot say the end was peaceful. The last thing I thought of gnawed at me inside, put my stomach in anguished knots. There was some unfinished business between me and a woman named Esperanza Morales. It was irresponsible to die before I had a chance to save her life.

PART ONE

Where the Devil
Lost His Poncho

PARTY AT THE PONDEROSA

The first thing Esperanza believes will kill her is the smell. It's a syrupy medicinal odor of disinfectant that comes from the blue liquid with which the floors are mopped in the morning and again in the afternoon. The smell is so hideous that at first, when she awakens at five A.M. for the prebreakfast body count, it brings bile to her mouth. If there were anything in her stomach, she would vomit. The odor creeps up her nostrils to the backs of her eyeballs, where it causes a wrenching headache for hours. And then she realizes that days have passed since she's last noticed the aroma. She has become used to it.

The second thing she thinks will kill her is the food: pink slices of gristle that leave a coating like Vaseline on her tongue, between slices of stale packaged white bread, smeared with rancid margarine. That's what they call a sandwich, with none of the condiments that embellish a *torta* at home—no mayonnaise, tomatoes, avocado, onions, jalapeños, or refried beans. Something else is served at least once a week, a flat brick covered in red paint with yellow powder on top. It's cold and flavorless—their version of pizza. And then there's "meat loaf" in "gravy." It's not clear whether there's any actual meat in it, and it tastes as if it's been thickened with sawdust. The entire saltshaker has been upturned in the sauce, which coagulates thanks to the same jar of Vaseline as the gristle sandwich. This is served alongside a ladleful of mushy kidney beans from an industrial-size can. None of it is ever hot, even when it's doled right out of the pot, pan, or oven.

At first Esperanza won't eat it, until she becomes hungry enough to remember those moments from childhood when, if the family ate at all, they shared a pot of beans or a pan of potatoes, tortillas divided into two or sometimes four. She remembers what it was like to be so hungry she would have eaten dirt. After a while she realizes that, if she does not precisely look forward to meals or eat them with pleasure, it's a relief how they break up the day at six in the morning, high noon, and five in the afternoon. She manages to choke enough of them down so that she—who has always run thin, who has been nicknamed La Flaca since girlhood—begins to put on a little weight. She no longer swims in her orange scrubs.

The third thing she thinks will kill her is the group of four women that attacks her one afternoon. It happens during the hour of recreation when the doors to the cells in her gallery are left open. Esperanza often forgoes the yard; the concrete slab frightens her, surrounded as it is by cement and razor wire, guards with guns and pepper spray, gringa and *morena* prisoners whose language she barely understands. She also likes to stay inside because Pamela, her cellmate, always leaves, and it is the only time of day she can be alone. She has been drowsing on her cot, the lyrics to an old song revolving in her head—*if this isn't a dream, you are my other half*—when she realizes that the four are standing in front of her bed. One of them, the stubby stocky one with the shaven head, talks quickly, saying things Esperanza can't make out. The woman has a smile on her face as if she is telling a joke. The others are grim. The tall dark one with the stud in her nose grabs Esperanza by the collar and pulls her to her feet. "*¿Qué haces?*" she asks, although none of them speaks Spanish. The tall one pushes her into the stubby one, who loses the smile and pushes her back against the others. And then the four of them are knocking her back and forth as if she were a volleyball. In a tight circle, they manage to keep her aloft in the small cell, until they decide they would prefer her on the ground.

Every year in Puroaire, for a week in the middle of July, there was a fair commemorating Santiago Peregrino, the town's patron saint. Esperanza's mother would take the kids to church, where the entryway had been festooned with balloons and crepe paper of red, green, and white, the colors of the Mexican flag. Sometimes a few pennies would be scraped together so they could go to the food stalls on the street by the chapel and share a *buñuelo*, a square of crispy, deep-fried dough bathed in sugar syrup and sprinkled with cinnamon, or an ear of roasted corn slathered in mayonnaise and powdered chile. But there was never money for the rickety merry-go-round or that other ride where they strapped you into a metal bullet that went around in circles.

Esperanza would have done anything to be one of the children screaming inside the bullets painted purple, green, or blue. One summer when she was six or seven she pestered her mother about it so persistently that somehow Mamá had found a few pesos—saved from what she earned sewing and washing, or maybe stolen from her husband's pants pockets while he slept—so Esperanza could be fastened into a golden bullet. The first moments of coasting were exhilarating, liberating, an experience so exquisite she wished the ride would last forever. But once the speed picked up, she regret-ted she'd ever been born. There was such violence to the velocity and the jerking of the cars that she thought her insides were being plastered against her bones, that her stomach would make its way out of her mouth. The fluorescent lights, the shouting toddlers, the painful jolts, all made her yearn for death. On the other side of the circle a boy, his black hair in flight like a bat's wings, cried out for the ride to be stopped, but people only laughed at him. Esperanza kept her mouth shut. If she could just withstand it a little longer, it would be over.

She remembers that scene as her head bangs against the concrete floor and the four women kick her. With one hand she tries to protect her head and with the other her sex. The tall one pulls her hair. The one with the snarling mouth kicks her buttocks, another her ribs. When she moves her hand to shield her side, the stubby one kicks her in the face, opening skin. If it were one woman, Esperanza might try to defend herself, even though she isn't a fighter. But what is she supposed to do against four attackers? They are a force of nature that can't be stopped, like one of those summer deluges in Puroaire that send the tin-roof adobe shacks cascading down the ravines. Or the other storm that brought her to a monstrous world of houses collapsed under the weight of their roofs, or stood upright but with entire walls missing, the rooms exposed like a gigantic doll's house.

They go through her pockets, find nothing, disappear. She lies on the floor, bent into a crescent, exhausted and bruised, silent tears blending with blood on the concrete. It is a relief to be alone again, until she realizes someone is standing outside the cell. It's Woodruff, the enormous officer, mammoth bones and solid curvature under the blue uniform, the one who runs her stick across the bars and makes sucking sounds, her tongue against her front teeth, one of which is capped in gold with the shape of a star cut out. Her hair, extravagantly curled and pomaded, is painted red.

"They been picking on you, baby? Don't make no nevermind. They only playing. Ain't got nothing better to do with their time." Esperanza has little idea of what the guard is saying but the voice, although stern, reassures her. She realizes she had almost stopped breathing and inhales deeply. "Now get your butt up off that floor, baby." She lies motionless. "Right now, girl," says the guard. She doesn't know what Woodruff said, but from the tone of her voice perceives the command and pulls herself upright.

All that happened months ago, weeks after the monolithic metal door painted the glossy green of an after-dinner mint slammed behind her with a frightening finality inside the jail in the Plaquegoula Parish Sheriff's Office. The first day: the shower, the cavity search, the insecticide spray, the baggy white underwear and the orange scrubs, the long walk down the green reeking hall to the cell block. The irreversible closure of that huge metal door, the impossibility of turning around and walking outside, the idea that she might spend the rest of her life staring at the concrete walls and never again see the sun or hear the chirp of a bird.

"You don't have any of those salty peanuts?" Pamela, her cellmate from Honduras, asks. "I like those salty peanuts." After her pronouncement Pamela begins to laugh and then rock back and forth on her cot. Esperanza nods without saying a word. She tries to be invisible before Pamela and responds only if it's absolutely necessary. Pamela will sometimes jabber in fragments of sentences. The words may be Spanish, but when Pamela talks she makes as little sense as the gringas and the *negras* yammering in English. She is thirty-five and flabby with lank brown hair. Her mouth is always open, her wide gums exposed, teeth as big as a horse's. Every day someone comes with a cart and gives her medicine.

Esperanza's first cellmate had been an unsmiling woman with a close-cropped natural and a dull gray finish to her skin, who read the Bible all day and never directed a word to her. Then she was gone, replaced with a *güera* with freckles, pimples, broken teeth, and greasy red hair, uncombed and creeping toward her shoulders. She was in her mid-twenties, about the same age as Esperanza, and because of her lax bathing habits had a sour odor. She spent most of the day directing invective toward Esperanza, words that became easy to ignore because she didn't understand them, and because the redhead never looked her in the eye when she said them.

The bowl of the seatless steel toilet is two feet from the cot where Esperanza sleeps. At first she panicked at the idea of using it in front of her cellmates. Even in Puroaire, with a dilapidated bathroom, she and the others in her family took care of their necessities privately. But to pull down her pants and squat before strange and hostile neighbors? She peed only when she couldn't hold it in any longer. Because of the starchy diet absent in fiber, a week went by before the institutional victuals caught up with her and she had no choice but to defecate. It was a thunderous, fluid, suppurating cascade of bile; it felt as if she was evacuating her internal organs and she couldn't stop herself from groaning. She caught her Bible-reading roommate gaping at her and glared back. When the other woman turned her head, Esperanza felt in a curious way triumphant.

"Maybe they'll give us that thing with the peaches tonight," Pamela says. She refers to a dessert in which a canned fruit encased in solidified syrup is perched atop a hard starchy chunk. The powers that be thought they were doing the few Spanish-speaking inmates a favor by pairing them up in cells. That is how Pamela entered Esperanza's life. Pamela, who growls gutturally and laughs when nothing remotely funny has been spoken. Pamela, who grinds her teeth and snores while sleeping. Pamela, who grunts as she begins to rub herself. Esperanza discreetly turns toward the wall. "You can look at me," Pamela says.

The noise never stops. Atop a cement bunk and an inch-thick foam mattress, Esperanza is constantly disturbed out of a fitful sleep by the bark of shouting arguments, the buzz of a radio, or the blast of a TV infomercial, a solo droning rap or the harmony of several voices in song. In Puroaire she was sometimes awakened by the arguments when her father came home drunk. That happened periodically but predictably; here she doesn't know from one night to the next what will wake her or prevent her from sleeping at all. Still, she has become more or less accustomed to the interruptions, to the fluorescent lights in the hall that are kept on through the night, to slumber in fits and starts. She wonders whether she is capable of getting used to anything.

She hears the sucking sound of Woodruff's tongue on her teeth. Sometimes the officer stops outside the cell and talks for a few minutes. Esperanza doesn't understand why; the words are almost entirely a mystery both to her and to Pamela.

"Where you at, Falanza?" the guard asks, peering into her cell. Esperanza nods. Woodruff has never learned how to pronounce her name so she more or less makes up a handle each time she addresses her. Esperanza can't say her jailer's name either. "How they treating you? Ain't no one been up in your shit lately?" She speaks playfully, but there is little comfort in the singsong tone; she holds her stick in a vertical position as if to warn Esperanza not to even think of defying her. "You getting to like partying here at the Ponderosa? They worst places in the world. Don't make no nevermind if you like it or not, 'cause you going to be on the inside a long time." She extends the word *long* in a breathy drawl.

Pamela doesn't like the guard. She gets up from her cot, begins to walk around the cell and mumble. In Spanish, she tells Woodruff that she is a fat idiot, and that she cannot cause Pamela any harm because she is protected by San Charbel. Soon the officer will be burning in hell where the devil will make her dance like Juana *la cubana*. Woodruff ignores her.

"I can't figure you out, girl," says the jailer to Esperanza. "Most of these motherfuckers up here is simple as shit, but you like a mystery."

The jailer fixes her gaze on Esperanza, who looks toward the floor.

"I seen all kind of freak-ass bitches up in here. Cutthroat hoes steal the yellow out of an egg or the white out of your teeth. Wack-ass bitches who give up all the pussy they got for five dollars worth of crank. Pimpstresses dumb enough to do two dimes for riding in a car with the soldier that pulls the triggers." Pamela stands next to the bars making faces at Woodruff, sticking her tongue out and barking like a dog. The guard barely glances at her. "And plenty that ain't right in the head, like you friend over there."

Between Pamela's bark and Woodruff's drawl, Esperanza is on the verge of a panic attack. What wouldn't she do to be back in Puroaire? How happily she would divide a tortilla in four just to see her mother's vanquished eyes once more, to taste a spoonful of homemade beans, to look over the valley and the trees and the sun in the spring. Was life hard there? Backbreaking hard, so hard it turned humans into ghosts by the time they were forty. But she had no idea what hard was until she came to *los States*.

"I get all that shit, but what I can't understand is a bitch like you that kill you own childrens." Woodruff shakes her head. Her eyes penetrate and her tone gets higher. "You must be out of your motherfucking conk, girl. How could you do that to you own baby?"

Since she arrived in the United States, Esperanza has worked with Mexicans, eaten with Mexicans, made love with Mexicans, and lived on the outskirts of a town in a neighborhood where nearly everyone was Mexican. Her whole life here has been in Spanish; the closest she got to speaking a foreign language was figuring out the slang of the Hondurans. Yet in her months in jail, through osmosis, she has learned enough English to understand the sum and substance of Woodruff's speech. It's true: Esperanza has been charged with killing an eleven-month-old baby, a blameless infant named Yesenia who spent nine months in her own belly before living a miserable and thankfully brief near-year until her death. The memory of holding the baby in her arms when she still gurgled with life fills Esperanza with a horror so complete that she freezes.

The guard begins to laugh. "Baby, you know she crazy and she don't mean nothing by it, but you best watch out for your friend.

She up in your drawers right now." She walks away, chuckling and banging the bars with her stick.

Pamela has indeed grabbed a pair of Esperanza's panties from the shelf and has them in her mouth. She pulls them with her hands, tears them to shreds with her teeth.

The Ponderosa may be a ghastly place, but no horror can compete with the death of Yesenia. Esperanza realizes that she isn't afraid that prison will kill her. She *wishes* prison would kill her. She wants to die. There is even a little comfort in the knowledge that, if the state has its way, she will be put to death. And still more in the assurance that, whatever Louisiana has in store for her, God will give her what she deserves.

WHERE THE DEVIL LOST HIS PONCHO

The house was squat and square, of cinder block and cement. One of these days they might get around to painting the facade. It was one story tall with rebar popping out of the roof. In towns like Ojeras, rebar represents hope: hope that one of these days there will be money to build a second story.

The woman behind the door was a foot shorter than me, her face crosshatched with wrinkles. Her gray hair was pulled back in a bun, the top button of a flimsy black sweater fastened across her chest. Although she looked like The Mummy's little sister, she was probably no older than sixty. That's how carefree life is in towns like this.

"Sorry to bother you, señora," I said, offering a pleasant smile. "I'm looking for someone who I believe lives in this town. His name is Juventino Escobar."

Although she understood me perfectly well, she was going to take as long as she needed to size me up before answering. Who was I? A slender gringo in need of a haircut, in black jeans and a carelessly ironed white shirt with the sleeves rolled up. A black backpack over my shoulder. My presence couldn't possibly mean good news. Did I want to kidnap Juventino? Arrest him? Sell him drugs, or buy some? Could she trust anyone who spoke with an accent like mine? Did I represent the CIA? The FBI? The DEA? Disneyland?

"Do you know Juventino by any chance?" I asked. I wasn't going to stand in her doorway all day, particularly in the early September sunshine that baked the earth after the rain. If she thought the existence of her neighbors was a state secret, there was always the next house. And the next one and the next one, each with its own plucky rebar.

"No," she said finally. "I don't know him."

"Okay," I said. "Many thanks, señora. So sorry to bother you." I turned my back. The taxi was parked across the street.

"But I know his mother."

I stopped in my tracks. "Excellent. Where does she live?"

"They say he might have come back. From *el gabacho*. I don't know." *El gabacho*. Also known as *los States, Norteamérica, Gringolandia,* or *el otro lado*.

Waving my hand, I motioned for the taxi driver to come over. Despite all the years I had lived in this country, I never understood when a Mexican gave directions. He would never send you left or right, east or west. It was always "up" or "down."

The cabdriver lived more than two hours away in Puroaire. He was slender with short hair and a winning smile. As the woman explained how he would have to go up there, and then down the other way, somewhere over the rainbow, he nodded sagely, as if he understood perfectly. He might have been to Ojeras before, but he didn't know it very well. He got us lost along the way.

"Did you get all that?" I asked, once we were back in the cab.

"Yes, absolutely," he said. After a pause, he added, "But if I didn't, we can ask someone else."

Sometime before the next millennium, the local bureaucrats might decide that it would be worthwhile to pave more than the two central streets of Ojeras rather than divert public funds into their own pockets. Don't hold your breath. Driving down the dirt streets, we kicked up a dust storm, passing more short and fat houses with rebar tilting toward the sky.

The town plaza was so tiny you could fit it in your wallet. It was ringed with trees, which had been pruned into perfect little squares like green marshmallows on sticks. There were iron busts of four men—*los hombres ilustres*—local poets, professors, politicians. The clock in the church's skinny spire read ten to three, 24-7.

Brown-skinned adolescents kicked a soccer ball despite the afternoon heat, wearing their caps sideways and pants that stopped at their knees. Two chattering girls barely out of their teens walked down the street, each pregnant. A lady in a blue apron waved the flies away from quesadillas she had fried in boiling oil for invisible customers, next to a white plastic table covered in a plaid plastic cloth. There were few men around. The absent were mostly in *el gabacho*.

The closer we got to the edge of town, the more primitive the houses became. Adobe or clapboard slats for walls, corrugated laminate for the roof. Sheets of torn plastic instead of windows. Bent, crooked doors fastened with a chain and a padlock, or with nothing at all. Finally we got to a huge crater covered in rocks and mud. It was a circle about three city blocks in diameter and fifty feet in depth, and it looked like the surface of an undiscovered planet. On the other side were more shacks.

"She lives up the hill there," said the driver. "Sorry, but my car won't get through that hole."

"No problem. I'll walk."

Clambering through the stones and mud was my exercise for the day. I tried to walk around the brackish, soupy puddles, some of which glowed with a rainbow chemical swirl. I had to go back and forth only once. Poor Juventino's mother had to do it day after day, if her son gave her any money for groceries.

I had high hopes for Juventino. He had been married to Marta, one of Esperanza's older sisters. The promising facts were that he was not an actual family member, that he and Marta had split up years earlier, and that he lived in another town. He had nothing to lose, no one to protect, no more diplomatic duty to perform. If I was lucky, he would have axes to grind. A witness like that can spill all kinds of dirt.

By the time I had traversed the crater, my black sneakers were covered in mud. The huts were so ramshackle they looked like they'd fall over if you leaned against a wall. A dry, hot wind kicked up a whirlpool of dust. If dirt were expensive everyone in Ojeras would be a millionaire.

Four dogs lay in the middle of the road, in shades of matted gray and beige. Mama was mangy and bloated with milk, and had about nineteen nipples. Her boys were lean. I could see their ribs, the flesh rising and setting with their breath. As I got closer they started to growl. What could they possibly have been protecting? Was anyone actually hiding a stash of something inside one of those broken-down shacks? The wrong questions to ask in a Mexican Podunk.

They snarled more loudly as I approached. The smallest one, a disheveled silver mutt, got up and yapped at the top of his high-pitched lungs. Why is it that the tiniest dogs always sound as if they'd swallowed a microphone? He scampered to my side. "It's okay," I said in a velvety but stern purr. I was perennially hopeful an utterance like that would shut up a barking dog, but it never did. He only bleated more loudly.

Let him yap. I ignored him and walked on. Dogs liked me—or so I thought until the son of a bitch set his teeth around my ankle and broke skin. I kicked him away. It hurt, but the shock was worse. I just stood there as he yapped, a *how could you?* expression on my face.

I bent over and pulled down my sock. I was bleeding. Not heavily. A steady, ladylike trickle. The defense team would get a kick out of this. If they needed any proof of my dedication, there it was written in red. Not only was I willing to crawl through dust and mud, I would suffer dog bites to try to save Esperanza Morales's life. I scowled at the mutt through narrowed eyes. He just kept yapping. I pulled back my leg as if I was going to kick him, but he didn't even flinch.

I realized I had an audience, outside the last house on the right. Another ancient sixty-year-old, her thick legs rooted in the ground like old oaks. Her flesh was a wobbly mass under a striped serape she wore despite the midday heat. Two other women, their middles swollen after multiple pregnancies, in jeans and T-shirts. One sat sifting through a bowl of dried beans, picking out the little stones; the other folded raggedy clothes she picked from a washline. A tiny girl stared. The three adults did not acknowledge the gringo in their midst inspecting his dog bite. I hoped that my victimhood would at least make them sympathetic to my cause.

I limped in a straight line to the old one. If she wasn't Juventino's mom, I was Pancho Villa. *"Buenas tardes,"* I said. "Señora Escobar? My name is Richard."

She just stared at me. Who the hell was I? How did I know her name?

"Juventino's mother?" I asked.

She wouldn't say yes and she wouldn't say no, not until I showed my cards. She just kept looking at me, her arms folded across her chest.

"Is Juventino around?" I asked. "We have friends in common in *los States*. I have regards from Esperanza Morales."

"Let me see if he's here," she said, and walked inside.

I turned around and smiled at the other women. They were Juventino's sisters, or sisters-in-law. One had her eyes on the bowl of beans, while the other's arm was wrapped around the child. Through enormous brown eyes the kid looked at me as if I were the Werewolf of London. *"Hola, guapa,"* I said, and waved. She buried her head in her mother's pubis.

He emerged from the adobe. Short, lean, muscular. A battered Dallas Cowboys cap. A thick black moustache like a hero of the Mexican Revolution, a three-day growth of beard. Watery black eyes. A gray T-shirt with multiple holes—who knows what color it had been when new? An emblem of the Virgin of Guadalupe around his neck. He nodded. I told him to call me Richard and shook his hand. "I'm here on behalf of Esperanza Morales," I said. "Could we please talk for a few minutes?"

"Sure," he said.

We were standing on the dirt path to his house. "Thanks," I said. "Where can we talk?"

"Here."

I looked down at my ankle. The blood was saturating the dirt and mud on my sneaker. "Could we sit down somewhere?" I said, adding, "I got bit by one of those dogs down the street. I'm bleeding."

Juventino looked around. "You can sit there," he said, indicating a pile of rocks with his chin. I could have stayed in Ojeras for ten years and he never would have invited me inside. I squatted on the rocks and removed a stenographer's notebook from my backpack, a pen from my pocket. Juventino stood over me like Zeus.

"You know that Esperanza's in jail, right?" I asked.

23

He paused before answering, as if it had been a trick question. "I think I heard something about that."

"She's in jail for murder in Louisiana, in *el gabacho*," I said. "The prosecutor wants to give her the death penalty, Juventino."

"*Ooff,*" he said, pointing his chin and making an ambiguous moue. He might have felt sorry for her, or he may have been impressed with her achievement.

What I had said about the death penalty simplified the story. She was charged with capital murder for killing a baby, which made her eligible for death. The prosecution had stated that they might seek the maximum penalty, but they always say that when the victim is less than seven years old. They could change their minds up to the last minute, even during the trial, even while the jury deliberated. Until the district attorney made up his mind to go for broke or to accept a plea bargain for a lesser charge, the state had to pay for my investigation.

I let the idea of the death penalty sink in for a minute, before saying, "I work for her lawyer. I'm an investigator. My job is to put together the story of her life, to show the prosecutor that she's a human being who deserves mercy. Who doesn't deserve to die." I spoke slowly and as quietly as possible. Juventino's mother and sisters were only two or three yards away, pretending not to listen. "You were married to Marta, right?"

"Yes."

"When was that?" He scrunched up his features, as if I'd asked him to solve a multivariable calculus problem. He didn't answer. "When did you and Marta split up?"

"A long time ago."

"Okay, but, like, how long?" No response. "A year ago? Five years ago? More?"

He nodded. "Yes."

For Mexican villagers, chronology was at best vague. Sometimes you had to let issues of time roll out with the tide. I hoped that Marta would be more specific when I caught up with her in Morelia. "Tell me about her family," I said.

"They were *buena gente*," he said. Good people.

They were always "good people." Most people who are facing death row come from families in whose bosoms there is systematic abuse, neglect, violence, and poverty to the point of malnutrition. If you hit the jackpot, you'll get learning disabilities, brain damage, or mental illness as well—that's good luck because according to the Supreme Court, you're not supposed to execute someone who is mentally ill. But to hear the witnesses tell it, they were always "good people."

"Good in what way?" I asked.

"Good people," he repeated, looking at me quizzically.

"Good how? Good, like hardworking? Good, like generous, like giving away their food and their money to people who needed it more than they did? Good, like petting dogs and cats?"

A list of questions like that is what is known as leading the witness. You are not supposed to do it. You are supposed to stand there through silences so long that you could drive a convoy of trucks through them. You are supposed to wait for them to answer until your hair turns gray and your teeth fall out and an archaeologist discovers your fossil in the desert after the next ice age. In the real world, at least with someone like Juventino, at times you have to give them a menu of answers to choose from.

"They worked very hard," he said. He removed his cap and scratched his black hair, brushed away from his forehead. "Don Fernando"—that was Esperanza's father—"he helped me to find work."

Reading between the lines: Don Fernando might have beat his wife and children with a skillet every Friday night after dinner, he might have stolen from his neighbors, raped his own grandchildren, and, on some Aztec nostalgia trip, cut out the hearts of his contemporaries and eaten them while they still beat four to the bar. But he helped Juventino find work spreading cement or picking beans. So he was "good people."

"And what about Esperanza? What was she like?"

"*Tranquila,*" he said.

How I grew to hate that word. *Tranquila*: Easygoing. Calm. Peaceful. Quiet. Every single Mexican in jail in the United States is, above all, *tranquilo,* at least according to their relatives and friends, colleagues and classmates, teachers and doctors.

"*Tranquila* in what way, Juventino?" I asked. Now he looked at me as if I were a moron. How many ways were there to be *tranquila*? "*Tranquila,* as in she was quiet and didn't say very much? *Tranquila,* like she was easygoing and helped other people? *Tranquila,* like if there was a difficult situation, she would try to solve the problem?"

Juventino stopped to consider the choices on the menu, and then something happened to his face. His brow relaxed, and the pupils of his eyes acquired a sheen of glaze like that which envelopes a Krispy Kreme doughnut. He gave up; this was too complex for him. I tried to reel him back.

"Remember, Juventino," I said. "The state of Louisiana wants to kill Esperanza. I'm trying to help save her life."

I rolled down my sock to get another glimpse of the wound. The teeth marks and the blood and the dirt were starting to look like the preliminary sketch of an abstract painting. I would need to buy a bottle of iodine on the road to Puroaire, maybe even see a doctor. They would be reimbursable expenses. For the moment, I was hoping against hope that the sight of the wound would help Juventino remember some salient detail about Esperanza or her family.

"She didn't say much," he said. Then he held up his hands, tilted his head to one side. "At least not to me. But she was good people."

For the next twenty minutes I tried every which way to get something, anything, out of the poor guy. I asked each question five times with slight variations, offered him every option I could think of. If his answers weighed in at three syllables, it was a miracle. Finally, I couldn't think of anything else to say. I just looked at him impassively, hoping the mirror of my face might inspire some memory.

He could tell I was unsatisfied. He only shrugged. "*¿Qué quieres que te diga?*" he said. In this instance, it was only a figure of speech. But I had an answer prepared for him.

"What do I want you to say, Juventino? You really want to know? Then here goes: I want you to tell me a story. And please, make it a horrible one. A tale of poverty and misery, of incest and abuse, of starvation and terror, of family violence so hair-raising and horrifying that anyone who listens to it will have nightmares forever. If you can include mental retardation, we're off to the races.

"It has to be a tragic Aristotelian narrative that corresponds to the fundamental order of the universe. There has to be a chain of cause and effect that begins the day Esperanza is born into wretchedness and has its inevitable climax at the moment she kills her baby. Which leads inexorably to her arrest, and for a denouement, the demonstration that she has been a saint in jail and is not only no longer a threat to society but a penitent and productive individual.

"You following me, Juventino? Most importantly, make the story devastatingly sad. The grief, the gloom, the desolation have to be so overwhelming that they will bring even the hardest-hearted, most vengeful Louisiana district attorney to tears. It has to be so heartbreaking that, after hearing it, jurors would rather cut their own throats than send her to the gas chamber."

Of course I didn't actually say any of that. I realized that Juventino had no story to tell, absolutely nothing to say about Esperanza or her family. Why should he? In half an hour, I tried to force him into what was probably more conversation than he'd had in the previous month. I asked him to reflect on things to which he'd never given a second's thought, things that had nothing to do with his existence or survival. In Ojeras, Juventino plants and harvests corn and beans in season, and during the intervals between farmwork, he tries to lay a little cement or hang drywall. That is, if he's not in California, Ohio, or North Carolina, hiding in the shadows while scrounging for any employment that will give him a little money to send home to his mother and sisters.

"Juventino," I said, "when I go home, I prepare memos for the lawyers about every conversation I've had with each person. I'm seeing a lot of people, and sometimes I realize I have forgotten something important. If that happens, would it be okay if I called you?"

"Sure," he said.

"What's your phone number?"

We listened to the birds warble in the trees for a while. Finally, he said, "I don't have a phone."

"You don't have a phone at home?" He shook his head. "A cell phone?"

"No."

"Okay," I said. "What's your address?"

He pointed to the adobe house. "I live there."

I nodded. "What's the name of this street?"

Another long pause. "Mamá!" he called. "What's the name of the street where we live?"

The wobbly lady in the serape shrugged her shoulders. That they did not know the name of their street is not as insane as it sounds. In towns like Ojeras, people tend to identify addresses not by names or numbers, but with a little travelogue: "It's down by the bakery," or "It's up where Lula's grandmother lives," or "It's next door to where the gringo got bit by the dog." It was the last house on the last street in the back of a one-burro town in the middle of nowhere. As they say here, *donde el diablo perdió el poncho*—where the devil lost his poncho. The street may not even have had a name. If there had been a sign, half the residents wouldn't have been able to read it.

"You can just say Ojeras," said Juventino, "in the municipality of Puroaire, the state of Michoacán, in México."

It crossed my mind that all this might have been an elaborate put-on. That Juventino was holding out on me, malevolently playing stupid for whatever reason he had up his sleeve: mistrust, perversity, petty revenge against Marta or Esperanza. But I looked into his glazed-doughnut eyes and my gut told me he wasn't clever or willful enough to withhold important information. He just didn't have any. Sometimes a potential witness can be a huge disappointment, but it's rarely their fault. They would help you if they could.

I put a hand on his shoulder. "Thanks for your help," I said.

"Para servirle," he said.

I put my notebook back in my knapsack, the pen in my pocket. I stood up to leave.

"What did you say your name was?" asked Juventino.

"Richard," I said.

"Can I ask you a question?" said Juventino.

"As many as you like."

He scratched his belly. "Is she guilty?"

People frequently ask me that. Most of the time, the answer is "hell, yes," but I would never say so. "I honestly don't know, Juventino," I said. "I wasn't there. There are a few things in this case that don't make sense. For now, I'm just trying to convince the prosecutor not to kill her. If we get death off the table, then there will be other options." Life without the possibility of parole, for example. Staring at metal bars and concrete walls forever, even if she lives to be two hundred.

He nodded. "I don't believe she killed the baby," he said.

I held my breath. You never know what little miracle they might have up their sleeves. "What makes you say that, Juventino?"

He shrugged. "Because she's good people," he said.

I limped back to the taxi. The driver put the car into gear and we began the trip back. There is always a moment of exhilaration looking out that flyspecked windshield as a town disappears and you hit the highway. It took two and a half hours to get here and would be another two and a half to get back. Plus an hour in Ojeras, another to write up the memo. Seven hours: seven hundred dollars. Not a bad day, if I didn't get rabies.

BAD COP, WORSE COP

He is thick with solid muscle, a body so dense that Esperanza thinks he might burst out of his stiff sky-blue shirt like *el increíble Hulk*. Two days ago he told her his name was Shepherd. He leans toward her so his face is a couple of inches from hers. Veins pulsate at his temples: he may whisper or he may scream. She can smell the pharmaceutical cologne mixed with his sweat, the chemical grease with which he tames his wavy hair into submission, the tobacco on his breath. There are pocks and pores in his sallow skin, red veins in his hazel eyes. His right eyebrow twitches. He needs a shave.

"How did you kill the baby?" he says. He speaks as if the question had occurred to him suddenly, as if he hadn't asked her 162 times over the past forty-eight hours.

Bobby, who is translating as well as transcribing the conversation, repeats the question in Spanish.

"I don't remember," she says in the tiniest of voices. Did he think she would say something else this time?

Shepherd's partner sits across from Esperanza. Shepherd introduced him to her as the Blob. Jelly-bellied and bullet-headed, he executes a two-fingered drum roll on top of the table. Esperanza registers him as Louisiana brown: a café au lait *moreno* who can't speak Spanish.

Straightening his body, pulling up his pants, snorting, Shepherd nods his head. "'I don't remember,'" he says, looking at his partner.

"She don't remember," says the Blob.

"You think she don't remember?" he asks.

"She says she don't remember," says the Blob. He snickers and scratches his dome.

"You know what? I'm sick of hearing that she don't remember."
Shepherd stares at Esperanza with boiling eyes. His hair is so black
it is almost blue, like a character from a comic book. Bobby neither
renders nor records the policemen's patter.

They are in a tiny room with a scratched Formica table, four plastic folding chairs, and a mildewed gray rug that smells of heavy Pay-
less shoes and the pavement they've beaten. Shepherd leans in until
he's an inch away from her eardrum and yells at the top of his voice,
"How did you kill that fucking baby?" As a consequence of all of his
screaming, Esperanza has a ringing in her ears that won't go away.
The Blob slams the flat of his hand on the table in front of her body,
in case further emphasis is needed.

"¿Cómo mató al bebé?" drones Bobby.

"Tell them I don't remember," Esperanza says to Bobby. There
are tears in her eyes. When they picked her up two days ago, she
was drenched from the pounding rain. She has a fever. No matter
how many times they scream in her ear or slam the table, it doesn't
get any easier. When is this going to end? When will they finally
kill her?

"She doesn't remember," repeats Bobby.

Shepherd begins to pace the room in a slow circle. "Oh, man,"
he says.

The Blob cracks his knuckles. "You having fun yet?" he asks.

"You think this is my idea of fun, you perverted Congolese boy
humper?" asks Shepherd. "I'm a family man. How can you say sick
shit like that?" He says to Bobby, "Tell her I got a three-year-old and
an eight-year-old and I want to go home and see my kids."

When Bobby translates Shepherd's assertion, Esperanza thinks of
tiny Yesenia, blue, cold, gruesomely disfigured, stiff as a baseball
bat. She wraps her arms around her torso and weeps.

"Shit, we lost her again," says the Blob. "Earth to Esperanza," he
yells, smacking his palm on the table to retrieve her attention.

"I'm supposed to feel sorry for her?" asks Shepherd to the air. He
looks at her with disgust. "Sick bitch kills her baby and what's she
want me to do? Call up the social work squad? Take her out for a
steak and a mojito?"

"She don't have to remember," says the Blob. "She says she done it. She came and got us. We can let the lawyers figure out the rest of it. Why don't we let a sleeping dog lay the fuck up? It's been two days."

"She remembers how she killed the fucking baby," says Shepherd. "Man, that kid was destroyed—burned, battered, and boiled. How can you do that to a fucking baby and not remember?"

"It's been two motherfucking days! She's a nutcase. If she remembered, don't you think she would've given it up by now?"

Sniffling, Esperanza runs a hand up her sleeve and scratches her upper arm. Her legs and torso also itch. It's as if the atmosphere were full of invisible fleas. When Shepherd and the Blob leave her alone, she curls up under the table and sleeps. She has been given no food or water since her arrest. She has not been allowed to make a phone call. She was advised of her rights to remain silent and to a lawyer. The first option went right over her head and Esperanza knows only rich people can pay for lawyers. "Rights" are, in any case, an abstract concept. She vaguely remembers hearing about them in school, but has no idea how they pertain to her.

"I'd rather give it back to the DA in a neat package," says Shepherd. One of these days I'd like to get a promotion."

"I say she would've given it up by now," says the Blob. He smiles at Esperanza, gives her the once-over. "She sure is fine, though. Mmm-mmm. Too bad that shit's going to go to waste on the goddamn lock-in." He narrows his eyes and says to her, *"La bonita."* He knows the words because they are painted on the side of a truck from which some enterprising Mexicans have sold tacos on a nearby side street for the past couple of years, since their work on the clean-up crews after the hurricane dried up. Then he adds to Bobby: "Kind of on the skinny side, though."

"I like them like that," offers the interpreter. It has been a long time since such a fetching suspect washed ashore in Plaquegoula Parish. She is tall, large-boned but slender, with caramel skin, wide eyes, and enormous lashes. Bobby imagines himself in a savage embrace with her, his fingers clutching the long wavy hair, kissing the wide mouth with its generous lips, now taut with fear. He doesn't recall ever seeing hands that size on a woman. She could cup a basketball in her palm. And although she's thin, she's got a shape. Everything is big about her: the eyes, the teeth, the fingers, even the tatas. Especially the tatas.

Shepherd leans in toward Esperanza once again, inches from her face. "Listen," he says. "Play ball with me and they'll feel sorry for you. They'll give you manslaughter or something. They'll cut you a deal and you won't get nothing but fifteen for the baby. You'll be in and out in eight and a half, maybe less. By that time you'll be what, thirty? Thirty-five? You'll still be young enough to have you another one if you wanted it. Hell, you could have two or three." Bobby more or less translates these words of encouragement for Esperanza. "But if you don't cooperate, you know what's going to happen to you? We don't fuck around in America, baby. Sure as shit we give you the lethal injection." His patience wearing thin, Shepherd listens to Bobby mumble his words in Spanish. "You know about the lethal injection, don't you?" Shepherd asks. "We stick that shit in your arm and your insides will broil like a crown roast in a slow oven." He opens his jacket and removes a needle and syringe from the inside pocket. He holds the apparatus in the palm of his hand while staring Esperanza in the eye.

She is exhausted, having only slept fitfully under the table. Her skin is burning. She looks at Shepherd and then in Bobby's eyes.

"Tell him to give it to me now," she spits out in Spanish.

"What?" Bobby asks.

"Tell him to kill me now." If that is going to be her fate, *santísima virgen*, then let's get it over and done with.

"What's she saying?" asks Shepherd.

"She says she's ready for that lethal injection right now. She wants you to give it to her."

"Ah, shit," says Shepherd. "Fucking refried fruitcake."

The Blob begins to laugh. "Go on, bro. She got her arm stuck out and everything."

Shepherd shakes his head. "They must grow them Tootsie Fruits and Brazil nuts in her part of Mexico," he says.

The Blob stands up and slaps his partner on the shoulder with the back of his hand. "Excuse us for a minute," he says. "We have something important to discuss." He pulls Shepherd out the door by the arm. It's almost one in the afternoon. Outside the police station in the blistering heat, they light up Marlboros.

"What do you want for lunch? You want to go to Subway again?" asks the Blob.

"How about some of those spicy wings at Popeyes?" asks Shepherd. "Or we could go downtown to the Piggly Wiggly and get the stuffed peppers."

"Whatever," says the Blob. "One thing's for sure. I ain't eating off of no Mexican taco truck. That greasy shit will give you a heart attack. A Mexican's hungry enough he'll eat his own donkey. You think they call them burritos for nothing?"

Bobby—gray hair side-parted, round shoulders, a loose shirt and a striped tie fraying at the knot—offers Esperanza a weak smile. He would like to say something consoling. If anyone is going to relieve her, it's him, especially now that they're alone. They don't play good cop, bad cop in Plaquegoula Parish. They play bad cop, worse cop. Dirty Harry would be the compassionate one around here. But what can he say? "Everything is going to be all right?" Nothing is going to be all right for this baby doll. Besides, the minute he opens his maw to say something nice to a woman, he gets in trouble. He's living in the house of one of his exes, paying her a fat rent, while shelling out three mouths' worth of child support to the other. If it weren't for his personal payroll he wouldn't be working for these creepy cops any longer.

Esperanza shivers. He thinks about getting the jacket out of his locker and putting it over her shoulders. Shepherd and the Blob would never let him live it down.

The Blob opens the door and finds Esperanza and Bobby sitting in silence. He takes his seat in front of her and stares. She sees the perspiration that has formed on his scalp and brow in pear-shaped droplets. She can hear him wheezing.

"You look like a princess," he says finally, adding, *"La bonita."*

He leans toward her with an outstretched arm. She jerks her head away before he caresses her cheek with the back of his hand.

HOW I LEARNED
TO LOVE NESCAFÉ

I woke up in what may have been the finest three-hundred-peso hotel room in all of Mexico. There was a firmish mattress and a newish
bedspread in a repulsive yellow-brown print. The walls were char-
treuse stucco, the light fluorescent and buzzing like a mosquito. The
room was equipped with telephone and TV, hot and cold water, a
ceiling fan and even air-conditioning. The latter seemed like a good
idea in Puroaire, a town situated in an area that extended across
three states called Tierra Caliente.

It was given that moniker long ago because of the tropical heat
and merciless humidity, but since drug traffickers claimed it as part
of their turf a few years ago, the tag had taken on a more sinister
connotation. The cooling system turned the room into a meat locker
in five minutes. I turned on the fan and lay naked atop the synthetic
sheets. After a while I got used to the smell of insecticide fluid, a
shield against cockroaches the size of roof rats.

When I got off the bus in towns like Puroaire, I would ask a cabdriver to point me to the best hotel in town. He'd tell me to hop in,
drive around for about ten minutes, and drop me off somewhere in
the vicinity of where he picked me up. At $100 an hour I could be a
sport about such extortion. The "best" lodgings were mostly along
the lines of the Hotel Central, where I was spending the night in
Puroaire. A doctor in Mexico City wrote me a script for Xanax for
nights in places like this. Three tequilas and half a pill usually took
care of me for a few hours.

I woke a little before seven and pulled on yesterday's clothes. The
hotel was built around an open-air patio with a gnarly Guadalupe
palm in the center. At a desk by the door a heavyset man dozed in
an office chair, despite a TV on his desk noisily broadcasting a grisly

car crash in Mexico City that morning. He had curly salt-and-pepper hair and slept in his black-framed eyeglasses. An unbuttoned guayabera exposed thatches of swirling body hair. His prolonged snore discharged in a continuous dissonant volley.

Trying not to wake him, I looked around the patio to see if I could find coffee. I was useless before I had caffeine in the morning. Without it, I was on irritated automatic pilot, a day of the living dead.

Suddenly the honking cascade ceased. "Can I help you?" asked the large man, folding his arms across his chest in an attitude of utter officiousness.

"Is there any coffee in the hotel?" I asked.

"Yes," he said.

I nodded, waiting for additional enlightenment. None was forthcoming. "Where might it be?" I asked.

"On top of the table over there," he said. "Monday through Friday. When the girl comes in to make it." He smiled and shrugged. "Today's Saturday. *Sorry*." He said the last word in English, trilling the double *r*.

"Is there anywhere open this early where I can find a cup?" I asked.

"The market."

I enjoyed crossing the plazas of these little towns so early in the morning, before the heat rose. There was no activity in the church, the town hall, the police station. One or two enterprising women in aprons mopped the sidewalks outside the storefronts with plastic brooms, but the shops and the banks were dead to the world.

After seven a few of the dreamy-eyed began to set up their stalls in the market. With long wooden poles, they hoisted hangers with made-in-China jeans and blouses, attaching them to the upper rungs of the metal mesh stalls. The market people believed the barely perceptible morning breeze contained harmful toxins, so they wore sweaters and knotted scarves at their necks.

Around the corner, in a storefront adjacent to the market, I saw her: my patron saint. The woman who arrives earliest and sets a table to serve fresh orange juice; bananas mashed with milk, sugar, and cinnamon in a mixer; or, for the belligerently health-conscious, blended concoctions of weeds, raw beets, and quail eggs. Her wavy hair was colored dark red. She had smooth olive skin and was about my age, maybe a couple of years older. There were laugh lines beside her eyes. She wore a yellow sweater and tight nylon pants.

"Good morning, señora," I said, sitting on a square plastic stool.

"Good morning, *joven*." Her smile exposed strong white teeth. She didn't call me "young man" because of my youthful appearance. Unless she knows us, all of her customers are *joven* or *señorita* or *caballero*. Unless and until we are friends, she is *señora* and I am *joven*. I will be *joven* until I am about seventy, at which point I will graduate to *señor*.

"Have you any coffee?" I asked.

"Of course." She poured hot water from a huge percolator into a Styrofoam cup and set it before me, along with a barrel-shaped jar of Nescafé Clásico and a white plastic spoon.

"Cream?" she asked, pointing to a blue plastic bucket full of powder. "Sugar?"

I opened the jar of pulverized brown particles. I loved the generosity of handing over the whole bottle. If I had started to eat the Nescafé out of the jar, spoonful by spoonful, she probably would have encouraged me, like a mother feeding her baby. I dropped one heaping spoon, and then a level one for good luck, into the polystyrene. I stirred and smelled the bitter blend through the little cap of sand-colored chemical foam that formed at the top, even without the benefit of compressed "cream." I was in heaven.

When I was a child in Brooklyn, my father used to take the subway to Greenwich Village to the only store in all of New York that roasted its own coffee beans. He would get a special blend, three-quarters of a pound of dark French roast and a quarter of milder Colombian. That was the first coffee I drank, from the age of twelve, when my parents allowed me to mix a few drops into my milk, until later in adolescence, by which time the proportions had been reversed. As a result, I grew up to be a complete coffee snob. In Mexico City, I bought organic coffee from the highlands of Chiapas. I would order a fine grind, which I prepared in an octagonal Italian espresso pot. Any woman who spent the night with me would get a cup of that in the morning, mixed with milk I heated on top of the stove.

But in a one-burro Mexican town, all bets were off. In some of them, you might have been able to get a cup of flavorless brown water at the local cafeteria. I would have jumped over a thousand cups of that swill to get to some Nescafé—particularly if I were handed the jar and allowed to do my own loading. After stirring in a little sugar I took that first familiarly vitriolic sip. Pure pleasure.

"*Qué rico*," I told the lady with the vibrantly painted hair.

"Is it?" she asked through her smile. "I don't drink coffee."

"Not even in the morning?"

"*Nunca de los nuncas.*" She fluttered a hand by her bosom. "It gives me palpitations."

"To your health," I said, raising the Styrofoam cup.

She tilted her head, a twinkle in her eye. "What are you doing in Puroaire, *joven*?"

"Just passing through," I said. "I have some Mexican friends in *el gabacho* and they have relatives around here." She looked at me as if she expected more. "It's beautiful—the hills." I always tried to change the subject as quickly as possible. For discretion's sake, I never trumpeted to locals that I was around to help one of their neighbors' kids who was facing death row in East Buttfuck, Kentucky. What's more, explaining what I did for a living involved taking a deep breath and expending a lot of wind.

"It's pretty quiet in Puroaire," she said. With a long wooden stick, she stirred sugar, corn flour, and water in a pot to make a breakfast drink called *atole*.

"That's not what they say."

"What do they say?" she asked, a smile on her face.

"You know. That there are a lot of conflicts. That it can be dangerous." I seldom referred directly to drug trafficking. That was supposed to be one of my strategies to sneak quietly into old age.

She smirked. "Take a look around. Do you feel threatened here?"

"No. Last night I took a walk and there were old people and kids all around the plaza."

"That's the way it is," she said.

"Good morning, Doña Inés," said a woman in her early twenties, skinny with long eyelashes and protruding teeth. She joined the older woman behind the table, removed her jacket, and put on an apron. "Sorry I'm late. Panchito has colic," she said.

"Don't worry," said Inés, stirring the *atole*. Her young assistant began to slice oranges in half. The morning light glimmered off the freshly cut flesh.

"I went to Cucaramácara last night to see the Los Dandys concert," said Inés. "And you know what? They didn't even show up."

"Don't tell me!"

"It took me an hour to get there. They had to give everybody their money back."

"How rude!" The assistant began to place each orange half in a hand-operated contraption that squeezed out the juice, half by half. Mexicans refer to their true love as their *media naranja*—their other half of the split orange.

I sipped my Nescafé and enjoyed the slight breeze. Within an hour, the air would stop moving in Tierra Caliente, and the temperature and humidity would squeeze us all in an oppressive embrace. I would be trying to get Esperanza's siblings to tell me heinous, painful, and humiliating secrets about their mother and father. But meanwhile, savoring the coffee in the market, listening to the women gossip, and watching the vendors set up their stalls, I was happy.

One of my virtues was that I didn't have to become miserable in order to ruefully recall that in the distant past I had been content. When I felt good, it was tangible, palpable—I could hold the feeling in my hand. My work was demanding and intense, but it was full of what I came to think of as "stolen moments." These were the instants when somehow, despite the desolation and misery that I was documenting, I recognized a feeling of serenity, or even joy. I noticed them all the time. When I ate or drank something that tasted good, when I felt the reprieve of a breeze against my skin, when I saw a breathtaking landscape, or when a pretty waitress turned her head to give me a second look. I enjoyed a free hour to walk around the broken-down houses and unpaved streets of an unfamiliar town. When I told people about my work, they tended to assume that it overwhelmed me with sadness. On the contrary. Being so close to other people's tragedies that I could kiss them was a constant reminder of how fortunate I was.

"You don't even know Los Dandys," said Inés to her assistant. "Your generation doesn't listen to those songs." She smiled, closed her eyes, and began to sway her hips. *"You are like a precious stone, a divine jewel, truly valuable,"* she trilled, her arms posed as if she were dancing with a lover. *"If my eyes don't lie, if my eyes don't deceive me, your beauty is without equal...."* She stopped abruptly and laughed, and, although facing her helper, she glanced at me from the corner of her eye.

"Gema" was Inés's siren song. Maybe she was my *media naranja*. I could marry her, settle down in Puroaire, and get all the Nescafé I could drink. I looked at the curve of her neck, still smooth and lovely. Her hips had not yet spread egregiously and her stomach was only slightly rounded. She had not let herself go. Her children were probably grown. It would just be the two of us in a small cinder block house, probably on the outskirts a mile out of town, with plastic window curtains and an embroidered picture of the Last Supper in the living room.

I am not saying I was any great prize, but how many like me passed through Puroaire in a day, a month, a year? Inés would probably be happy and even grateful to have a man who didn't beat her, who had a modicum of patience, who listened to her when she gossiped about her customers. I vaguely remembered in a novel—was it written by García Márquez?—a description of two old people, after many decades of marriage, in their dotage coupling like two little earthworms. Would Inés and I merge our bodies like that in twenty or thirty years? What would we talk about?

"I'm working for the lawyers who are defending your sister," I said when he came to the door. "May I come in?"

Joaquín, Esperanza's eldest brother, opened up without a word. He was a little taller than me, an inch or two over six feet, and lanky. At fifty-three, his thick wavy hair was more salt than pepper, but his heavy eyebrows were black. The flesh in his face was beginning to fall. He could have packed for the weekend in the bags under his eyes. I found his house on foot, about ten unpaved blocks from the market.

I walked into the living room. There was a modest table and four chairs, a sagging sofa, a framed image of the Virgin of Guadalupe. A boy of about three or four with a bowl-shaped haircut stood in the doorway to the kitchen. Joaquín's son? His grandson? Beyond the boy, a somber, heavyset woman dried her hands on a dish towel. She stared at me with impassive, almond-shaped eyes.

"Could we please speak privately?" I asked.

He led me through two more rooms. Each had furniture of unadorned wood with the kind of cushions that began to slump before they got home from the store. Still, by the standards of a town like Puroaire, Joaquín was doing well. We got to the last room. Through a screen door, I glimpsed an overgrown patio, a deflated soccer ball, a tricycle on its side as if it were napping.

"Take a seat, *licenciado*," he said, pointing to a sofa covered with an old blanket. He sat in a wooden chair, his hands on his knees. That he called me *licenciado* meant that he thought I was a lawyer. During my investigations, Mexicans called me *licenciado* all the time. At first I tried to disabuse them of that notion, insisting that I wasn't a lawyer, merely an investigator who worked for lawyers. Yet even after the explanation, they continued to call me *licenciado*. Finally I realized that they wanted to believe I was a lawyer. Who was I to spoil their illusion?

He wore a checked shirt with snaps for buttons, untucked and with the sleeves rolled up, jeans and snakeskin boots. While he exuded masculinity, he was not your garden-variety macho. He was quieter, more introspective.

"This is a nice house," I said.

"Thank you."

He'd hardly uttered a sound. I hoped small talk might warm him up. "What do you do in Puroaire?"

He let the question sink in before he answered. "What do I do? Nothing," he said. "I sit around the house."

43

"Okay." I smiled. "Nice work if you can get it."

His gaze was penetrating. "This house comes from Montgomery, Alabama," he said, "where I washed dishes and cooked at Marcello's Italian Restaurant. This house comes from Millersville, North Carolina, where I picked tobacco, and Tar Heel, where I worked twelve-hour shifts killing pigs in a slaughterhouse. This house comes from planting and picking cotton in Mississippi, sorghum in Missouri, and corn in Kansas. I was a cabinetmaker in Iowa. I built doors and bookshelves. I worked for Fleetline in Nebraska, moving houses with trailers." He made the speech in a flat monotone. "This house is twenty years of my life, away from my family in *el gabacho*."

"I understand," I said, and took a deep breath. "Look, Joaquín. I am what is called, in English, a mitigation specialist. There is no reason for you to know what that is because you come from a civilized country where there is no death penalty." Those bags under his dark eyes and the lines around them made him seem exhausted, or ineffably sad. "You know that the prosecutor's office in Louisiana is seeking the death penalty for Esperanza?" I asked.

He said nothing, but there was a slight intake of breath that assured me he'd had no idea.

"My job is to put a human face on Esperanza. I put together the story of her life and of her family. Whenever the prosecutor arrests someone in the U.S., he makes up a story that he has captured a monster—Hitler, Jack the Ripper, and Hannibal Lecter rolled up in one. I try to show him that Esperanza is a human being who may have made mistakes but who nevertheless deserves mercy and consideration. I try to help convince him to take the death penalty off the table." I paused to see if Joaquín had any questions. "If that doesn't work, and in the worst of cases there is a trial and she's found guilty, we tell the story to the jury. To convince them that Esperanza's life is worth saving. Do you understand?"

After a moment, he nodded. It's a terrible lot of information to absorb in a couple of minutes, particularly when it pertains to someone you love. I'm not trying to get them to understand the gringo justice system. I'm just trying to get them to trust me.

"All I ask is that you tell me the truth, Joaquín. The good, the bad, and the ugly. *Todo se vale.* Okay?"

Once again, he nodded.

"I'm going to ask you to go back to the days when you were a little boy. Maybe six or seven years old. Tell me about Puroaire back then. What was it like here?"

He looked at me, then up at the ceiling, and then back at me. He inhaled deeply through his nose. Putting the palms of his huge hands together, he brought his fingertips to his mouth. He tried to say something but there were no words. Tears came to his eyes. "It was hard, man," he said finally, his voice cracking. "It was hard."

In my heart I thanked him a thousand times. He had conjured a memory from before I was born. More than forty-five years later, it still broke his heart. Now we were getting somewhere.

MORE ERRANT
THAN KNIGHT

Seated in a tiny booth, a smudged window separates Esperanza from her lawyer. She looks at Catherine's straight brown bangs, her watery blue eyes, her bee-stung lips. Squeezed into her side of the booth, Catherine has brought a man with her. Esperanza imagines he is some other *licenciado*. Lawyers, cops, detectives, interpreters, investigators, consular officials, and their respective assistants have all come to visit Esperanza in the months since her arrest. The meetings are brief and intense and then they disappear. She has seen few of them more than once.

"How you making out, Esperanza?" Catherine asks, in a voice honed by tequila and Tareytons into a commanding musical rasp. "Everything okay up here?" Esperanza gets the gist of the lawyer's questions and nods in assent. "This is Richard," says Catherine. "He's on our team. He's one of the good guys."

Esperanza looks at the man's egg-shaped face—the unruly curls spilling onto his forehead, the heavy-lidded eyes, the square chin. He has a generous lower lip but almost no upper lip at all. A crooked, jumbo spade-shaped nose spares him from notable beauty. He looks at Esperanza and smiles as if apologizing. In Spanish, he says, "Catherine told me to tell you I'm one of the good guys. I will be working on your case with her. It's a pleasure to meet you." He speaks Esperanza's language well, even if his accent is jarringly, comically thick.

"You haven't had any more problems or troubles in here, have you?" asks Catherine.

Richard makes the inquiry both more specific and more general, asking if any guards or inmates have "interfered" with her. "No," she says quickly. No good can come from answering "yes." What are they going to do, join her in the cell and protect her?

"I know things are moving slowly," says the lawyer. She speaks loudly, as if with that tactic she could break the language barrier. "But that's the way things work in Louisiana. And it's actually a good thing, honey—if nothing is happening, then nothing bad is happening, you know what I mean? It gives us more time to maneuver." Catherine smiles sweetly, and Esperanza takes some comfort from the voice. The lawyer stands and smoothes the skirt of her gray suit.

After Richard translates, Esperanza says, *"Muchas gracias."*

"I put twenty dollars into your commissary, Esperanza," says the lawyer. "I bet that's okay with you, isn't it?"

The prisoner thanks her again. This will buy her a couple of bars of soap, a stick of deodorant, some Styrofoam cups of, once hot water is added to their contents, noodle soup.

"I've got to be going now, dear," says Catherine. "Richard is going to ask you some questions. Please tell him everything he needs to know. Remember, he's one of us."

He looks at Esperanza through the window, lurching awkwardly in the tiny stool. Catherine smiles at Richard. "Do your magic, buddy," she says. "See you soon, dear," she tells Esperanza, who watches the attorney leave, taking long strides in the gray skirt.

Richard expresses regret for the discomfort of having to speak through the window. Usually prisoners can meet with their legal representatives in "contact rooms" where they sit together, but none is available that afternoon.

"Let me explain who I am and what I do, Esperanza," he says. She observes that his shoulders are broad, that he is slim, and that he has no woman to iron his shirts. "The system of justice is very strange in this country." By retracing the steps of her life he hopes to come up with a narrative that will talk the prosecutor out of trying to give her the death penalty. He looks into her black eyes. "If you have any questions, let me know." She nods.

He removes the notebook from his knapsack. "Where were you born, Esperanza?"

"Puroaire."

"That's in Tierra Caliente, right?" She nods her head. She is surprised he has any idea where it is. "I've lived in Mexico City for the last six years," he says.

"You have?"

"Yes. All of my cases involve Mexicans in trouble," he says. "So far, none of them has been put to death."

She smiles out of the side of her mouth. "So many of us are trying to come over here and you went to live there," she says.

"That's right." He nods.

"Why?" she asks.

"I don't know," he says. "I like it there. People treat each other more warmly in Mexico." She smiles, and then an expression of regret clouds her face. "How old are you, Esperanza?" he asks.

"Twenty-six," she says, reflecting that she has already had one birthday in jail.

"Are both of your parents alive?" he asks. She nods in assent. "Are they both in Puroaire?"

"My father is in Huetamo, and my mother lives with my sister María Concepción in Morelia."

"How many brothers and sisters do you have?"

"Nine, *licenciado*. And the one who died."

"Do any of them live in Puroaire?"

"My oldest brother, Joaquín. And my sister Elena."

"What was Puroaire like when you were a child, Esperanza?" he asks.

Esperanza thinks of dirt floors and water carried in buckets, drawn from a hose outside the house. She was the youngest of the litter, and by the time she was born her mother was spent. Her father was more concerned with drinking than raising any more children. Esperanza was darker-skinned than the rest of her brothers and sisters, and although she matched his pallor almost exactly, he'd always had a sneaking suspicion that she wasn't really his. Once in a while he would take a crack at her mother for her implied infidelity and the shame it caused him. Although he never said so, he had no doubts she knew why he hit her.

Esperanza remembers her maternal grandfather's homemade sandals, the soles fashioned from flat tires. His thick and hoary toenails, ugly as those of a rhinoceros. He used to squat on his haunches and stare into space. Esperanza would help her mother cook and wash clothes and sweep with a straw broom. Sometimes she played with the hairy black pigs that her grandfather kept in a dirt pen encircled by cinder block behind the house, until the day they were big enough to sell and slaughter.

She conjures a picture of the sweeping view of the valley in the early autumn, sun-dappled but still wet from a thundershower. "It was beautiful, *licenciado*," says Esperanza.

"Beautiful in what way?" asks Richard. She stares at the hands in her lap. He runs his hand through his hair and looks at some of the words that other prisoners have scratched into the walls on her side of the glass partition. Esperanza has no idea what they mean: RAT. SHIT. INNOCENT. HELP. FIGHT. LA. KILLS. When she doesn't answer his question, he tries another: "Tell me about the house where you grew up."

She has been unsure about most of her visitors, sometimes unable to distinguish between those who are defending her and those who are against her. Richard is one of the few people who has come who she feels certain is not a policeman. Still, she doesn't understand why he is asking her all this. She knows he wants to help, but can't fathom how talking to him about her childhood will do her any good.

"How many rooms were there, Esperanza?"

She is ashamed to say there were only two, plus the kitchen. She stares at the wall behind his head.

"Esperanza, I know that I am asking you to tell me things you don't usually talk about. Things that you might prefer not to remember. And I'm sorry about that." He adjusts his seat so it is harder for her to avoid his gaze. She looks at the floor. "And I know that we've just met. I don't expect you to trust me. I know I have to earn that trust." She looks up at him and is surprised to find that his heavy-lidded eyes are a little wet. His sentiment annoys her. What reason can he possibly have to be sad or sorry? He's not the one with a dead daughter. He's not in jail.

After taking a deep breath, he says, "I just want to say something about talking about yourself. I don't usually talk about myself either. We all have armor, some kind of protection. Like these clothes we wear. They protect us from the cold, the rain, the elements. But if I walk out of here and I get hit by a car, and I have a wound, and the doctors have to dress the wound—even if it means stripping me naked in the middle of the street—I wouldn't care. It would be all right, because they would be trying to save my life." She imagines him, naked and bleeding, on a stretcher being led into an ambulance. "Louisiana wants to kill you. If you want us to try to save your life, you are going to have to expose yourself a little bit."

She imagines herself naked on her side of the glass. Unlike many of her other visitors, she is not afraid of the *licenciado*. She thinks he may desire her. When he averts his eyes, it is as if he has read her mind. For a moment she feels dominant, which in turn gives her a sense of freedom. The oddity of feeling liberated while inside jail makes her body tingle.

"You don't have to talk to me if you don't want to. Just think about it," Richard says in a stumbling voice. "I will come back and visit you again, but I can't force you. *No te hago manita de puerco.*"

Literally, that means "I won't make you a little pork hand." It is Mexican slang for "I won't twist your arm"—an expression from her grandparents' generation. Coming out of his mouth, with that impossible gringo accent, it sounds ridiculous. She bursts out laughing, and once she gets started she cannot stop. She covers her mouth, turns red. She cannot remember the last time she has laughed. She cannot remember the last time she has forgotten how miserable she is.

He wipes his eye with a finger, smiles, and puts his palm against the glass that separates them. She stops laughing. She is not ready to join her palm in his.

FICTION

Gustavo's pockmarked face was crumpled. His Donald Duck voice cracked with emotion. "That scene where little Marcel can't fall asleep," he said, his tongue heavy in his mouth. "He rolls around and around in bed. He just lays there all night." Twenty years ago he studied French literature at the National Autonomous University and he thought this made him a *chevalier des arts et des lettres*. "He cannot fall asleep until his mother comes in and kisses him good night." He grasped his curls with both hands. "My God, he was the greatest. *Qué chido, güey*."

That was the most insightful observation that Gustavo—an editor at one of Mexico's most prestigious monthlies—could quack about Proust: the Mexican equivalent of "Awesome, dude."

Armando shook his graying head. A novelist from Culiacán, up north where men are putatively men, he needed to put things in perspective. Passing the back of a hand across his beard, he said, "I read that book. Kid can't sleep without his mother's kiss? What a fag."

I looked at the bottom of my cylindrical shot glass, hoping there would be an overlooked last sip of tequila. "I could have done without the first two hundred pages about the hawthorn bushes," I said. "But the middle section? Where Swann goes after Odette? That is the greatest depiction of obsessive love that I have ever read."

Mandarino, whose novels established him as the premier cynic in a city of twenty million of them, said, "I don't know about your love life, my dear Richard, but that story isn't like any kind of love I have ever known." And he'd known a lot, at least to hear him tell it. However, the tales of his exploits were a bit bewildering to reconcile when you considered his pear-shaped body, his jowly face, and his infrequent bathing habits, evident if you sat anywhere near him. He held up two fingers. Lola the waitress—sixty, gold teeth, *cuerpo de boiler*—saw him and nodded. The signal had nothing to do with a drink order. She would disappear onto the rainy sidewalk for a few moments and bring back Mandarino two grams of cocaine.

"My dear Gustavo, do you know what Walter Benjamin said about your beloved Proust?" asked Mandarino. He adjusted the brim of his green porkpie hat. "That he died of ignorance, because he didn't know how to build a fire or open a window."

Most of my friends in Mexico City were writers. We usually drank enough for me to drown out their sexism, homophobia, and machismo. I thought they were funny and heroically quixotic—according to a survey, Mexicans on the average read a half a book per year. Still, sometimes their company made me restless. Didn't they have anything else to talk about besides books?

We were in Mi Oficina, the tiniest bar in Mexico City. On the ground floor of an abandoned office building whose upper stories were consumed by fire a decade ago, it was a low-lit overheated room with five tables. Behind the bar was an unpolished wooden rack with bottles of cheap rum, tequila, whiskey, and a popular variety of Mexican brandy with which I wouldn't have disinfected a toilet bowl. The toothless bartender slept on a stool, next to a tiny altar to the Virgin of Guadalupe. Mi Oficina's chief attractions were its bargain-basement prices and Lola's phantom sidewalk connection.

"Ah," quacked Gustavo, "but if you read Adorno's letters to Benjamin about Proust...."

I considered going somewhere else to get another drink until Lola returned. My friends may have pitied me, but their brand of blather made me relieved rather than regretful about my status as a silenced scribe.

You may have wondered about my life before mitigation. Maybe you vaguely remembered my name. Could you possibly be among the brave and happy few who read either of my books? I was a writer nearly all my life. While growing up, it never occurred to me to want to be anything else. From early childhood, my parents sent me to the library around the corner to get me out of their hair. I began to fill journals at the age of ten, and wrote stories long before I had any to tell.

I wasn't the only one convinced that the world needed another narrator. A piece of paper in the back of a closet attested that I had an MFA in creative writing. It may have come from a liberal arts college in Maryland rather than Stanford or Iowa, but they took care of every cent of my tuition and gave me a stipend to boot. They even funded a semester in Mexico for "research."

By my mid-twenties, I was being published in literary magazines, some of them prestigious. My first book managed to make a little noise. Published when I was twenty-nine, it was a collection of short stories about Mexicans who cut lawns and worked in restaurant kitchens, sleeping in shifts in shadowy furnished rooms in Long Island. Before the book came out, the story about Rodrigo, the gardener who has AIDS, won a prize given by *Embolalia*, one of the best literary magazines in the country, which I hoped would consolidate my destiny. At the end of the year, the *New York Times* blessed it as a Notable Book of the Year. The reviews were solid, some even splendid. It barely sold two thousand copies and never came out in paperback.

Although initially dismayed by the sales figures, I took them on the chin and moved on, imagining them to be a peculiarity of the publishing industry rather than a harbinger of the world's indifference to what I had to say. My illusions were encouraged by Rhoda, my agent, and Lucien, my editor. *Wait for the next book,* they said in an angelic mini-chorus. *You need to write a novel.* Everyone loved the story about Rodrigo, and Rhoda and Lucien backed up my decision to supersize him to 335 pages. It took me four years but the novel got written.

I envisioned a world waiting for it with open arms. After the book was published, life would be a cruise on the *Queen Mary*. There would be awards, royalties from editions in dozens of languages, speaking engagements, adoring fans. And the jewel in the crown, a cushy teaching job in a small university, where I would shovel the same shit that had been thrown at me in Maryland, while I wrote the next one and the next one and the next one. By that time I was married, to a Mexican named Carla, whose steady salary kept us afloat until my ship came in.

The book came out on September 12, 2001. The day before, nineteen demolition men named Mohammed toppled a couple of buildings downtown, and there disappeared every clap of thunder that was meant to herald my novel. You want a deadly accurate rendering of how little the world cares about you? Try publishing a book the day after the first terrorist attack on U.S. soil. Poor Rodrigo sold eight hundred copies.

Hope springs eternal. I rolled up my sleeves and ground out another one, in a little over a year. By the time I finished, Lucien had quit editing, gone upstate, and opened a B&B with an antiques store attached. No one else at the publishing house was even vaguely interested. Rhoda sent it to thirty-seven editors, one by excruciating one. None of them bit.

That's when I decided it was time for a break, an auspicious moment to consider what story I may have had to tell. The greatest writers in the world didn't write 365 days a year. Even Flaubert lived it up a little, at least while he was young. If I always believed I was a talented writer, I never realized how incredibly good I was at *not* writing. The world proceeded apace, even though I had ceased to record its progress. The sun kept rising and setting, and if you got far away enough from the city to see them, the stars continued to shine.

I needed a job. Aside from an occasional magazine assignment or piddling fees from teaching a creative-writing workshop, Carla supported me with her salary. Though she rarely complained, it was a source of tension. A friend named Sharon Bromberg, an activist journalist who straddled the border between Tucson and Nogales, had just begun to do mitigation investigations and got me involved. "They're desperate for people," she said. "There are fifty Mexicans on death row and another couple of hundred charged with capital murder. There's hardly anyone out there qualified to do the Mexico cases."

There is no school for mitigation. Although most of its practitioners have backgrounds in social work, law, or psychology, I was as close to a natural as the lawyers were going to find. I had some experience with magazine reporting, which left me unafraid to knock on a stranger's door looking for a good story. I'd studied Spanish since childhood. I had spent as much time as possible in Mexico since I was seventeen, when as a high school senior I was part of a student group that went to a tiny hamlet in Oaxaca to build latrines and teach dental hygiene. Most of the villagers preferred to use the woods for their toilette, and few had running water with which to rinse out their mouths after flossing and brushing. (Instead, some of them dutifully used Coca-Cola.) But I felt more at liberty and alive in that village than I ever had in Brooklyn, and through the years, on vacations and work trips, I went to Mexico every chance I got. In Mexico City, I instinctively knew I'd found another home. After I got a letter from Rhoda wishing me luck at finding another agent, and Carla miscarried and disappeared, I got an apartment in *el D.F.* and never looked back.

It wasn't as if I never wrote at all. I was perhaps the greatest memo writer in the English language. The lawyers for whom I worked got detailed accounts of every interview I conducted, and longer painstaking ones explaining the life of the family of the accused, the places they were from, and a theory as to what in our client's life brought him to the moment where he found himself charged with murder. I explained who would make a good witness and why, and which of them would be repellent to a jury of pious, closed-minded trailer trash. I alerted them to the concise menu of what might be a mitigating circumstance: mental illness; great promise thwarted; violence, abuse, and neglect; toxic waste in the well water; previous good deeds heretofore unpunished; a line of people willing to testify that they would be devastated if the client were put to death.

Still, without a writing project of my own, I felt unmoored, unmanned. It was only after I had worked on a few death-penalty cases that I began to feel like I might possibly have a significant story to tell. Every day, matters of life and death were handed to me on a silver platter. If I were to take the project on, whose story would I tell? You could hardly find a better one than that of Roberto, my first case. It happened in Harris County, whose county seat is Houston. It should come as no surprise that about half of my cases came out of Texas, which is not only home to countless Mexicans, but has distinguished itself as the Death-Penalty Capital of the Universe. They could sell T-shirts and coffee mugs with electric chairs on them. At the time I was chosen for Roberto's case, more people had been sentenced to death in Harris County than any other in the world.

Roberto was undocumented, one of the millions of nameless, faceless Mexicans doing the odd jobs that most people born in the U.S. believe themselves too delicate to negotiate—planting and harvesting, gardening, roofing, maintenance. He was twenty-four, and had distinguished himself with some prior convictions, including a couple of DUIs, possession of a tiny bag of marijuana, and indecency before a minor. (He was busted for that one after consensually French-kissing a fifteen-year-old hillbilly. Her mother, whom he had been screwing, got jealous and pressed charges, which resulted in his deportation back to Zacatecas. Within a few months he had returned to Texas. His rotten luck.)

When Roberto tried to stick up a Dunkin' Donuts, another customer—an off-duty cop—pulled a gun. Roberto blew his brains out. Sadly, this was not any old cop, but a cop beloved in his community, decorated for bravery, who'd left behind a widow and three sons. We were in such deep water with Roberto that I wanted to ask Donna, the attorney who hired me, why we were even taking the trouble. A Harris County jury would put him in a toaster like a slice of Wonder Bread and turn the dial to burnt.

Donna was extraordinary. If only they were all like her. She ran me ragged all over Zacatecas. Like a bulldog on a short rib, she would not let go of any lead. I got Roberto's brothers to open up about how their father had been in *el gabacho* when he was born and constantly taunted him by denying that he was his son. To emphasize the point, he systematically beat the crap out of Roberto. (If anyone deserves the death penalty, it's usually the father.) I found a beatific nun, a woman whose faith was so palpable that an aura of light surrounded her, like those images of the rays emanating from the Virgin of Guadalupe. She had given Roberto classes in Bible studies when he was seven, and she told the jury she was sure he'd had a calling.

I found a Mexican criminologist who testified about the murders committed by policemen in Zacatecas, and the mistrust nearly everyone in the state felt toward them. I got the hospital records from when he fell off the roof as a seven-year-old and busted his head open. A bunch of his schoolmates testified that he lost consciousness after banging his conk against the goalpost in a soccer match. Goal: Donna found a doctor who swore before the jury that his behavior was consistent with frontal-lobe brain damage.

They gave him life without parole. He will be in jail until he dies, no matter how many years. But the state didn't kill him. In this business that's victory.

"When Durex did an international study about sexual satisfaction," said Mandarino, "Mexican women said they were the most unfulfilled and disappointed on the planet." Apparently there were other things to talk about besides Walter Benjamin. "They are more miserable than Chinese women who bend over for five minutes in a rice paddy. They are worse off than women in Finland, for whom a fuck only means a respite from seventeen hours of darkness. Eskimo women are blissfully happy compared to ours, and all they do with their men is rub noses. We are so rotten in bed that we even have to call in reserves from other countries. We had to get Richard over there to come and help us out."

There is no death penalty in Mexico. (In truth, there is no need; in this country people settle their scores with each other on the street in broad daylight.) So my work was only an abstraction to these guys, who saw me first and foremost as a failed writer, someone who published a couple of books that had something to do with Mexico a long time ago, and then dried up. I was their gringo mascot.

Trying to sound casual, Mandarino said, "I think our dear Richard fucked Victoria Díaz last Tuesday." There had been a party. He didn't like that she liked me. "I bet you got an incredible blow job, right, Richard?"

"That's your fantasy," I said. "We just flirted a little bit."

Lola arrived and took Mandarino's right hand in both of hers: the cocaine delivery system, each gram folded inside a tiny piece of paper.

"I've been waiting for you forever," I said, holding up my empty shot glass. "Could you please make it a double this time?"

"Why not, *mi amor*?" she said, running her fingers through my curly hair. "Anything I have is yours." As she took the drink orders for the rest of the table, a woman walked into Mi Oficina. Somewhere in her twenties, because of her diminutive stature, she looked about twelve. She had fetching bangs, huge eyes, and wore patterned black tights under a miniskirt. She went straight for Mandarino and gave him a hug.

"This is Olivia, gentlemen," he said, a proprietary arm around her slender waist. "Where have you been, *mi vida*?" he asked. "I've had to suffer the company of these brutes for hours waiting for you." And to us: "I gave a workshop at the School for Dynamic Writers and Olivia was by far my most gifted student. One of these days I might even get around to reading something she's written."

Lola pulled up a chair for Olivia and set it in between Mandarino and me. She merely nodded when I introduced myself, preferring to engage in obligatory banter with her teacher and the other writers. In Mexico City, there are poor benighted women who like writers. Most have ambitions of writing a book themselves, which if it ever gets published will be one of those books read halfway to the finish line by fifty or a hundred people. Some of them might even read the other half the following year.

Armando from Culiacán asked her what she was working on. "My first book is about to come out," she said, her eyes alight. "It's a book of essays about Cinderella." There is something jarring about a grown woman who looks like a child writing essays about a fairy tale; no doubt Olivia understood this. "I describe the differences between each adaptation: Perrault, the Brothers Grimm, the Disney version." She was losing him but knew how to reel him back. "And what they all have to do with contemporary sexuality and eroticism."

"Excellent," said Armando, having heard only the last three words.

A half hour later, after her conversations with the others ran out of gas, she turned to me and asked, "Are you a writer too?"

I pursed my lips and shook my head.

"Thank God," she said, having co-opted some of Mandarino's cynicism. "The last thing the world needs is another one of us. What do you do?"

Most people can describe their work in three words or less. I had to take a deep breath before I let you have it. After, most of the time I had to listen to your position about the death penalty. There were only three: yes, no, and maybe, under certain circumstances. Everyone stated these opinions as if they were the first to have considered them.

In the U.S., I tried to avoid those conversations. Sometimes I told people I was a driving instructor, just because it is such a boring job and, as such, people changed the subject as soon as I'd declared it. However, in Mexico, talking about my work had its advantages. I looked at Olivia's eyes with their hopelessly long lashes and conjured a vision of how the night could end. "I try to save people's lives," I said. Her brow wrinkled. "Don't worry, I'm not a priest."

"You're a doctor."

"Not even vaguely." I took that deep breath and told her about how I tried to stop her countrymen, one poor devil at a time, from being injected with toxic poisons in U.S. prisons. How I traveled from hellholes in Texas, Oklahoma, and Alabama to others in Michoacán, Chihuahua, and Durango to piece together the stories of their lives. Little by little she began to melt. I imagined waking up in the morning, her slender frame against mine, running my fingers along her ribs. I could have stared into those eyes for the rest of my life.

"Qué chido, güey," she finally uttered. "Thanks." She looked at me as if I were Mother Teresa of Calcutta.

When I started out as a mitigation specialist, I made sure to tell Mexicans that it was a job and I was paid to do it. I didn't want them to get the mistaken impression that I was Mother Teresa. Nonetheless, they would continue to look at me with admiring, watery eyes, and keep saying things like *"qué chido, güey"* in choked voices. And just as I came to understand that they wanted to believe I was a *licenciado*, even after I explained that I was not, I also realized they liked to imagine I was a saint. Far be it from me to disappoint them.

Olivia wet and then bit her lower lip. "That's sounds like a tough job," she said.

"It's a great job," I replied. "I get to go places and meet people I never would otherwise. And I am never, ever bored." I looked toward Lola and held up one finger.

MEDIA NARANJA

Before booking Esperanza in the Plaquegoula Parish jail, the police took away all of her possessions. Aside from the toiletries she can buy with what Catherine has put in her commissary, she has nothing. All she owns—all that they cannot take away from her—are her memories. In her mind they are in a constant orbit.

Lying on her cot, she recalls not knowing how to drive, but nonetheless once in a while finding herself behind the wheel of her brother Joaquín's pickup truck, a hacking black heap with flaming orange racing stripes that he picked up across the border. At first there is a terrible sensation of panic as the vehicle hobbles down the rocky, unpaved side streets of Puroaire, kicking up dust clouds in its wake. But as the truck climbs onto the blacktop highway leaving town, Esperanza's hands are on the steering wheel, tentative but confident, and she finds that she is driving. Smoothly, expertly; above all, inexplicably: no one has ever shown her how, and she is, after all, only twelve years old. Coasting along the road to who knows where, she is engulfed by feelings of accomplishment, confidence, and hope for the future. It has become a recurring dream, and always a disappointment to wake from it.

Now she remembers opening her eyes on a flattened cardboard box atop a dirt floor, her bony body covered by a flimsy fraying sheet and surrounded by a dozen others—brothers and sisters, cousins, relatives whose names she can't always remember—snoozing on their own cardboard rectangles. Her grandparents occupy the only bed in the room, a foam mattress above the sagging springs of a spindly cot. There is another tiny room where her parents sleep, so small that the lumpy mattress barely fits inside. The rasping thunder of her father's snore is loud enough to be heard through the whitewashed adobe wall. Her mother wheezes, her eyes pointed at the corrugated plastic ceiling.

Before climbing to her feet, Esperanza closes her eyes. Can she trick her consciousness into returning to that pickup truck? Or to the other dream that returns periodically, in which she falls from the top of an enormous banana palm high in the sky? This dream also begins with a panic, but as she plummets her plunge brakes to slow motion, as if she were coasting, even flying, to the ground, and she lands on her feet unhurt. Again, with a feeling of triumphant self-reliance. Once in a while the ruse of shutting her eyes works for a blessed few minutes of extra sleep. But if the roosters outside cawed with words, this morning they'd be saying, *Not today, not today.* Esperanza's eyes adjust to the darkness and she looks up at the seven black crosses that occupy a high mantel overlooking the sleeping family, then at the wooden statue of the Virgin of Guadalupe and the towel with the picture of the Last Supper adorning the wall.

In battered plastic flip-flops, an enormous sweatshirt that was a gift from a neighbor after her husband left her, and pajama pants that have been handed down so many times they are threadbare, Esperanza sleepwalks down the dirt alley behind the house on the way to the latrine, passing the pen where a couple of pigs are being fattened for the market (one snorts as she walks by), stepping over the hose that serves as the family's outdoor shower. The stench of the toilet is overpowering. Once, Esperanza made a comment to her mother, Consuelo, about how badly it smelled. Consuelo replied that it was better than having to walk to the woods to fulfill their necessities, which the family had to do before Esperanza was born.

She breathes through her mouth as she enters the cinder block cubicle, lowers her pajama pants, and squats over the seatless commode. When she finishes, she fills a pail with water to rinse out the toilet; the flush handle is mere decoration. One of the advantages to getting up before everyone else is that Esperanza has no competition for the privilege of the fetid privy.

She makes her way to the narrow kitchen—more dirt floor, wood slats instead of cinder block walls, a thatched roof—and washes her hands. With a plastic cigarette lighter, she sets afire the split wood and kindling she placed in the hollow of the adobe stove the night before. Atop the metallic grate, she balances the pot of beans that have been soaking in water since the previous night. She salts the beans, which will be ready in an hour or so when the rest of the family wakes up. This moment, when suffocating woodsmoke begins to fill the kitchen, is the only time Esperanza has to herself in the house. After the rest of the family wakes, its members will wend their way to the toilet, to the screeching song of the *chachalacas* in the trees and the honking of the pigs. Esperanza sits, resting an elbow on the table, which is covered in red plastic so old it is cracking. She feels an itch and sees a small colony of tiny ants crawling around her arm. Had she forgotten to clean the table the previous night? It doesn't matter. The ants come and go without regard to her ministrations. She wipes the table with a wet rag and they provisionally vanish.

Behind the ancient clay cooking pots she has left a paperback book, its frail parchment wrinkled from having been left out in the rain. It's a square comic left behind by her brother Bernardo before he went off to *el gabacho*, whose protagonist, El Cholo, is a heavily muscled, shaven-headed tough with a black Pancho Villa moustache and a scorpion tattoo on his neck. El Cholo was born in *los States*, to Mexican parents, and easily passes across both sides of the border. He gets by dealing drugs to the gringos, whose ingestion of them is as renowned as it is ravenous, and spends much of his time dispatching his rivals with a submachine gun. If he's caught without his weapon, he'll take care of them with whatever is at hand—a baseball bat, a bread knife, a tire iron, his bare arms.

El Cholo has Carmencita, a beautiful wife in California, but when he is in Mexico and he's not fighting criminals, he is often seen in the comic's panels entangled with other women, all of whom have cascading hair, voluminous hips, projectile bosoms, and tiny waists. In most of the images, he wears no shirt, the better to show off his wide shoulders, broad back, muscled hairless chest, and brawny biceps. From time to time Esperanza has pondered what it would be like to be overpowered by a body like El Cholo's. Her sexual experience is nil; the thought is an abstraction. No one in Puroaire looks like the characters in the comic. Adults are short and brown. A few men manage to stay slim, but most of them develop potbellies early on. The women have children young and the spread of their bodies is all but inevitable. If you are slender, like her mother, Consuelo, it's an indication of ill health.

Esperanza knows it is a stupid book, but it's the only one in the house, and as such she has read it countless times. When she was in primary school, her teacher, *la señorita* Ana, complimented her for her reading skills and told her to ask her mother for books. Consuelo asked her daughter from where she thought the money for books was supposed to come. Any available cash was needed to feed all those bodies sleeping on top of the cardboard in the other room.

Soon her mother will wake up and Esperanza will pour boiling water into a cup, retrieve the jar of Nescafé from its hiding place behind the pots, and stir in half a teaspoon. The coffee and one cigarette are Consuelo's two daily indulgences, enjoyed before the rest of the family awakens. Esperanza will watch her mother ingest the steaming acrid drink and position the tobacco between the wrinkled lips of a mouth missing its upper front teeth. They are supposed to be pleasures, but Consuelo never looks happy as she inhales the missile and sips from the cup. In fact, she appears to suffer as she indulges in the supposed treats. Her wheeze is semipermanent, a consequence not just of the daily tobacco but the constant inhalation of woodsmoke as she cooks.

Her husband would wallop her if he knew that she spends a precious peso per day to buy the cigarette, a loose single dispensed from an orange-painted street stall whose owner also sells candy, Kleenex, and chewing gum. It would make no difference to him that it is Consuelo's peso, earned from washing and ironing the neighbors' clothes, or money sent to her from their sons in *los States*.

Esperanza remembers being woken from sleep the previous night by Consuelo's muffled screams after her father came home. Everyone else pretended to sleep. They argued but it didn't sound like he was beating her, which still happens periodically despite their advanced age. Esperanza would like to get up and defend her mother, but what could she do? She is a skinny twelve-year-old, small for her age. The elder brothers and cousins who remain at home do not interfere. Esperanza is terrified of her father's violence, even if it does not flare up as often as it used to when she was little. She remembers he broke a chair once, and several times threw plates of food that displeased him. Periodically he would knock Consuelo to the ground and kick her. One of Esperanza's earliest memories is of hearing her sister María Concepción scream as she ran into the kitchen. She clutched her curly black hair, her hands and arms dripping with blood.

After sharing the beans with her family, Esperanza will walk for twenty minutes in her cracked flip-flops over hills and craters of mud and rocks until she gets to the two paved streets at the center of Puroaire and arrives at the secondary school. She still thinks about *la señorita* Ana, and remembers how she told her she should stay in school and maybe one day could be a teacher herself. *La señorita* Ana wears eyeglasses, is short and shapely, and has cream-colored skin, her hair dyed auburn and worn in a flip. She was Esperanza's favorite teacher. Esperanza likes children and thinks it would be fantastic to be a teacher, but how? Joaquín and Bernardo send money from *el otro lado* but it's never enough. María Concepción left for Morelia but isn't earning sufficiently to send any money home.

Children in Puroaire are supposed to finish secondary school (it's the law), but not all of them take the trouble. As soon as she graduates—if not before—Esperanza will probably have to go to work to help the family. She cannot yet figure out what she will do. Only boys shine shoes in the square or sell chewing gum at the traffic intersections, like her older brothers used to do when they were still toddlers. Maybe she can carry people's parcels home from the market, if they are not too heavy. She can always babysit. Consuelo said she would teach her to sew and iron.

On her way to school a song invades Esperanza's mind. It is being played so relentlessly on the radio, on jukeboxes, on TV, streaming out of neighbors' windows as you walk down the street, that it has been embedded in the brain of every budding adolescent in Puroaire, indeed in all of Mexico, from the border with *el gabacho* to the other with Guatemala.

*I touched the moon, thanks to you....*A few days ago she was sent to the store to buy a hundred grams of lentils, and stopped to watch the video of the song broadcast on the television above the cash register. Esperanza likes it when her mother sends her to the store to pick up something because of the opportunity to watch for a few minutes. There is a television at home but its picture is grainy, and her family talks while the TV is on so you can never really concentrate. The video captivated her.

*Maybe my carnation-red mouth brought you here, clean as the April rain....*The song is intoned by a lovely person with the budding body of a very young woman but the blameless expression of a child, honey hair to her shoulders, eyes as wide as ten-peso pieces and the color of the sky after that rainfall she sings about. She has an adorable smile—a little overbite and perfect white teeth—and skin the color of a white peach. And her own room and a green telephone and a closetful of clothes with which her two girlfriends, her handmaidens, dress her for the lover who made her touch the moon.

Those clothes. The singer wears a dozen different outfits in the course of three minutes. She wears what the characters on soap operas wear, what Esperanza imagines you can find in the stores if you go to Morelia or Guadalajara or Mexico City....plaid shirts and baggy jeans (not just blue, but white and orange and even striped), a red velvet vest left unbuttoned, a baggy black shirt that the singer ties around her silky, level midriff. Brand-new sneakers and thick socks almost blinding in their whiteness.

You, my complement, my media naranja, *I love you, without saying a single word, if this isn't a dream, you are my other half.* At the end of the song the actual lover appears—a slender person neither boy nor man but as nubile as the singer—with a timid expression. His black hair, held in place with gel, contrasts with his pale skin. He wears a black shirt unbuttoned, a white T-shirt underneath. Hanging from his trim frame are a pair of jeans pale not from a hundred washings but because they came that way from the store, complete with an upside-down triangle on the back pocket.

He caresses her hand and her wrist before they take off in a black convertible at the end of the video. It's anyone's guess where they are going, but everyone knows that they are off to cement the act that underpins the message of every teenage video: that innocence is the most highly overrated of supposed virtues in human history.

Esperanza often finds herself singing "Media Naranja" on her way to school. The songs that stream from the windows are a clue that life holds possibilities as yet invisible to her. Will their potential be fulfilled? Or are they merely dreams, like the one in which she drives a truck?

ALL THIS

The call came at about six thirty in the afternoon. I was in my hotel room taking a nap and luckily not in a cantina, where I wouldn't have heard the cell phone's discreet purr.

"I just wanted to see how you were doing," she said.

I'd hoped she would call. *Come to papa,* I thought. "I'm fine," I said. "How about you, María? Everything okay?"

She paused for a long time. I imagined her as a pink snapper, circling curiously around a minnow baited to a fishhook. Finally she said, "I want you to meet me in church tomorrow."

That was a new one. "I can do that. Which church?"

"La Basílica de Nuestra Virgen de la Soledad." It was close to downtown, where I was staying. "Can you be there at five in the afternoon?"

"Of course," I said.

"We're going to pray together."

"Yes." There's a first time for everything. A witness had never before made such an indecorous proposition. But at a hundred dollars an hour, I would have rendezvoused with her at the Vatican.

I first met María Concepción earlier that day, in a tiny box of a house in Altos de Mofongo, in the misery belt on the farthest outskirts of the city. Her mother lived there, along with her sister Marta and her brother Bernardo. María Concepción lived nearby with her own family. The community, one unpainted cracker box after another, had sprung up in the last ten or fifteen years, to accommodate people fleeing the poverty and violence of the *ranchos,* villages, and towns in Tierra Caliente.

The house smelled of dust. There were a couple of small windows just for show; no sunlight came through. In the center of the living room, an unvarnished wooden table and six chairs. Dishes and cups piled atop a dresser. A calendar with a picture of the Virgin of Guadalupe.

I explained who I was, that I was trying to help Esperanza, and, so that I could keep track of who told me what, that I wanted to speak to each of them individually. This was not the absolute truth. I liked to talk to people one by one in the hope that by themselves they would speak more freely than they would if they were talking in front of others. In any case, I said, whatever they told me would be in the strictest confidence, only to be shared with Esperanza's lawyers. I never repeated to any family member what the others had told me.

However, as there were only three small rooms in the house, privacy was impossible. I asked who would like to speak first, and Bernardo volunteered. Consuelo was so tiny and frail that Marta and María Concepción practically carried her into the bedroom, without even bothering to shut the door. Even if they weren't listening to Bernardo and me—fat chance—there was no way they couldn't hear us.

Bernardo was heavily muscled and shaven-headed, with a tattoo of a skull in a sombrero on his forearm. Clearly a hard case, but with sad, exhausted eyes and an incipient potbelly. He wore a T-shirt and tattered khakis. His heavily accented English was a good sign: his mother and sisters probably wouldn't understand. "I spent almost twenty years in *el gabacho* until they deported me back here," he said.

"Tell me about Puroaire, Bernardo," I said. "What was it like when you were a kid?"

"First, tell me about Esperanza. Have they got her in County? What kind of a bargain can you get for her? Do they do splits in Louisiana? Can you get her a two-for-one?"

He was trying to impress me with his knowledge of the criminal justice system, no doubt picked up from a scratch-ass Legal Eagle in the next cell in jail, where Bernardo had done most of his sightseeing in the U.S. "I wish I could answer you," I said. "But we have to take it one step at a time. Right now, all I am trying to do is to help convince the state to take the death penalty off the table. If we accomplish that, then we can look at other possibilities."

He looked me in the eye. "Can you do it?"

The standard response: "Some things are in God's hands. But Esperanza has very good lawyers. They're doing everything they possibly can."

He nodded at the floor.

"Where did you do your time?" I asked.

"Cook County," he said in a small voice that gave me goose pimples. "And Menard State." He might as well have said "Buchenwald" or "the white hell of Pitz Palu."

It had been a drug thing. When they let Bernardo out of jail, Illinois state marshals escorted him to the airport with a one-way ticket home, paid for by Mexico's foreign ministry. Now he worked as the night watchman in a car dealership in the prosperous part of Morelia, where the politicians and the narcos lived.

He gave me some good material about how the other kids laughed at him and his brother Joaquín because they wore hand-me-downs and sometimes had no shoes. How they began to work almost as soon as they could walk, carrying packages home from the market for housewives, shining shoes, selling Chiclets in the town square. He didn't have much to say about Esperanza. When he left to cross the Rio Grande, she was still a little girl.

Marta was thin and wore too much makeup, a turtleneck sweater and polyester pants. She answered phones in an office, a tremendous step up from her unpromising beginnings. Yet even though she was only about my age, her face had set into a bitter mask. Gravity pulled the corners of her mouth toward the ground. Joaquín had told me that their father had been particularly rough with her.

When possible, I avoid leading the witness, or at least try to do it subtly. "You have all those brothers and sisters," I said. "How did your father maintain discipline in the home?"

She looked at me crosswise and shrugged. "He was very easygoing," she said.

"All parents sometimes get impatient with their kids," I suggested.

"Not mine."

"Even if you misbehaved?"

She gave me a look that said, *You're being intrusive, even insolent.* Which, of course, I was. "We never misbehaved."

"Tell me about your father."

"He's good people," she said. "He did everything he could for us. He worked very hard." She began to describe a being with the combined qualities of Saint Francis of Assisi, Mahatma Gandhi, and Santa Claus. This was so at odds with what Joaquín and their sister Elena in Puroaire had told me that I was close to speechless. It was more important to protect that bastard's honor than to save her sister's life. I began to hate Marta.

Until she began to describe growing up hungry. "When you went to school in the morning," I asked, "had you already eaten breakfast?"

"Sometimes. A little. Usually we ate when we came home."

"That must have been rough, trying to concentrate on math and history on an empty stomach."

She exhaled, shaking her head. "There were so many of us. We ate every day but there was hardly anything. Sometimes just beans," she said. "Or tortillas."

"Those days when there were only tortillas, Marta. How many were there for each of you?"

"Sometimes we had to divide them in two. Sometimes in four." She looked toward the bedroom where Consuelo waited with the others. "Sometimes my mother wouldn't eat anything at all, just so there would be a little more for us. It hurt my stomach to eat those beans when she ate nothing." Tears came to her eyes. "I remember times that I asked for something, anything to eat. She would say, 'How can I give you something when there's nothing to give?'"

I kept my mouth shut as she cried. You want to let them go the distance. There might be more details on the way. And this time, there were. In a voice barely above a whisper, Marta told me about the rain falling through the holes in the ceiling. Meals of cactus and *quelites* that grew wild in the woods. Her mother going door-to-door begging from the neighbors. The rotting fruit scavenged at the end of the day from the market. And the candy bar her father had brought home one day. When she opened the package there were more worms than chocolate.

"You have to understand," she whispered, and then seemed at a loss for words.

"Understand what, Marta?" I asked.

"When I was growing up, we didn't have all this." She gestured around the living room.

All this. A concrete bunker. A matchbox. A mousehole. But it was a mousehole with a cement floor. And a toilet that flushed. With windows instead of sheets of plastic, doors with knobs that actually shut. A mousehole in which she slept on a bed with a mattress, a sheet, and a blanket, no matter if it was alongside her mother, and so close to her brother on the living room couch that she could hear him breathe. At least she didn't have to share the space with insect colonies or barnyard animals.

Consuelo was tiny, fragile, wrapped in multiple sweaters and wheezing through a wrinkled gnome's face. She had no front teeth. Although only seventy-one, she looked ninety, with one foot through death's door. She answered my questions in vague, distracted monosyllables. I wondered whether senility had set in, or if she simply denied what she'd prefer not to recall. We weren't getting anywhere. You needed patience and a willingness to visit multiple times. I would have to try to see each of them alone, either outside the house or when no one else was around. After a few minutes, I thanked her for her time.

"Joven," she murmured in a tiny voice. Young man. Suddenly she looked at me with intention and leaned forward.

Maybe there was something she needed to say. Urgently, before her Timex stopped ticking. Something she didn't want her children to hear. "Yes?" I said, leaning toward her.

She whispered, "Have you got a cigarette?"

In the house, I noticed María Concepción staring at me through the bedroom door while I talked to the others: her plump dark face, the eyeglasses with the tilted plastic frames, her hair pulled back in a braid. Yet when she moved into the living room, she didn't say anything that her brothers and sisters hadn't already told me.

And there she was the next day, on her knees in a hoodie and sweatpants, in a pew in front of an elaborate seventeenth-century altar. In the baroque style, it was made of wood trimmed in gilt, about forty feet high, with a statue of Christ at the top and the Virgin in the middle, surrounded by dozens of carvings of angels and saints. All that gold was magnificent, a monument to how much the Spaniards were willing to spend to dazzle the locals into servitude. To the right, there was a mural with a panorama of monks in brown robes and with bald spots, surrounding the baby Jesus.

We were the only ones in the church, except for an old man in a white straw cap, taking his siesta in another pew. Why were we alone? I wondered. Wasn't this place in the tourist guidebooks? I guessed that visitors would all be in the cathedral in the central plaza, the one with the famous pipe organ.

I didn't want to interrupt María Concepción's prayers, so I sat in a pew a few rows back. I was determined to enjoy the stolen moment. I was happy inside that peaceful empty church. The shining gold on the altar, the streaming sunlight from the stained-glass window, the plaintive eyes on the statue of the Virgin—even if you're not a believer, you're going to feel some sense of tranquillity and serenity. I wondered about White Cap. I imagined him coming here for his nap every day after a late breakfast. If I lived here, I might join him.

When she finished, María Concepción said, "Let's go outside." There was a shady courtyard next to the chapel, away from the street. It was almost as peaceful as inside the church. We sat on a bench across from a stone fountain. "My family doesn't want to say anything," she said. "There is a lot that they don't want to remember. But if it can help my sister, there are some things I have to tell you."

I made it clear that I was all ears.

"I was fifteen years old. I had been working for a señora. I cleaned, cooked, washed and ironed the clothes. One night she made me stay late because some people came for dinner. She wanted me to serve and wash the dishes after. I hated to go home late at night. It was the other side of town and most of the streets were completely dark. The farther away you got from the center, the more you were surrounded by vacant lots.

"There were three of them. The Mendiola brothers. Everyone in Puroaire was afraid of them. One of them grabbed me from behind and clapped his hand over my mouth so I couldn't scream.

"I didn't tell my parents. When I got home my father had been drinking and he was furious that I came home so late. He wore a thick brown belt that he used more for beating us than to hold up his pants. He chased me around the living room, even though the whole family was sleeping on the floor. I don't know how many people we stepped on, but no one made a sound. Finally he cornered me in the kitchen and let me have it. It might have been on purpose or a mistake because he was drunk, but he was hitting me with the side of the belt with the buckle. The next day my back was covered in welts. After he hit me in the head, I grabbed my hair, and I think he only stopped because he saw the blood run down my hands and arms. No one tried to stop him. No one even said a word. Except for Esperanza, who ran into the kitchen and watched. She cried for him to stop. I don't know if she would remember. She was just a little girl, maybe three or four.

"After a few months it became obvious that I was pregnant. When he found out he locked me in the closet. He made me stay there until I gave birth. He would only let me out when he was drunk, to beat me and tell me I was a whore. When he was working in the fields my mother would let me out to give me some food and use the bathroom. After José, my first child, was born, my father threw us out. He said he wouldn't shelter sluts and bastards. I stayed for a little while with one of my mother's sisters, and then I came here. I was the first in the family to come to Morelia. Esperanza stayed with me for a while, and then my mother and Marta when they couldn't stand living with him any longer. Bernardo came when he got out of jail."

By the time she got to this part of the story she was weeping. The tears streamed from under her eyeglasses and her shoulders trembled. This is one of the trickiest parts of the job. I ask people to remember precisely what they would most dearly wish to forget, to relive the worst experiences of their lives as if they happened the day before. I am not made of stone. I reached into my pocket looking for Kleenex, but she was crying so hard that it seemed like a ridiculously inadequate gesture. So I took her body into my arms and patted her back like a baby's. She sobbed into my shoulder.

Nevertheless. Hers was precisely the sort of story that could inspire a jury to save a client's life. Graham Greene once said, "There is a splinter of ice in the heart of a writer." You could say the same thing for a mitigation specialist. When I was working on my novels, I thought I understood what he meant, but in moments like these, the statement truly came home. Of course I felt terrible for María Concepción, but in my heart I was jubilant.

THE GIRL

Esperanza feels as if she is all gangly brown arms and legs in the uniform, a pale blue dress with short sleeves and a white lace apron sewn to the front. The señora explained that the dress, small for Esperanza's frame, belonged to the *muchacha* who worked for the family previously, but who one fine day, without so much as a smoke signal, disappeared from the face of the planet. The señora wondered out loud why they couldn't make them all the same size in a factory—not the uniforms, but the *muchachas*. She made the remark with a straight face. Hours later, Esperanza wondered if the señora might have been joking.

In the first few days of her employment, the señora would follow Esperanza around and emit a continuous monologue while the new girl made the beds, dusted the furniture, cooked, and washed dishes. The señora told her that it set her teeth on edge to think of the rudeness and lack of gratitude that propelled the previous girl to simply evaporate without even waving good-bye the day after payday. Commonly, she noted, *muchachas* are thought to be *la felicidad del hogar*, but in the señora's experience, most of them provoked more problems than they provided relief. However, she did say she considered herself lucky that, only a few days after the other girl flew the coop, a neighbor told her that María Concepción, who also cleaned houses, had a sixteen-year-old sister who was looking for work. At the time, Esperanza was fresh off the bus from the *rancho*.

She wakes up a little before six in the morning, so she can quickly wash her face, put on the pale blue dress, and prepare breakfast for the señora's three children before they go to school. Ten-year-old Julieta likes *huevos a la mexicana*, scrambled eggs with tomatoes and onions but minus the slivers of jalapeño, as her poor little palate is sensitive to chile. Next to the eggs, the *muchacha* spoons a dollop of refried beans—only a bit, because the señora has read about the epidemic of childhood obesity. She told Esperanza that she would rather shoot herself than be responsible for fat progeny. Alejandro, eight, likes his eggs scrambled with ham, along with packaged white bread, toasted with the crusts removed and cut into triangles, with the beans spread on top. Little Amanda would staple her lips together before touching a scrambled egg, so Esperanza slices up papaya, cantaloupe, and pineapple and serves them to her with yogurt and granola. For the whole family, she heats sweet rolls and serves them in a basket under a cloth that keeps them warm.

The señora likes tortillas toasted dry in a frying pan (she told Esperanza that they contain only fifty calories each—according to the advertisement, the same as half a pear), accompanied by a drink with cactus, apple, watercress, and a tablespoon of sugar mixed in a blender with water. When the señor comes downstairs, dressed for work in a suit and tie, he asks Esperanza to prepare whichever breakfast his whim dictates.

One morning, at the table, the señora tried to convince him to make the girl's life a little easier by having the same breakfast every day. He answered that, since he pays the bills, when he wakes up in the morning he'll eat *lo que se le hinchan los huevos*. Esperanza was so embarrassed by the coarse remark that she would have liked the earth to open up and swallow her.

After he left for work, the señora told Esperanza that her husband thinks her life is easy, but he doesn't realize the incredible amount of work and all the attendant anguish that is involved in running a household. For example, she mentioned that in these first days she'd had to teach Esperanza how to use the stove and the blender. You'd think that in the *rancho* where she came from they're still foraging for berries and killing oxen with arrows! The señora opined that she thinks the girls should pay *her* for teaching them how to use appliances; it would stand them in good stead later when they got married. But she complimented Esperanza for picking up her lessons quickly and keeping the kitchen immaculately clean.

Esperanza notices that when the señora talks to her husband, he has an expression on his face like a TV that's been turned off. She told Esperanza that at least Dr. Figueroa understands her and prescribes antianxiety medication. Esperanza tries not to notice when the señor stares at her legs while she reaches for dishes in the cabinets, or at her chest—the other girl's uniform is too tight across her breasts.

On her third day, the señora sent Esperanza to the corner store to pick up a liter of milk and a pack of Marlboros, stressing that she must count the coins carefully to make sure she has been given the correct change and to bring the receipt. Esperanza passed the test, but the señora accompanies her to the market twice on her first week.

The señora explained that, although she can order groceries to be delivered from the supermarket, the fruits and vegetables are fresher in the market. However, the vendors in the market think this is still the era of the Aztecs and they don't give receipts. The señora told Esperanza that she made the previous girl bring a notebook and write down how much she spent on tomatoes, how much for bananas, how much for onions, and so on. The señora would do the math to make sure it all added up. Just to make sure the *muchacha* was giving her a legitimate accounting—and not adding a couple of pesos to each item and pocketing the difference—the señora would accompany the girl to the market every once in a while and make it clear she knew the price of a kilo of mangoes or a bunch of asparagus. Would Esperanza be able to handle a trip to the market herself? the señora wondered out loud. Esperanza was terrified that her math skills would fall short.

When the señora drives the kids to school, Esperanza washes the clothes in the machine and then climbs the stairs to the roof of the house, where she hangs them up to dry on clotheslines. The next day she can do the sheets and pillowcases. While the clothes are drying, the señora will supervise the girl as she cooks lunch for the children, which they eat when they come home from school at two.

Why has God plagued her with offspring with such distinct tastes? the señora wonders. Julieta likes tortilla soup, but Alex won't touch it—it's got to be chicken soup (but without any chicken in it! only vegetables) or nothing. Amanda likes tomato soup from a can or *sopa de letras* from a package. Sometimes the señora thinks she should be in the restaurant business. She compliments Esperanza for learning so quickly how to make various dishes. Her food has *sazón*, says the señora, which gives Esperanza a sense of relief, until she adds that it's never as tasty as it would be if she were to make it herself. Unfortunately, she laments, one person can't do everything.

Esperanza had been working in the house only a few days when, from the kitchen, she spied the señora deliberately spilling some of her Diet Coke on the coffee table, after she had already cleaned it. As soon as the señora left the room, she wiped the spill clean. Similarly, the señora has dirtied ashtrays, left lipstick-stained Kleenex on otherwise immaculate surfaces, and strategically placed dirty laundry on the bathroom floor. Esperanza cleaned them, threw them away, placed them in the hamper where they belonged. She believes that these are tests the señora is administering, to make sure she is conscientious about the job.

After the children have finished their lunch, the señora will leave them under the girl's supervision for a few hours while she goes to the gym or meets her friends. She tells Esperanza that when she gets together with her *amigas*, they go to the shopping center and have a couple of drinks or a dessert (she allows herself these indulgences as she usually skips lunch) at the restaurant with the hanging plants and picture windows. When she returns home, sometimes she shows Esperanza a scarf or a skirt that she bought, or lets her smell the sample of the new Dior perfume, or shows her the cream that supposedly makes the bags under your eyes disappear. She tells Esperanza she should thank God that her skin is so smooth and enjoy it while she is young—soon enough, she'll have the same kind of trouble with wrinkles that the señora does. The girl polishes silver or wipes dust off the furniture, until the señor comes home and she prepares a supper for the couple.

Esperanza can tell that once, while she was cleaning or washing clothes, the señora went into her room behind the kitchen. Esperanza lives out of a vinyl bag—there is no closet—but the room is so small that the señora would have had to crouch in a corner in order to open it and examine its contents. What is there to look over? A few T-shirts and two blouses with collars, a couple of sweaters for the cold, some jeans. One skirt, socks, a couple of bras, five pairs of panties, white or pale blue and conventionally cut.

The señora has also made encouraging remarks to Esperanza about how she answers the phone correctly (*"la casa de los Sánchez Rodríguez"*) and leaves messages on the notepad hanging from the refrigerator door. Her spelling is far from perfect, the señora notes, but at least she can jot something down on the paper. The last girl was hopeless—practically illiterate, it was impossible to understand her writing, and she never remembered who had called, even a half hour later.

Esperanza is speechless when the señora confesses that she is jealous of her. "No, really," she says, "you *muchachas* live rent-free and all your meals are provided." No one's life is perfect, but the señora believes that the *muchachas* have a carefree existence, gliding through their days without having to worry about food or mortgages. If Esperanza only knew how traumatic and stressful it is to run a household like hers!

The previous evening, while the señores were having dinner, the señor mentioned that he liked the *milanesas* and the pureed potatoes that Esperanza prepared, and asked for a second cutlet. Esperanza heard the señora smashing out her cigarette in the ashtray and could imagine the way the señor was looking at her.

The following day, to Esperanza's surprise, the señora brings her a uniform that fits a lot better than the one that belonged to the previous *muchacha*. In fact, it is a relief that it is too large and hides her figure. Her days are long in the household, and by nightfall, when she finally washes the dishes of the señora and her husband's dinner, she takes a shower and sprawls on her narrow bed. She is glad that she doesn't have to depend on anyone and is earning her own money. Or will be, whenever the señora gets around to paying her.

INDEPENDENCE DAY

She said her name was Rosana. When I asked if she wouldn't mind wiping off her lipstick, she looked at me as if I were a pervert. "Why?" she asked.

"Because I want to kiss you," I said.

She smiled with relief as she reached for the roll of toilet paper. I wasn't a deviant. I wouldn't try to cut her throat. I was just a bit sentimental. "No one's ever asked me for that before," she said.

Could it be true? How could a man look at that face, the eager black eyes with the long lashes, the wavy hair, the high cheekbones, and especially the wide mouth, and not want to kiss her? She was young, but not a child. "How long have you been working here?" I whispered.

"Just a couple of weeks," she said, as if she were unsure whether the revelation would disappoint.

Moving the threadbare spread out of the way, we sat on the bed. Rosana wore a cheap baby doll made from a smooth black synthetic trimmed in flouncy lace. It was too big for her, and didn't so much reveal her body as leave it a mystery. I took her in my arms. She gave me tiny kisses, like you would give to a baby. I put my hands on either side of her face and gave her a longer, although similarly gentle, kiss. "You drank before you came here," she said, with an accusatory laugh. "To give you courage." How cheeky. Is that why I drank? I would have said I'd gone to the cantina because I was happy, because I was satisfied with the day's work, because María Concepción had been kind and brave enough to share painful memories.

I liked being at liberty, finished with the day's duties. With nothing left to accomplish, I would take the bus back to Mexico City in the morning. But there was still the night. In a one-horse town I would have had to content myself with a book or the hotel room's TV set.

But Morelia was the state capital, a colonial city with a population of more than half a million. And its attendant temptations. The cantina, practically empty, had walls painted a glossy institutional green, decorated with photos of Pancho Villa. You see his picture in so many cantinas in the provinces. What could he possibly mean anymore? What kind of revolution does a Mexican dream of these days? In the front pages, on TV, in whispered warnings, Mexicans are constantly reminded of weapons, but today they are AK-47s, not the Winchester repeaters and bandoliers of bullets draped across their chests with which Villa and his band conquered so much of the country by 1914. The bartender was gruff and unsmiling, but by the time I ordered my third drink, the rest of the patrons had gone and he became friendly. Ultimately he suggested I go four blocks south, make a left at the corner, knock on the green door with the two-way mirror.

Stripped of the baby doll Rosana was busty, but thin enough that you could count her ribs. I ran my fingertips along the bones. Her skin was soft as a pillow and the color of walnut shells. I exhaled warm breath from my nostrils along the back of her neck. "You're so tender," she said. She let me give her a real kiss and returned it. I tried to lose myself in her skin, touching, smelling, tasting the sweet, the dry, the moist, and the acrid of her body. After I got a rhythm on, she seemed to enjoy herself, or at least to put on a good show of it. She dug her nails into my shoulder and held on to me as if afraid she was going to fall, whispering, "*Sí, papi,*" into my ear. Then she turned me on my back and took over, let me disappear inside her. For a fleeting moment it crossed my mind to ask her to marry me. I thought, *If the sex is this good, then we could somehow manage to find a way to work out everything else.*

I know what you're thinking. A loser. A saddy. A gringo. Who uses his economic privilege to take advantage of a vulnerable young woman (how old was she, anyway?) from a "developing country," a nation that offers women with no education, no money, and no connections a stinking series of options from which to choose. You know what? You're right. I won't even try to defend myself. All I would suggest is that after you have lived through as much death as

I have, to the point that death has become your way of life, after that, then come back and judge me. At that point, we might actually run into each other in the corridor of the same brothel, looking for some sensation to offset all that loss and despair, something that reminds us we are still alive.

Rosana left me alone in the room while I dressed: the musty carpet, the walls dejectedly naked, the wooden table with the roll of toilet paper and the baby wipes. I thought that I had chosen her because she was tall, and had wavy hair and a twinkle in her eye, but after she was gone, I realized that I'd picked her because of her similarity—the height, her hair, that mouth—to Esperanza. I shivered at the thought. Probably I'd considered marrying her because she reminded me of Esperanza; it had certainly never crossed my mind with a prostitute before. On the way out, I passed Rosana in the corridor gossiping with a couple of her colleagues. I smiled at her warmly. She nodded, glancing at me through dead eyes, as if we might possibly have met years ago.

I liked the feeling of well-being that alcohol, in the right measure, could inspire, the carefree fiction of readiness for anything the world might offer. But as much as I enjoyed drinking, I hated to get drunk. I couldn't stand the sloppy discomfort, the woozy loss of control. That night in Morelia I went a little too far. After what I considered a lovely encounter with Rosana, I wanted to erase her resemblance to Esperanza and her casual glance at me, the reminder that in truth we were strangers. I went to another cantina and had a few more. By the time I got to the Plaza de Armas, I was not roaring drunk, but my empty stomach and the neon lights of the fair made me dizzy.

There were hundreds of people in the plaza, many of them waving Mexican flags. The entryway to the cathedral with the famous pipe organ had been festooned with crepe paper the colors of the flag—red, green, and white. From tables covered with orange tarpaulins, they were selling *pambazos*, huge bread rolls dipped in guajillo chile sauce, stuffed with potatoes and sausage, and then fried in oil. There was a rickety merry-go-round and another ride in which they strapped children into little metal bullets that went around in circles. They went so fast that looking at them made me nauseated.

Some scaffolding had been set outside the cathedral, with a platform on top. A bunch of bureaucrats, male and female, listened to a man make a speech. It was about eleven, and I realized it was September 15, the night that Independence Day is celebrated in Mexico.

The man on the platform was making the traditional speech, known as the Cry of Dolores, supposedly similar to the one shouted in 1810 by a skinny, bald-headed priest named Miguel Hidalgo. The padre's call declared the war of independence from Spain, and was uttered from the small town of Dolores in Guanajuato. On the night of September 15, in every plaza in every settlement in Mexico—from the one-burro *ranchos* to Mexico City—some pen pusher or another gets up and yells *"Viva México"* to the multitudes, about an hour before midnight. Everyone gets the day off on the sixteenth, which is the actual Independence Day.

The man making the speech was no doubt a big-timer, maybe the mayor or governor. His hair was slicked back and he had a bounteous mustache. He wore gray polyester pants, a shirt and tie, accented with a green windbreaker in an unconvincing bid to prove that he was, after all, a man of the people. His words, a politician's blather, came out as an undifferentiated jumble.

Instead of listening, I was thinking about the story María Concepción had told, and the doors it might open to save Esperanza. I remembered the first time I got a phone call from a paralegal telling me that a jury had sentenced a client to life without parole. He'd never leave jail but had been spared death. It was Roberto the cop killer—my first case. I had thought that he was unsalvageable, that those coldhearted cowboys from Harris County would squirt him with hot sauce, throw him over the coals, and barbecue him. The work of mitigation suddenly made perfect sense to me. If Roberto could be saved, then anyone had a chance. I was jubilant.

"Long live the heroes of the fatherland!" shouted the governor.

"Viva!" shouted the throng in response. The sounds of firecrackers and cherry bombs were a form of punctuation.

Helping to save Roberto's life gave me a sense of accomplishment I had never felt before. It was was as good as having my books published. It was as good as sex, maybe better. It was as good as when Carla, my wife, told me she was pregnant.

"Long live national independence!" screamed the pencil pusher.

"*Viva!*"

Death-penalty defense can be addictive. You help to save one. In your head you understand you can't save them all, but in your heart you begin to wonder: *How many?*

"*Viva México!*" shouted the politician.

"*Viva!*" we all shouted back. I am not a nationalist, and of course not even Mexican, but I was happy and screamed along with the flag-waving crowd.

"*Viva México!*" once again.

"*Viva!*"

Whoever gives the Cry of Dolores shouts "*Viva México*" three times. After we in the crowd gave our final "*Viva*" rejoinder, I heard the grenades explode.

At first I thought the detonations were part of the party, but then the plaza filled with smoke. People began to shriek from terror rather than joy. Much of the crowd ran away from the center of the plaza toward the periphery. As the smoke cleared, I saw a woman in a yellow sweater who clutched the spreading red stain on her side as she limped along. A bald-headed middle-aged man, who had somehow lost his pants, crawling on all fours, trailing blood. A woman shrieking next to a gory heap that may or may not have still breathed. In front of the platform, dozens of people helplessly kneeled next to, or stood over, the dead and the wounded. Many lay on the ground covered in blood.

The next day I would read in the paper that the grenades had been filled with shrapnel. Eight dead and a hundred wounded, some of whom lost eyes or limbs. Yet that night, amid the carnage, it didn't even occur to the bureaucrats on the platform that they might want to stray from the script. They continued the festivities and began to warble the Mexican national anthem. They were the only ones who sang. The rest of us were in a state of shock.

SIDEBAR

D.A. Undecided about Death Penalty for Baby Killer
Louisiana States Informer
January 25, 2009

MUGRERO—Esperanza Morales, 25, was charged with capital murder at the Plaquegoula Parish Courthouse Thursday. A statement from the district attorney alleged that the illegal alien, a Mexican national, brutally murdered her 11-month-old baby. Morales is being held without bond.

"Wednesday night a 25-year-old Mexican female stopped a squad car in Mugrero," Detective Victor Shepherd told reporters after the hearing. "It took us a while to figure out what was going on, because the person involved didn't speak good English." Police went to a predominantly Hispanic neighborhood near Interstate 22 and found the defendant with the lifeless body of her baby. The infant girl, named Yasenior, had multiple bruises, abrasions, lesions and burns on her face and body, and may have been beaten with "a blunt instrument of some kind," according to official sources. "We are still trying to determine what weapon was used to kill the infant," said Detective Shepherd. The medical examiner has not yet filed a report.

Although a conviction for capital murder can result in the death penalty, the district attorney has not yet made a decision whether to seek the ultimate punishment for the accused baby killer. "For the moment, all I am prepared to say is that we will consider the evidence and will come to a decision in due time," said Assistant District Attorney Sarah Pendleton. "However, given the cruelty and viciousness of the killing, we may quite possibly seek death. In Plaquegoula Parish we take crimes of a horrific nature with the utmost seriousness."

Defense attorney Catherine Crowley entered a plea of not guilty for Morales but declined to go into details about the death of the baby. She said that the defendant came to Louisiana in the wake of

Hurricane Katrina to participate in the cleanup. The lawyer said that thanks to Morales, as well as thousands of other Mexican nationals, the equivalent of thirty-four years of accumulated garbage was cleaned from the streets of New Orleans in the two years after the hurricane. Most of those Mexicans were illegal aliens, who had no permission to be in the United States.

---

9 Readers' Comments
View: Oldest first

Ibstrokinoff January 25, 11:05 am
Bring back old Smokey. Bitch kills a baby and they're still making up their minds about the death penalty? She deserves to fry. Might discourage the next greaser thinking about fricasseeing her children.

Our eyes on you January 25, 1:16 pm
Hang 'em high. In the town square. Use the same rope over and over until it breaks, it's cheaper that way.

Zipadeedoodah January 25, 3:22 pm
Where was the border patrol when this chic crossed the river? Why cant they stay in thier own country and kill thier own people on thier side? A bullet through the brain would be too good for this Mexican peace of crap.

Bob the slob January 25, 4:42 pm
They come in here illegal and get the same rights as we do. How come she's getting three hots and a cot for nothing while I go to work every day? WTF?

Billiam January 25, 5:46 pm
In this country, the law says she's innocent until proven guilty. If it wasn't for people like her south Louisiana would still be deluged in garbage.

Our eyes on you January 25, 6:15 pm
You mewling pinko commie crybaby. Why don't you join her in jail? You can wash her feet and make her chicken soup. They'll give it to you up the chute without the grease in there. Then maybe you'll wake up and smell the coffee.

Justmyopinion January 26, 6:08 am
The ten commandments says judge not lest ye be judged. I know it's tragic that a little baby girl will never get to get to eat a Happy Meal, go to her first prom, or have her daddy take her down the aisle to give her away. But her mom's where she should be, in the Grey Bar Hotel, and surely she'll get her just desserts.

Had Enuff Y'all? January 26, 8:17 am
All those stinking Mexcrements took thirty thousand jobs away from hard-working Americans by working cheaper than we do. This death could have been prevented with an electric fence across the whole border with Greaseland.

Sherlock Jr. January 29, 12:19 pm
The American people deserve everything they got. Wasn't the patriat act supposed to protect us? We got lied to after 911 when the boarders was supposed to be closed to all those Muslins that wanted to get us but they still open to all this baby killing scum from Mexico. You understand why I say this? I'm fed up with their lies and with the ignorance of the American people. Stupid is as stupid does, you get what I'm saying. Or how else would we end up with a black Muslin terrorist that was born in Egypt for a president.

PART TWO

Welcome to the Club

A HALF ORANGE
AMONG LEMONS

Esperanza has been working for the señora only a month before she goes downtown for the first time, and when she arrives at the Plaza de Armas she stops breathing. Nothing she has seen in Puroaire—not the adobe shacks and ramshackle houses, the concrete school with its peeling paint, the central square with its windowless town hall—prepares her for the magnificence of the cathedral. It is enormous, with matching baroque towers and a bulbous dome in between. "*Qué lindo,*" she says, and *qué lindo* she keeps repeating to Hilda, the maid in the house next door to where Esperanza works, who dragged her there on their Sunday off. Everything is *lindo*—the wrought-iron balconies and wood-framed windows of the government palace, the thick stone archways of the buildings around the plaza, the waving flags and wine-colored awnings of the pink sandstone Hotel Virrey de Mendoza, where tourists tuck into enchiladas at the tables of its sidewalk café. Echoing the owner of the house where she works, Hilda tells Esperanza that all of it was constructed in the seventeenth and eighteenth centuries. It is the first time in her life that Esperanza has seen a building worth admiring. Indeed, every structure she has seen before seems shabby in comparison.

Esperanza and Hilda are not the only *muchachas* downtown that Sunday. By the dozens they spill into Morelia from *pueblos* and *ranchos* all over the state to find work as maids. They step down from sagging second-class buses at the station, they clamber off the backs of turnip trucks, they arrive on foot from unpaved roads in plastic shoes. And once they settle into employment, they don't have many options for entertainment on their Sundays off.

Particularly Esperanza, who does not retain much of her earnings, which are by no means extravagant. When the señora remembers to

pay her at all, she gives Esperanza two thousand pesos a month. She
sends half to her mother back in Puroaire. With the remainder, she
can buy a pair of sneakers that say ABIBAS or NIKKE on the side, a polyester blouse or an acrylic sweater, or some new socks or underwear.
Or she could acquire a backpack or a handbag, or else some soap
and shampoo. She could go to a convenience store and buy some
minutes for her cell phone, so she can continue to send messages
back home, or to her sister María Concepción across town. What
she could never do—what would unquestionably define luxury for
her—would be to pay for all those things at once.

Three years later, Esperanza has not yet seen a movie. She would
like to go to a *cine* for once in her life (there are no movie theaters in
tiny Puroaire), but she couldn't justify squandering forty pesos on a
ticket, particularly when pirated DVDs of the same films are sold in
plastic envelopes by street vendors for ten. After she had worked in
the house for a year, the señora left a tiny television set in Esperanza's room, after it had been discarded by her youngest child. Maybe one day Esperanza will save up for a DVD player—the cheapest
one costs three hundred pesos. The family had one in Puroaire for a
while, until it broke.

Once she browsed in the book section at Sanborns and was
shocked that most of the paperbacks cost two hundred pesos or
more—what she keeps of a week's wages after sending money back
home. No wonder her mother looked at her like she was crazy when
she came home from school and asked for books.

Esperanza spends every other Sunday with María Concepción and
her husband, Juan Pablo, and their children, Pedro and Brenda, plus
José, the product of when María was raped in Puroaire. Esperanza
is commandeered to help María Concepción cook, although once in
a while Juan Pablo springs for *tortas* from a stand, or a spit-roasted
chicken from a nearby bakery.

On the alternate Sundays, Esperanza goes downtown in the company of Hilda, who comes from Cucaramácara, a *rancho* a few miles
from Puroaire. She and Esperanza became friends as soon as they

met: their lives are almost identical, except that Hilda left behind an infant son with her mother back home. They go to the Plaza de Armas and walk in circles. For lunch, the girls gorge on grilled hot dogs from a cart on the street, at three for ten pesos, festooned with mustard, mayonnaise, ketchup, and chopped chile peppers. Hilda cannot resist *morelianas*, cookies named after the city, two disks of flattened flour with caramel in between.

After eating, they sit on a green wrought-iron bench outside the cathedral and watch the world go by. There are families whose children munch on apples coated in *dulce de leche* and chopped nuts, or wispy whorls of cotton candy in pink, lavender, or blue. There are other *muchachas*—hundreds of them, it sometimes seems, walking without going anywhere, just like Esperanza and Hilda. Most are short, like Hilda, although there are a few as tall as Esperanza, and one or two even taller. Some are slender, some are doughy around the waist, while some are already fat and making matters worse by eating fried *chicharrón* doused with lemon and hot sauce, also sold on the sidewalk. Some dress in jeans and T-shirts, others in skirts and blouses. Some deck themselves out in polyester dresses in bright red or blue and high heels, with three colors of eye shadow blended on their lids, as if every one of their days off were a *quinceañera* party. Many cross themselves each time they pass the cathedral. Without exception all are brown-skinned.

Those who apply eye shadow have put it on for the benefit of the boys who come out to flirt with them. The boys who have approached Esperanza may have reached legal age, but in their souls they are still *muchachos*. She and Hilda wouldn't give them the time of day. Some are gawky, with bodies so slender their jeans slip from their hips. Others are short and sturdy, with arms and shoulders strong from moving crates or hauling piled boxes on a handcart in the market. Some are cross-eyed or bucktoothed, some wear moustaches as thin and wispy as a moth's wings. Some are so chubby that the curves of their bellies peek out from where their T-shirts meet their pants. Despite their youth, the hair is already disappearing from some of their scalps.

Most wear jeans and T-shirts. A few take the trouble to put on shirts with collars and buttons. Sneakers are the preferred footwear, although some wear the scuffed work boots in which they labor through the week. Some sport baseball caps worn backward or sideways.

A few of the *muchachos* are even handsome—tall, well proportioned, with slim waists and hair they have taken the trouble to comb. They have recently washed their jeans and perhaps turned up the collar of a polo shirt. Unfortunately, their contemptuous expressions indicate that they know too well how they measure up to the competition.

Through narrowed eyes they stare intently as Esperanza and Hilda walk past, as if they were sizing up how much the girls would cost if sliced and sold by the kilo. The most heinous make a noise with their tongues against the roofs of their mouths (*thwack!*) or a sibilant serpentlike hiss: *Tssssssssssssssss!* Others make insinuating remarks, such as "I could go with you all night long," or "Mamacita!" The jokers repeat come-ons that are tired even to Esperanza's nineteen-year-old ears: "Your name must be Alice because you come from Wonderland," or "Do you believe in love at first sight? If not, I can come back tomorrow."

The *muchacho* who stops Esperanza in her tracks catches her off guard with one word: *"Amiga."* Slender, shorter than she but taller than Hilda, he wears a neat black shirt with the sleeves rolled up. He has wavy black hair, earth-toned skin, dark and soulful eyes. Hanging from his trim frame are a pair of jeans, neat but pale from countless washings. He says that word to her—*amiga*—as if it were a preamble to a stern message or an urgent warning.

"Yes?" says Esperanza, betraying only slight impatience.

"You have pretty eyes," he says, and smiles.

His smile begins around his own eyes, accentuated by the raised black brows, the heavy lids, the dark moon-shaped slivers underneath that suggest he may have stayed out too late the night before. It extends to his generous lips, revealing a row of reasonably straight white teeth. The smile appears as if it were the sun emerging through reluctantly parting clouds. Esperanza can feel its sudden warmth on her skin. Her face reddens and goose bumps appear on her upper arms.

"I've seen you here before on other Sundays," he says. The "you" is singular; he barely acknowledges Hilda with a glance. Esperanza stands there dumbly. She feels she should say something, but what? Her mind struggles but no words appear. "You know what I thought when I saw you?"

She shakes her head. "What?" she asks.

"I thought, *This is a woman I could look up to—always, for the rest of my life.*" Esperanza knows he is flattering her, but doesn't quite get what he is talking about. Her body temperature has risen, as if she were feverish. "*I would have to,*" he adds, "*because she's taller than me.*"

Hilda laughs and Esperanza follows suit. He is half a head shorter than she, but it is as if, after taking possession of the fact with a joke, he now towers over her. "What are your names?" he asks. "I'm Leonardo." The girls introduce themselves. "Where are you from?" he asks.

"Cucaramácara," says Hilda.

"Puroaire," says Esperanza.

"You don't say," says Leonardo. "I have cousins in Cosquicheo." Another *rancho* in Tierra Caliente, barely forty miles from their homes. "But I live here now and work at Taller El Gordito, the auto repair shop on Calle Hidalgo."

He offers to buy them a soda. At the same moment, Hilda consents and Esperanza refuses. They look at each other, perplexed, and all three begin to laugh.

The boy has reduced Esperanza to a jumble of mixed emotions. She wants to stay and have a soda with him and Hilda, but she is afraid she will be speechless throughout, or that even worse, she will say something wrong. She can't stand the way that Hilda, who is only one year older than she, effortlessly carries on a conversation with Leonardo.

"We live in Lomas de las Camelias," Hilda says, mentioning the prosperous neighborhood, a fifteen-minute walk from where they stand, as if they were the señoras of the house and not domestic employees. "I've been here for four years. And Esperanza for three."

"Do you miss home?" asks Leonardo.

"Sure, but what can you do?" says Hilda. "There's no work there."

"How do you like Morelia?"

"You're never bored here," Hilda says, smoothing her curly hair.

So jealous is Esperanza of the ease with which Hilda chats away that she says the only thing that occurs to her. "It's nice to meet you, Leonardo, but we have to go."

"Where?" asks Hilda.

"Don't you remember? To see my sister."

Hilda tries to bargain between allegiance and ambition. "Do we have to go this early?"

"I said we'd be there by lunch."

"But it's not even two o'clock yet."

"We have to help her cook." She can feel the wheels turning in Hilda's head, her eyes alight under the curls. Her friend is wondering whether she should abandon Esperanza, let her go "to her sister" by herself and fly off to drink a soda alone with Leonardo. "We promised her," says Esperanza weakly.

Leonardo looks at them with an amused smirk. "Don't worry," he says, looking directly in Esperanza's eyes. "I'll see you here next Sunday."

As she and Hilda walk away, Esperanza turns to glance at him. He is standing in the same spot, the self-confident smirk still on his face, as if it's next Sunday already and she is nestled in his arms.

SIXTY-NINE MOTIONS

"Adultery is an opportunistic crime," said Catherine, fishing in her handbag for her Tareytons. "It's based on an unintended circumstance that comes up unexpectedly, but isn't necessarily likely to be repeated."

"It could become habitual," I suggested. "If I had anything to do with it."

She lit up and replaced the Zippo in her handbag. "Don't even think about it," she said, and returned to bed. She lay on her back and began to blow smoke rings toward the ceiling. We were in a nonsmoking room in a chain hotel in a strip mall near Intercontinental Airport, charged to my credit card. I would have to go downstairs later and buy a can of air freshener. If the maid smelled smoke when she cleaned the room the next morning, I would be charged a $200 fine. This had actually happened once before. Catherine told me to bill it to the state of Texas when I submitted my invoice. I think she was joking.

I poured a little more tequila from a pint bottle into the hotel's cardboard crockery at the bedside. The skin around Catherine's belly was smooth and a little slack with an almost imperceptible coating of peach fuzz under her navel. I brushed my lips along this sweet spot, caressed her thighs with the backs of my fingers. She was about ten years my senior, but I would have happily married her if she didn't already have a husband. She never talked about him. Word on the street was that he was filthy rich.

Even if she were single, I doubt that Catherine would have considered me husband material. She had pigeonholed me as a reliable colleague with whom she had the occasional assignation. On that particular night, the flight between Houston and New Orleans was canceled. (American Airlines, as usual; I kept reminding myself to book Aeromexico next time.) As there were no more planes until the following morning, I rented the room and called her. This gave us not only a chance to commit an opportunistic crime based on a contingency, but to have a professional conference about our client. Technically, I could have billed the state of Louisiana an hourly rate for the rendezvous, as we discussed the case intermittently. I didn't, but wondered if Catherine did.

She had long curling lashes over huge eyes of gunmetal blue. She spoke with a heavy Chicago accent, and had had a distinguished career as a death-penalty defense lawyer in Illinois, until 2003, when George Ryan, the governor at the time, granted clemency to everyone on death row. At that point, Catherine hotfooted it for Houston and became licensed in Texas. After Hurricane Katrina, many lawyers left south Louisiana, so she took the bar there too, to take up the slack. Along the way, she also picked up a license in Oklahoma, and was highly sought after as a consultant to death-penalty defense lawyers around the country. I had done investigations for some admirably dedicated people, but none who worked as hard as she.

It's so much less stressful to work for a good lawyer than a bad one. I had a case in Alabama, and every time I traveled there, the lead attorney and his co-counsel were more concerned about whether the Crimson Tide would win the following Saturday's football game than if the client lived or died. I worked that case for over two years, and I don't think they visited our guy in jail more than five times. I am certain they never read my mitigation memos. It's only because the prosecutor was similarly lazy and didn't want to spend the county's money on a trial that they came to a plea agreement.

Apart from her skills as a lawyer, Catherine's body temperature was two or three degrees warmer than everyone else's. As she reached orgasm, she made a guttural growl that sounded like an espresso pot as it comes to a boil. I moved to kiss her, but she put a hand in my hair and moved my head away.

"I need to know where you're at, Richard," she said. "What are you going to do while you're in Louisiana?" They say that men are good at compartmentalizing, but Catherine was the mistress of the game. If there is a time and place for everything, she had them measured to the nanosecond.

Not that it was a bad idea to concentrate on Esperanza's case. I'd been working on it, off and on, for close to a year and a half, primarily interviewing the family, friends, classmates, colleagues, and teachers in Mexico. There was an overwhelming amount of work to do on the Mexican side of the investigation, and as such, aside from visits to Esperanza, I had been lax about the U.S. part (which I'd regret after it was too late). You needed to constantly revise the mitigation story, redefine what you were trying to achieve, make sure you were on the same page as the lawyers.

"It's a long shot, but I'm hoping to find people who worked with her and the boyfriend after Katrina. Maybe a foreman. Maybe I can find employment records, although they were almost certainly working off the books. Or a neighbor, but even that's a long shot. All those Mexicans went to the Gulf Coast after the hurricane, but after the work dried up, most of them left."

"Knock on every door in that project where they lived. There's got to be someone left."

"Where are you at?"

She took a long drag of the cigarette. "On Friday afternoon I filed sixty-nine motions on behalf of Esperanza, just to give the judge and the prosecutor severe headaches on their way home for the weekend."

"Sixty-nine?"

She held up her cardboard cup of tequila. "In your honor, Richard."

"What did you file?"

She ran a hand through her brown bangs. "A motion that Esperanza never be seen by a jury in shackles or in jailhouse scrubs. Not that anyone's ever said she would be, but that's grist to grind the headache. A motion to lower the charges from capital murder to felony murder. A motion for a fair trial. A motion that, if we ever go to trial, Esperanza sits at the table closest to the jury." She took a deep breath. "A motion for more funding for you. A motion for funding for a neuropsych who speaks Spanish to take a look at her. A motion for funding for one of your Mexican cultural experts to examine her. A motion for funding for a videographer so you can get movies of that *National Geographic* town where she grew up, and get the big brother to cry on cue."

During her summation to a jury Catherine could bring herself to tears, all the more powerful because her raspy, throaty voice never cracked. She put even the toughest prosecutors on edge and many were panic-stricken at the idea of going toe-to-toe with her in a courtroom. She negotiated most of her cases, and it was because of her that I had some hope that Esperanza might get a plea bargain without going to trial. Esperanza herself wasn't helping much. I wondered whether it mattered to her whether she got the death penalty.

"That reminds me, Catherine. I was reading through one of the manuals about defending people who are mentally impaired. There's case law on this that I think is pertinent to any Mexican defendant, no matter whether there is anything wrong with them." My computer was already on, and I looked for the relevant information. "In 1988, *Patterson v. Illinois*, quoting *Moran v. Burbine*, says that for an intelligent and knowing waiver of constitutional rights, a defendant must have 'a full awareness of both the nature of the right being abandoned and the consequences of the decision to abandon it.' And according to *Johnson v. Zerbst*, whether a waiver is knowing and intelligent is determined by the particular facts and circumstances of the case, 'including the background, experience, and conduct of the accused.'"

"What are you getting at?"

"They're talking about mental impairment. But here's what I'm saying. There are people who are not mentally impaired at all who do not have an awareness of their rights, or the consequences of abandoning them. This is where background and experience come in. A poor Mexican, even one with a perfectly functioning brain, doesn't understand his Miranda rights. He didn't grow up watching *Law and Order* reruns, so he doesn't know the drill. 'You have the right to remain silent' means absolutely nothing to him, because in one-horse Mexican towns—even in Mexico City—if you're picked up by the cops, you better have a good story and you have no choice but to tell it. The only people who get away from the cops are the ones with enough money to bribe them. Not only are there no Miranda rights in Mexico, but I'd say poor Mexicans don't really know that they have any rights at all."

"Put that in an e-mail to me."

"I already did."

"A judge won't pay it any mind, but that's motion number seventy. A bigger headache for them."

"Who have you got lined up for the neuropsych?"

"I like Madrazo." Based out of Fayetteville, he was originally from Hermosillo and worked a lot of cases with Mexican clients. "But he's booked up for six months. I'm hoping that will be cause for a continuance."

"Catherine, I have a question for you."

She sipped her tequila. "This is where you're going to ask me what if she didn't do it."

"Sort of. But not yet."

"Okay. What do you want to ask?"

"What kind of a woman kills her children?"

She swirled the tequila in the cup. "Usually one who's been wailed on since she was a kid. She wails on her kids until one day she loses it and goes too far."

"And if she doesn't have any history of wailing on her kids?"

"A variation on the theme. It's still one day she loses it and goes too far."

I shook my head. "It just doesn't add up." Every time I visited Esperanza in jail, I couldn't believe she was guilty. This would be meaningless for Catherine, because I had no basis for the belief. It was something I saw in Esperanza's face. Nor did I believe her story that she didn't remember what happened at the moment of the murder.

"Now ask me what if she didn't do it."

"How do you know I want to ask you that?"

"Because you always do."

"And you always say they did it."

"Most of the time they always did. I know you'd like to believe she didn't."

"Why do you say that?"

"Because you've never worked on a case with a woman as a client before. Because she's beautiful. Because she's brown, and if you exonerate her that makes you a white knight. I don't want to burst your bubble, but in fact it's most likely she's guilty. Remember, she made a statement that says so to the cops."

"She said she didn't remember what happened, which you know isn't the same thing. And what if it was coerced? Isn't it a good thing to remind yourself that the possibility exists?"

"Yes. To what end? Whether she did it or not, we have to be prepared to give her the same defense at a trial. If we don't have another guilty party, or an alibi as tight as a closed fist, there's not a whole hell of a lot we can do with 'What if she didn't do it?'"

"Okay."

I think she felt sorry for me because I'd put on a sullen expression. "But run with it, Richard. If she didn't kill that baby, who did?"

"The father."

"She said the father split two months before."

"What if it was an accident?"

"*An accident?* That poor baby was brutalized, Richard. That child was FUBAR." (Lawyers tend to use acronyms for sophisticated criminal classification. FUBAR is short for Fucked Up Beyond All Recognition.) "You saw the autopsy pictures—there were marks all over her poor little body. Think about what a jury is going to feel about Esperanza when they see them."

"What if there was someone else involved?"

"Same question. Who?" Catherine tossed her butt into the "ashtray"—another cardboard cup with an inch of water in it. "This is your first dead baby, right?"

"Right."

"Usually there's a couple involved. Mommy and Daddy. The cops arrest them both immediately. They play Mommy off Daddy. They lean on her with all they got: 'He did it, right? Either he did it or you did it. If you did it, we fry you, but if you tell us everything about how he did it, we get you out of here in time for breakfast tomorrow.' And they do the same thing with him and see what sticks. But without another party, they're kind of hamstrung. They don't have anyone to play off anyone else."

"Usually who did it?"

"It could be either one, Richard. A lot of the time they're both involved. In some way. One might have done the actual HAC acts"—that's Heinous, Atrocious, and Cruel—"but the other enabled."

"But wouldn't acting and enabling be the difference between life and death in a case like this?"

"It damn well could be, if we had any evidence that she enabled but didn't act. But we don't have any, at least not so far, that there's anyone else involved at all. The difference between life and death could be a lot of things. You've already come up with a history of poverty, neglect, abuse, violence. All that's good stuff. Likewise that she's got no criminal record anywhere."

I wondered if I was out of my depth working a dead-baby case at all. "Is there any way to develop a theory of criminally negligent homicide? What about with forensics?" I was grasping at straws, thinking of *CSI* episodes I'd seen in hotel rooms in Texas and Arkansas.

"Good question. If there's any possibility to sow seeds of doubt that this wasn't a murder, it's because the medical examiner's report is flimsy. I filed another motion to appoint an expert to go through it with a fine tooth comb, and if we're lucky, piss all over it. The truth is we don't really know how that baby died. I've subpoenaed every possible document that has anything to do with the report, and I've got an investigator looking into the ME herself."

"Which expert are you hiring?"

"I want to get a guy named Beremberg." She explained he was a doctor who often testified for the defense in dead-baby cases. He tended to call into question the science of the autopsy reports, which all too often were carelessly prepared and repeated whatever story the police had concocted. "He's also backed up with other cases, so between him and Madrazo, we've got a better chance at a continuance. The judge may ask me to hire someone else."

"If you establish that she never harmed the baby before, can you get her a discount because it wasn't CCP?" (Cold, Calculated, and Premeditated.)

"That's one of many tools in the kit." She stood up and walked to the sofa, where she had left her clothes in a pile. She wrapped a black bra around her body backward, fastened the clasp and then revolved it to its rightful place. Wearing nothing but the bra, she lit another cigarette. "When you get to Louisiana, set up a meeting with Burt Sands. He's been appointed co-counsel."

Every death-penalty defense team has two lawyers, but it had taken a ridiculously long time to get another one appointed. Almost five years after the fact, New Orleans was still going through its post-Katrina personnel shortage. "Is he any good?"

She had a funny expression on her face that wasn't from swallowing straight tequila. "He's what we got," she said in a grave tone, the one she used to alternately persuade and intimidate jurors and prosecutors. "I don't even know him. I think I might have met him at a death-penalty workshop I gave in Shreveport once."

Leaning against the headboard of the bed, I asked, "What if I can find the boyfriend?"

She looked magnificent, sitting on the sofa in nothing but that black bra. "Then you'll be my white knight," she said, and began to blow smoke rings.

A SUNDAY KIND OF LOVE

Leonardo has no cousins in Cosquicheo, but he does have relatives in Maravatío, in another part of the state. (So his father told him. He's never met them.) Since he has relations out there somewhere, when he tells girls from Tierra Caliente about his invented cousins in their part of the world, it doesn't feel like an out-and-out lie. If his back were to the wall, he would say these "relatives" are a kind of shorthand he uses, which means, *I'm a* paisano, *you can trust me*. It was just the first strike with Esperanza. She was enchantingly shy; he knew he would have to be patient with her. You don't get a girl like that by snapping your fingers.

He invited her out four Sundays in a row. The first time, they took a long stroll from the plaza to the park in Lomas de las Camelias, but poor Esperanza seemed terrified that the señora for whom she works would pop up out of the bushes. The second time he took her to the other park on Calzada Benito Juárez, and even sprang for tickets to the zoo. They watched a jaguar pick at the scarlet scraps of a bone, a seal fly out of a pool to catch a fish in its mouth, and, behind a fence, a flock of flamingos that, as if by magic, transformed the entire landscape pink. The third Sunday they had their first kiss on a narrow lane with sandstone buildings called El Callejón del Romance. Their lips tasted of the ham and egg *tortas* he had bought them for lunch.

He was born and raised right here in Morelia. From infancy, Leonardo used to spend Sundays with his father and older brother. They left the women behind at home and walked all over town. His father would stop on certain street corners and emit something between a warble and a blast on a trumpet, executing as best as he could "Usted Es la Culpable," the only tune he had ever halfway learned. Leonardo's brother, Mario, just a couple of years older than he, would try to keep time on a little drum fastened with straps around his shoulders. Leo's task was to approach passersby with an upturned baseball cap and, with imploring eyes, wait to see if they would drop some coins into the headgear. He remembers with happiness the adventure of those Sundays, the complicity of the exclusively male companionship.

Sometimes another man would appear from one of the houses on the street where his father had stopped to emit the constipated volley of notes. The man would exchange words with Papá, who would enter the doorway and look for something in his knapsack. They would always press palms before they parted. Occasionally one of these men would say something to Leonardo or Mario—"What's going on, champ?" or "How quickly you're growing!"—but most often the boys would be ignored, as if there was nothing but air in the space they occupied. Leo didn't mind. There was an element of edgy mystery to the world of men, far from his mother and sisters.

The masculine reverie of those Sunday afternoons came to an end when, to save his own skin, one of those "friends" from behind a doorway ratted out Leo's dad. Three cops stopped him and the boys in an alley of two-story cinder block houses. Leonardo can still remember the violence with which one of the uniformed men, as frightening to him as a wild animal, threw his father's trumpet to the ground before grabbing the knapsack with its incriminating contents. As one of the cops squeezed father and sons into the back of a squad car, Papá asked meekly if he could retrieve the instrument. The officer in the driver's seat told him he could go and get it, but only if he'd stick it up his ass and play "Solamente Una Vez." In the backseat Leonardo got on his knees, and through the window he saw the trumpet shining in the sun as they drove away. A single tear rolled down his father's cheek. It was the first and only time he saw the man cry.

Leonardo spent the next two years—from the age of six to eight— sleeping on the floor of his father's jail cell, along with Mario, their two sisters, and their mother (if Papá wasn't in the mood for her to share his narrow cot). They snoozed atop flattened cardboard boxes, sharing flimsy moth-eaten blankets. The boys' and the girls' heads were shaved monthly as a preventive measure against fleas and vermin, and as they slept, everyone did their best to avoid the prison's rodent population. Some of Morelia's most upstanding citizens considered it a humanitarian measure to allow the spouses and children of indigent prisoners to share their cells. In fact, it was a practical matter for those who had nowhere else to go.

Intermittently there was school for the children, although the teachers were absent as often as they turned up. Leo preferred to accompany his parents to toil in the jail's leather workshop, where Papá cut huge squares of pigskin into narrow belts. Mamá helped him, stacking the cut pieces and applying coating to their edges, and later attaching the buckles. Leo would measure them and, with a pencil, mark where the holes would be punched. Their labor was trancelike and silent, and a source of happiness to Leonardo, except on those days when Papá was in a bad mood and would turn one of the belts against him or Mamá. Optimistically, he hoped one of Papá's leatherworking colleagues would rise to his or his mother's defense. Instead, they pretended not to notice. Although he couldn't have put them into words, the experience taught Leo two lessons: that justice did not exist, and that even among those he loved he was alone.

After his release from jail, Papá disappeared. Leonardo's mother could not support all of her children, so she sent him to live with Jorge, who was not precisely an uncle, but a friend of one of her brothers. A wiry man who rarely shaved, he had gray hair and walked around the city in sandals, exposing chapped feet and gnarly toenails. The night that he moved in, Leonardo told the man that he was hungry.

"I'm not going to give you anything to eat," Jorge told him. "I'm going to do better than that. I'm going to teach you how to eat." He instructed the boy to go to the market the following morning and offer to help ladies carry their packages home. He told the boy to be patient until he found a woman who had avocados in her bag, and showed him how to cup one in his little palm and slip it into his pocket. Then he told him that if he were to stand outside of the bakery and cry, someone would give him a bread roll, which cost less than a peso.

"How am I supposed to cry if I'm not sad?" asked Leonardo.

The old man slapped him hard across the face, on both cheeks. "Remember what that feels like and then you'll cry." As the boy quietly whimpered, the old man added, "A roll and an avocado will fill your belly the whole morning. Plus you'll probably get a few pesos from the lady after you bring her groceries home. That's how you start to make your way in the world."

Esperanza is sweating bullets because finally she has brought him to the house of her *patrona*. The family has gone for an overnight visit to relatives in La Piedad. She is so rigid you'd think she'd seen a ghost. They sit on the bed that almost occupies the entire tiny room. "Relax," he says with a laugh, and moves her long hair away from her neck so he can give her a soft kiss under the ear. She lays an awkward hand on his shoulder, staring at the door as if certain that someone will burst through at any moment. *"Amor,"* he says, taking her chin between two fingers and pivoting her head so she looks at him. "You are so lovely," he says, and brushes his lips against hers.

When he takes Esperanza in his arms, Leonardo can feel her heart through the cotton of her short-sleeved white blouse. The rapid beat is like a challenge to him: *come on, come on, come on*. He puts his palms on both sides of her face and kisses her again. She will have to loosen up sooner or later—or not, because he has made up his mind that he'll have her today, the fourth Sunday of his courtship. He begins to unbutton her shirt, his gaze resting on the white bra, the bony frame. He caresses her soft, nut-colored skin with his palms. "This is your first time?" he asks. She doesn't answer.

After relieving Esperanza of her bra, Leonardo realizes he has never been with a woman so beautiful, and cannot take his eyes off her brown nipples, round as the setting sun. When he was in his teens, he would go every evening at nine o'clock to a tiny store where a skinny widow who laid on her makeup with a trowel sold sweets, cigarettes, cold drinks, and newspapers. He would take out the garbage, help her stack boxes and bottles, and close the shop for tips. One evening she brought him home and told him she was going to show him how to make any woman his slave. He is determined to reveal to Esperanza every one of those tricks, and pull from his sleeve even more. He cradles her hips from the mattress so he can remove her white panties and bring his mouth to the sparse wavy hair under her navel.

He has never before entered a woman so slowly or gently, never made love to one so tenderly, as if she were a breakable object or a baby easily bruised. All the same, she does not seem to be enjoying his efforts, or even feeling them. Instead she stares at the door as if waiting for an army platoon to break it down. Still, she is gushing wet, which he takes as a sign of encouragement. He cups her buttocks in his hands, expels hot breath on her neck.

Before long Esperanza has one hand on Leonardo's shoulder and another on his back. She holds on to him as if for dear life and breathes heavily into his ear. This is a relief to Leonardo. After they finish, he will hold her until she stops crying, murmuring reassuring words into her ear, and offer to help her bleach the soiled and stained sheets in the stone sinks on the roof. Taking them up there will give him a better idea of the layout of the house.

SILENT SCREAM

From time to time I wondered what story I would have told if I were the murderer and had been called upon to mitigate myself. I suppose I would have had to start with my father in a rage, coming after me with a bamboo cane—a prop he'd bought me because I admired Charlie Chaplin. When he got angry, he was completely out of control; it was as if he were possessed. After the beatings, I would cry alone helplessly, enraged at the injustice. When these episodes occurred, my mother disappeared.

In a recurring dream I had in childhood, a boy (me?) and a girl (the sister I never had?) go to the Staten Island Ferry (the scene, in waking life, of both school trips and the occasional excursion with my parents). The boy and the girl (siblings) are unsupervised, which makes them outlaws, as they are too young to be alone—perhaps six or seven (him) and eight or nine (her). They run along the deck of the yellow boat, which strengthens their reprobate status—the first thing any semiconscious teacher or parent tells a kid before climbing aboard is *Don't run.*

The deafening moo of the foghorn. The murky water over the side, parted by thick foam as the craft makes its way across the river. Somehow it becomes clear that the boy and the girl never made it on board. (I know we just saw them running along the deck, but dreams have their own merciless logic.)

A subway grate on a concrete sidewalk. The rumbling roar of the train underneath, the warm air billowing up through the crosshatched metal. With sickening lucidity I understand that the boy and the girl have been crushed under the wheels of the train.

It wasn't until after my father died that I related that dream to an actual incident from when I was no more than five or six. This is what I remember. I was standing on a subway platform. My father was behind me, his hand pressed against my chest. As the train we'd just exited rattled behind us, he was screaming: *"You've got the wrong man."* Or something like that. But to whom? I cannot recall a body, a face, the recipient of his cry. In response, the person at whom my father screamed must have stolen away. And where was my mother? She was there, somewhere nearby, but at the same time not there, which was characteristic of her. His hand pressed against my chest: Was the gesture to keep track of me, so he wouldn't lose me in the scrimmage of the subway platform, or to use me as a form of protection? Who was shielding whom? The memory caused the same sensation as waking from the dream: utter panic.

The last time I saw him he was supine in a bed that had been propped up by a push button so he could receive visitors at Saint Vincent's Hospital. Six feet tall and ninety-seven pounds, his cheeks were sunken, his face shriveled and colorless. After countless chemo treatments, there were just a few wispy patches of white hair on his scalp. He was naked under a short gown, blue with a diamond pattern, loosely tied in the back. It had become his most frequent costume in those last months in which he died by inches, as one infection after another attacked his organs and even the skin that surrounded his bones. It became increasingly difficult to keep him at home. Once, just twelve hours after he had returned from the hospital, his temperature shot up to 104 and he began to fill the bucket at his bedside with bloody vomit. I called an ambulance. He begged me not to send him back to Saint Vincent's, but I was too afraid of what might happen at home.

One of his legs had swollen to the circumference of a tree. The lesions on it were purple, massive, hideous. Skeletal and wheezing, he was utterly exhausted. The antivirals kept him propped up and breathing, but only in the most literal sense of the word could he have been classified as "alive." He could no longer eat. He could swig a sip of a canned protein drink but would vomit before he could digest it.

He stared at the ceiling. After caring for him those last few months, I was pretty worn out myself and just sprawled in a vinyl chair, vaguely disgusted by the medicinal odor of the disinfectant with which the hospital floors were mopped. White plastic lilies in a vase, the terra-cotta brick building across Eleventh Street out the window. I hoped that my presence comforted him in some way. There was a great deal left for us to say to each other, but the moment had passed. There was nothing left of him.

I turned to face him. His mouth was agape. He shook his head no. Tears began to stream from his eyes. Even though he no longer had the power of speech, he was talking. I had no idea what he was saying, but a barrage of language was being produced in his brain and communicated through his gaping mask of dread and misery. I took his hand and he grasped mine with shocking strength. He began to howl. No sound came from his chest but I understood from that wide-open mouth, those despairing wet eyes, that he was screaming.

What could I say? "I know, Dad" was all I could utter. And "It's going to be all right. Try to get some rest." I couldn't bring myself to say, "Stop suffering. Let go. Give up and die." But that was what I was thinking. I kept repeating, "I know, Dad, I know." After a while, I disengaged my hand from his grip. I looked at that silently screaming countenance, stood up, and slowly walked to the door. I took one last look and said good-bye. His mouth had opened even wider. It was as if he were shrieking more loudly, although still mute.

Out in the daylight, I went to the closest bar, a black hole on Greenwich Avenue, and ordered a double shot of Irish whiskey. After I finished it, I covered my face with my hands and cried as quietly as possible. When I looked up, the bartender had set me up with another drink. He didn't even charge me for it. I suppose that, working around the corner from a hospital where battalions and brigades of people were dying of AIDS, he had seen weeping customers before.

After the second drink, I returned to the hospital. My father was gone. It was 1990. I was twenty-two, he was sixty-three. If he had lived a little longer, he would have been able to take the cocktail of chemicals that have helped so many people with AIDS to survive. He probably would have outlived me.

As a young man, my father moved to New York City from Meridian, Mississippi, to become a playwright. He often had a manuscript at one agent's office or another. He was certain that their repeated rejections were due to an impenetrable gay Mafia from the Yale School of Drama that controlled whatever ultimately saw a first-night curtain climbing heavenward. He made his living as a public relations man, a job he despised. Perhaps it shouldn't have surprised me that he was gay, or some permutation of bisexual. But it had never occurred to me until he was diagnosed with AIDS.

After he died, I began to wonder what the incident on the subway had meant. He didn't tell me, but I was a writer, so I invented a version. Who was the man at whom my father screamed? (I assume it was a man; I can't imagine a woman would have threatened him so, at least in this context.) I imagined that my father had been addressed, or even accosted, by someone he had known in a gay bar, or perhaps the toilet in the very same subway station—a context that would have compromised his role as a husband and father. My father tried to ignore the man, who misinterpreted the attempt to snub him and became more insistent, perhaps made an importunate remark. Maybe he laid a hand on Dad's shoulder.

The touch made my father panic. (Panic was more or less his default mode.) He corralled me, the hand over my chest. The scream: "You've got the wrong man." Did he scream to be heard over the subway roaring behind us? The other man evaporates; my father collects my mother and me and acts as if nothing happened. We move on beyond the turnstiles, up a flight of stairs to the sidewalk and the light of day. Of course something happened. If the man disappeared, the unease lingered. A subway grate on a concrete sidewalk. The rumbling roar of the train underneath, the warm air billowing up through the crosshatched metal.

The reason that I never committed murder or needed to be mitigated is that, unlike my clients, there were saving graces to my upbringing. When my father wanted me out of his sandy hair, he sent me around the corner to the public library. Books, movies, music—all the arts and the worlds they took me to—made me realize that there were other possibilities to life than the one in which I was growing up.

And he wasn't just a closet case enraged at the world. When I did my homework in the first grade, it was my father's hand on top of mine, guiding me through the circles, lines, and curlicues of the alphabet. When I talked about the library books I'd finished or wrote reports about them in grade school, his eyes brightened. Despite his violence, I knew that he loved me. Had he lived long enough to know that I had been accepted into grad school for creative writing, it would have made him proud.

His AIDS diagnosis was a kind of liberation. I learned I was not the cause of his zero-to-sixty flashes of frantic rage. He had been harboring a pain that had nothing to do with me. After he died, when I thought of his ache, I felt sorrier for him than I did for myself, an indication that adolescence had ended.

He made me a writer. When I got to the master's program in creative writing, his death turned me into one of the few students who actually had a story to tell, as well as a character—the blithely bisexual Rodrigo, the tragicomic Mexican gardener who crossed the finish line to the pages of *Embolalia*: he was everything Dad wasn't and perhaps a lot of what I wished he had been.

Q & A

Striding purposefully down the street, Esperanza is preparing a list of questions. And she's going to make sure that Leonardo gives her some straight answers. Or else she'll snap his head off.

She wants to know if he robbed the señora's house—her jewelry, some laptops, the children's Xboxes, a TV, the good silverware. Was it him? Or people whom he tipped off, telling them the family would be away for the weekend? Or someone else entirely, someone he doesn't even know? She would be so relieved to find that he wasn't involved and that it was simply a coincidence that the crime occurred while she and the family were gone. But she knows better. She remembers him trying to seem casual when he asked those questions about where they were going, for how long, at what time they would be back.

Those *cuates* of his. There was a Sunday afternoon when she went to a little *fonda* with them, a hole-in-the-wall with walls the color of cantaloupe. Shifty-eyed buddies who drank beer from liter-size *caguamas* poured into plastic cups while they watched a soccer game on TV. She sat there primly sipping Coca-Cola through a straw that kept bobbing out of the plastic bottle. She could tell that, as a sign of respect to Leonardo, the pals were trying to be polite to her, but she didn't like their looks, particularly the short sneering one with the wispy moustache, who wore his baseball cap backward. She could have sworn that he was one of the guys who hissed at her in the plaza before she began to go out with Leo.

She would like to know if his intention was to rob the house while she and the family were away in Uruapan, to protect her from suspicion of involvement in the crime. Does Leonardo have any feelings?

Does he care what happens to her, or did he simply wait around for the right moment, no matter the consequences for her?

What she would really like to know is if he loves her—now or ever. They've seen each other at least two Sundays a month for several months. He has said he loved her. He has acted like he loved her. Was it all a game? She remembers when he made love to her in the tiny room in the señora's house, intense moments because of her insistence on furtive silence. And the handful of occasions when Leonardo had a few extra pesos and he would rent a room in a hotel *de paso*. It may have had a cracked mirror in the bathroom and that cloying little bar of pink Rosa Venus soap, but for a few hours it was all theirs in which to luxuriate, hours in which no one and nothing else existed. Their bodies and the bed and the color TV, the hot shower, and the beers and the Coca-Colas they brought with them were the entire universe. She would have happily spent the rest of her life with him in that room. How she hated to go back to her tiny cubbyhole in the señora's house afterward.

And there was the time in the car that belonged to a friend of his—a wide and wobbly forest-green Ford almost as old as the two of them put together. They drove to the outskirts of the city, then farther out on a dirt road to some fields between *ranchos*. Despite her protests, they moved to the back, where he leaned her over the front seat and took her from behind. Looking out the windshield into a field overgrown with weeds sun-scorched to a honey color, she felt ridiculous and uncomfortable. "Someone could find us at any moment," she said. "I know," he gasped, and she understood that was precisely what was exciting to him. She gave herself over to the circumstance, the location, to Leonardo, to show him that she belonged to him and would do anything he asked. They sprawled in the backseat afterward; he caressed her and whispered *linda* in her ear.

He paid for everything those Sundays. He rarely had an abundance of money, but he treated her to sodas and *tortas*, to popsicles from a rickety two-wheeled cart on the street, sold by a wrinkled man who wore a straw hat that looked as if someone had sat on it. After a few Sundays he began to recognize them. He called her *linda* too, and even remembered her favorite flavor was strawberries and cream, and apologized whenever he had sold out of it.

Leonardo talked about living together. He said he wanted to wait until he had saved enough money so she wouldn't have to work. If she left to live with him, the señora would fire her; the lady of a household needed someone who could live under the same roof with the family. Esperanza told him it didn't matter. She could find something else—a job as a waitress, or cooking in the kitchen of a restaurant, or selling fruits or vegetables from a stall in the market, or helping María Concepción to make tamales, which she sold around her neighborhood. "But what will we do," he asked, "when the children are born?"

He was the first to mention them. Leonardo was scrupulous about wearing a condom, or, if he didn't have one, exiting her body before he climaxed. He made it clear that he wanted to wait until he had saved this elusive money and felt more confident about his ability to support them before having any.

But the words—*the children*—had issued from his lips and established an intent. He would be *the father* of her children. She would be *a mother*. She could imagine them so clearly—cradling them in her arms, pushing them in a carriage, their toothless gums suckling at her breasts—that it was as if they already existed. She wished for a girl first, whom she would name Yesenia. She'd had a schoolmate with that name (her parents had been inspired by a character in a soap opera) and she thought it was the most pretty and exotic she'd ever heard. Girls are more responsible than boys, Esperanza thought, so Yesenia could help her take care of her little brother, who would be called....she wasn't sure yet. She thought she liked Ismael or Israel, or maybe even Itzli, which she remembered from *la señorita* Ana's class was the name of the Aztec god of sacrifice. Perhaps Leonardo would have his own ideas about what he wanted his son to be called. She would name the daughter and he could name the son.

A few days after the robbery, the señora asked her to get in the car with her. Esperanza thought they were going to the supermarket, but the señora surprised her by saying they were on the way to the police station. "It's just a formality," the señora explained, her eyes staring straight ahead at the traffic. "In cases like this they need to speak to everyone who lives in the house that was robbed." Esperanza resigned herself to the idea that uniformed cops might lock her in a cell. Instead, in a small office a man asked her to sit in front of his desk, on top of which were heaps and mounds of folders and loose papers. He wore a striped shirt, had unkempt graying hair, and what appeared to be egg yolk on his blue tie, loosened at the neck. He looked like he hadn't slept in a week. Sitting behind the desk, he clasped his hands in front of his belly and reclined. He stared at her in silence. She wondered whether he was going to say something or take a siesta.

"I am Inspector Gómez," he finally said. What was her full name? Where was she from? How long had she lived in Morelia? Did she have family here? Esperanza observed that he didn't write down any of her answers. Had she seen anything unusual in or around the house in the last couple of weeks? Anyone she didn't recognize coming or going? Anyone lurking nearby? Did she have even a vague suspicion as to who committed the robbery? The inspector scratched his mussed gray hair with all ten fingers and then, in the most offhand way—not that differently from how Leonardo had inquired about the family's plans to go away that weekend—he asked if she had a boyfriend.

She looked him in the eye and said no. It was a surprise to Esperanza how easily the lie came to her. She wondered if she had spoken too quickly or categorically, and if he believed her. Wasn't he a professional at catching people who lied? Could he see a lightbulb flash when the untruth emerged? The inspector repeated that it was only a formality. They had some leads as to who robbed the house and he was sure they would catch the little rats. It would be better for them if they confessed, and if they returned what they had stolen the court would be lenient. Esperanza restrained herself from asking him any questions about their supposed leads. Would Leonardo end up in jail? If he was responsible, that was where he belonged. But everyone knew that cops weren't any good at catching criminals. She doubted there were any leads at all.

"Thank you for coming in, Esperanza," said the inspector, absently fingering the tip of his blue necktie, noticing the egg yolk for perhaps the first time. She wasn't sure if this meant that she was free to go so she stayed seated. His phone began to ring and he looked around the mountains of paper on his desk. He held his hands above, as if through vibrations his palms might divine the phone's location. He seemed to think better of answering and looked at her again. "A pretty girl like you," he said with a smile. "*Linda.* Are you sure you don't have a boyfriend?" This time she blushed, but stuck to her story: "No, señor." He told her she could go, but to let him know if any information was revealed to her.

A week after the interview, Esperanza thought she was in the clear. There were much more serious crimes happening every day in Morelia; Hilda told her that four people had been murdered in one night a few days earlier, the result of a shootout around the corner from the federal police station that went on for twenty minutes and left hundreds of bullet shells on the surrounding streets.

But as Esperanza was rubbing a damp cloth over the dining table, the señora told her that after she finished work that day she must pack her things. Esperanza stood there clutching the rag in both hands. "You've been a very good *muchacha*," said the señora, "but the girl who worked for us before is coming back." She removed a long, slim cigarette from its packet and set it aflame with a gold lighter. "She was like a part of the family, but she had to leave to take care of her sick mother. Her mother finally died, so she can return to us," she said with a malicious smile. "I'm going to give you two weeks' pay—a thousand pesos for nothing!" Smoke billowed from both nostrils. "Isn't that nice?" As she held the cigarette to her mouth, Esperanza got a good look at the glimmering stones—green, red, transparent ice—set in the new rings on the señora's fingers.

At that moment Esperanza hated her, and wished she could slap the señora silly, take the rings from her fingers and sell them to the same crook to whom Leonardo had fenced the family's goods. Instead, she meekly went to pack her things. The señora humiliated Esperanza further by standing in the doorway as she put her few possessions in the vinyl bag.

On the twilight bus to the outskirts where María Concepción lived, Esperanza reflected how, by dint of ceaseless work and attention to detail, a measure of trust had been built between her and the señora in the three and a half years since she had come to Morelia. That was what hurt her most about getting fired. She remembered how, at first, the señora had accompanied her to the market to supervise her purchases, but after a while she let Esperanza go by herself, as long as she came back with an accounting of her purchases. There had been afternoons when, while Esperanza mopped the floors and dusted the furniture in the living room, the señora would lie on the sofa, a slice of cucumber over each eye (the vegetable was meant to prevent wrinkles), and unspool her anxieties.

Julieta had become sullen and evasive, and she wondered if there were "bad influences" among her classmates at high school. Girls grew up so much more quickly than they had when she was a child. The señora also lamented that she had gone straight from her family's house to her marriage with the señor, and never had a chance to use the degree in administration she had earned from the University of Morelia. Somehow, despite being temporarily blinded by the cucumber slices, the señora knew when the ash on her cigarette was growing long. When she extended her bangled arm, she never missed the ashtray.

When Esperanza arrived at her sister's house lugging her vinyl bag, María Concepción let out a sigh—a sigh that acknowledged another body that would occupy the scant space of the two rooms, meals that would have to be stretched yet further to feed one more mouth, another bout of unemployment that had to be surmounted. It was a sigh informed by the Sisyphean existence of a family like theirs, with no education, no connections, and no money—every step forward obstructed by mangled sidewalks, potholes, police barricades. This was the way the world worked for people like them. It was inexorably frustrating, disappointing, and impoverished. María Concepción embraced Esperanza, who cried briefly while listening to the chirping of a neighbor's parrot.

Her pace growing more decisive, she is determined to tell Leonardo that she won't be able to live with her sister very long. She will say that she doesn't know where else she can go or what prospects she has for another job—good ones like she had with the señora don't grow on trees. She will make it clear that he has ruined a perfectly good situation that she developed through time, patience, and, above all, hard work.

What will he say to her? She can imagine him looking at her through those black Nescafé eyes, saying, *"Amor,* I am so sorry you lost your job, but I had nothing to do with the robbery. The night that it happened I was in the *fonda* with my friends drinking beer and watching soccer—my friends, and the other customers, and the waitress and the proprietor can all corroborate my story. And, *linda,* if the señora is such a bitch that she fires you over the idle suspicion of your involvement in a robbery of which you had nothing to do, then she can go fuck herself! Come here into my arms, *hermosa linda,* I will take care of you, I will protect you, you and Yesenia and.... well, we'll name the boy later. I will take care of you until you can find another job, and if you can't, stop worrying. As long as we are together you will never have to worry again."

Even if he would say anything that remotely resembled that fantasy speech, could she believe him? No. In her heart she is sure he was involved in the robbery, that it may have been those very same hands, those fingers that caressed her skin and brought her so much bliss, that grasped the señora's bracelets and necklaces, Xboxes belonging to innocent children, silverware that had been a wedding present—that stuffed them into a bag and then fled with them in the night. A thief. A rat. A viper. A merciless *cabrón* who preys on the vulnerability of others, people he doesn't even know. The man she loves.

There are so many things she would like to say to him, but he isn't answering his cell phone and she doesn't know where he lives. All these months he has neither taken her to his home nor mentioned an address. But he has spoken about his job at Taller El Gordito, a few blocks from the plaza where they first met. He pointed out the place to her while they were walking one Sunday, in the late afternoon after it had closed. It is not her preference to confront him at work but he has left her no choice. She walks with determination down Calle

Hidalgo, past the sandstone buildings, the little square with the co-coconut palm and the fountain, the internet café and the bargain store. Finally, as the shops and offices begin to disappear and the neighborhood becomes more residential, she arrives at Taller El Gordito: a musty locale with oil stains on the sidewalk and only enough space to work on two cars. Indeed, there he is under the body of an old Chevrolet Shadow, his ankles peeping out. She recognizes the jeans, the sneakers. She feels her heart will explode inside her chest.

"Leonardo," she says. He ignores her and continues working. She lets a few seconds pass and says his name again. This time when he pays her no heed she becomes enraged and looks around for some kind of a weapon with which to beat his ankles. Instead, she screams, "Leonardo!"

The body, on a wheeled dolly, emerges from under the car. It is a body similar to Leo's, but belongs to a man who is shaven-headed, wears a goatee, and whose face, arms, and clothing are smeared with oil. The *taller* may be called El Gordito, but it cannot possibly belong to this man, because he is no *gordito*—he is in fact skinny, with pale, pasty skin. The expression on his face is both quizzical and annoyed. "Leonardo who?" he asks.

TRUE BLUE

To mitigate myself, of course I'd have to paint a portrait of my mother. Her only indulgences were coffee and cigarettes. Sadly, she didn't seem to take much pleasure from either. She drank her coffee black and acrid as soon as she got out of bed and, along with her cup, lit the first smoke of the day. That was the breakfast combo. During the last year of her life, my strongest memory is of her sitting in a faded floral housecoat, staring out the window at the white brick wall that the living room overlooked. The skin around her lips would wrinkle as she inhaled, and while sipping the sour coffee she would wince slightly, as if it had been straight vodka going down her throat. I may have picked up her coffee habit, but her evident displeasure from cigarettes is what stopped me from ever smoking.

Until those last days, she wore bright red lipstick. Scarlet stains garlanded the white filters as the butts accumulated in the ashtray. She smoked True Blues, a cigarette that came on the market around the time I was born. They're still out there, although I understand it's not so easy to find them anymore. The big drawing card for the brand was that it has less tar and nicotine than any other smokes out there. It also has a "recessed filter"—inside the plastic mouthpiece, the filter is set a little way back from the smoker's lips, like a built-in shallow cigarette holder.

True Blues are so low in tar and nicotine that the people who smoke them have to inhale more deeply to get any juice out of them. If you smoke them long enough, you'll probably end up with a network of creases around your lips, like my mom. And if she was any indication, there is so little satisfaction to True Blues that you have to puff on one after another to feel as if you're smoking at all. She went through two and a half packs of those babies every day.

She lasted a little over a year after my father died. Lung cancer got her, so technically you could say it was death by cigarettes. But I wonder whether that would be disingenuous. She told me many times that she wanted to die. In her old country accent, almost as thick as it had been when I was a child—perhaps only a few degrees more assimilated than when she emigrated as a teenager after World War II—she would say, "I wish I could find a doctor who would just give me a pill." She said this so often that once I called her bluff and suggested, "That could probably be arranged." She let the comment dissipate into the air like cigarette smoke.

After my father died, she took early retirement from her social work job at an old-age home and spent her remaining year collecting a pension, sitting around the apartment, and smoking. She ate once a day, and the meal—a reheated piece of spit-roasted chicken with some defrosted vegetables I'd bought for her in a market around the corner—was consumed without pleasure, choked down as if it were a punishment. She had always groomed herself impeccably, but at that point she let go. Several days would pass before she took a bath, dressed, or even brushed her wavy hair, no longer dyed, white as whipped cream. Seeing her unkempt, without the red lipstick, was almost as disarming as it would have been to see her naked.

A doctor said she had suffered a "mild stroke." Although only sixty-one, she was extremely depressed and completely befuddled: her short-term memory was shot. Time after time, after saying she wished she were dead, she would add, "I have no one, no one in the world," and sometimes, "I should have married another Lithuanian." These remarks were a dagger in my heart. The first erased me from existence, and the second made clear that, had her wish come true, I would have never been born.

These feelings, or at any rate similar ones, were not entirely unfamiliar. As a child I remember her as affectionate and attentive—until suddenly she wasn't. In an instant she would disappear, although still in the room, lost in a reverie about which she never spoke. It was an eerie feeling, her being there and not being there. There were times when she would hear an innocuous song on the radio—"Those Were the Days" or "Yesterday"—and tears would well up in her eyes. After an instant she would go silent and compose herself. When she pushed away her emotions it was a palpable sight, like a sated diner pushing away his plate after a meal.

Something was inaccessible—dead, buried, frozen solid—in her center. When I was a child, my father told me that she had been "in the war," but that was as far as it went. It wasn't discussed. However, even as a little boy, I understood an absence enshrouded her; she had no relatives. When I was nine or ten, I saw a documentary in school about the war, black-and-white images of starving skeletons in striped uniforms, of dead bodies piled in heaps on top of one another. The corpses gave me nightmares; I understood that some of them might have been my family. When she lived among those corpses she had been a child, just as I was a child when I formed a limited understanding of her past. This nightmare awareness formed whatever symbiosis we had.

It wasn't until I was a teenager that she went into a little more detail, and only because I prodded her insistently. She offered only a handful of facts. When the Soviets invaded Lithuania in 1939, she was nine. Her entire family was wiped out—parents, three brothers, and a sister. Her father was a Jew who had converted to Catholicism to marry her mother, but when the Nazi mobile units invaded Vilnius in 1941, they were both thought good enough to be killed— not shipped to a concentration camp but shot through the head by neighbors. She saw one of her brothers, who resisted the Nazis, beaten to death on the street.

If some of her neighbors were patriotic enough to kill her parents and siblings, she survived much of the war hidden by others, living in a closet. They let her out for some meals and a weekly bath. At the end of the war, the Soviets occupied again and she spent the better part of a year living in the forest as an appendage to two other families. After the war ended, the U.S. wanted to save the world from communism. Thousands of refugees from the Soviet-occupied Baltic nations were allowed into the U.S., and in 1948, after marking time in displaced-person camps, she became one of them.

And that was all she would tell me. When I asked more questions she would raise her voice in a heavily accented complaint: "Why are you torturing me? I don't remember! I was only nine years old!" Sometimes she would look daggers at me; sometimes she would shed tears. Obviously I felt mortified to have caused a woman who had suffered so much even further anguish.

In Chicago with no family, she had an unparalleled opportunity to live the American Dream, or a variation of it: a wholesale reinvention of herself, a complete erasure of the blackboard of the past. As an intelligent war refugee she found scholarships to Lake Forest College in Chicago and then the Columbia School of Social Work in New York. Her first job was with the New York Association for New Americans, assisting immigrants like herself to acclimate to the New World. She looks beautiful in photographs from those days: wavy black hair down to her neck, bee-stung lips, a mischievous smile, a voluptuous body.

Was there ever a time when she experienced joy or happiness? Or any more pleasure than drinking black coffee on an empty stomach? I can only assume that no matter how successful she was in spinning off a new life, the old one would keep popping up, like a jack-in-the-box with a horrific face. Was she haunted by the ghosts of her dead brothers and sister, her parents? Did she wake up in a cold sweat from nightmares? Did she miss Europe, despite it being the scene of her family's destruction?

Few men go into social work. I can only imagine that she married my father—a man who relentlessly criticized her, who I never saw touch her with fondness or affection, who showed no interest in that voluptuous body and with whom she shared a loveless bed for more than twenty years—because no one else asked. They touched at some point in their lives. I have a photograph of them with their arms around each other on a vacation in Puerto Rico, during which I was conceived. She was thirty-six when they married—in 1966, an old maid—and thirty-eight when I was born.

For the last ten years of her professional life, she attended to the needs of a moribund population at the old-age home: the infirm, the feeble, the baffled, the terminal. Much of her time on that job was spent working on a ward of terminal patients known as Scheinbaum Seven. Perhaps Scheinbaum had been a significant donor to the home, while Seven meant the seventh floor. "After Scheinbaum Seven, you go to heaven" was the general joke. Perhaps working there helped prepare her to die. How exhausted she looked that final year, although she had smooth skin; aside from the network around her lips she had few wrinkles. "I fucked up my life," she would say in a cloud of cigarette smoke. There was no self-pity in her tone; she was stating a fact like the color of the sky or the sum of two and two. "I had a terrible marriage. I have no friends, no relatives. I have no one." She would ask, "Why have I suffered so much?" and add, "I hate my life and wish I were dead."

Sometimes your dreams come true. She began to cough unceasingly. There were severe chest and stomach pains. She stopped eating; she hacked up blood. She could barely get out of bed. Her skin was cool and blue. The doctors said it was too late for chemo. The cancer spread to her bones. It was horrible, but quick. The worst of it lasted less than six months.

After she died and I went to study creative writing, it occurred to me to try to fashion something inspired by her experience, the same way that my father's death resulted in Rodrigo's story. But when I began to read about the war years in Lithuania—literature I had studiously avoided while she was alive—I was shocked and overwhelmed. If you look at Germany in World War II, it's a snap to distinguish the good guys from the bad guys. But the Baltic nations were a free-for-all. The Germans who were there, the Soviets, the Lithuanian army, but especially the ordinary citizens—all barbarians.

Even the Nazis were amazed by the alacrity with which the Lithuanians slaughtered the Jews. The first day in the library I read the account of a Lithuanian survivor who remembered some of his neighbors *sawing in half* a screaming Jewish child and leaving her in two bloody parts on the sidewalk. They were not even soldiers; they were just the folks next door. And it didn't stop in 1945. Lithuanians who weren't lucky enough to escape had the pleasure of living through a guerrilla war and skirmishes against the Red Army that lasted well into the 1950s. If you didn't have that kind of fun, maybe you got to spend your winter holidays in Siberia after being deported.

I was twenty-three when she died. I tended to keep this thought to myself most of the time, because of the horrified looks I saw on people's faces when I said it out loud. But I knew my parents did me a favor by dying when I was still a young man. They allowed me to close the book on their lives and begin mine. Like my mother the new American and my father the former Mississippian, I was free to reinvent myself as an orphaned young writer. They gave me the liberty to stop worrying about them. Their early deaths taught me that survival is a miracle, not a curse.

Being my parents' son wiped out any illusions I might have had about the world, which I recognized from early on as an unjust place. Caprices of geography and history—being born in Lithuania in 1930, being gay in New York in 1990—can have deadly, dire consequences. Being their son prepared me to live in Mexico, a country where half the people are born in poverty and destined to die in it, where justice exists only as an abstract concept in black and white, where survival is arbitrary.

Although I didn't remember a single day in which it was easy to be her son, I missed my mother—the elegantly polite manners, the thick accent, even the tragic cloud that always hovered above her, mixed with the cigarette smoke. The melody line of my life was the consciousness of death, and I was indebted to her for that. Because of her experience, I understood that death always lurked around the corner—indeed, I ingested that from her breast milk, before I had a consciousness.

MORE *MEDIA NARANJA*

"You don't want to go to trial, Esperanza. Believe me, it's always better to make a deal."

"Why? What difference does it make?"

They sit on folding chairs at a plastic table, their feet on unclean carpeting the color of dust. She listens to Richard sigh, watches his eyes look up at the fluorescent light, where the cinder block walls meet the pasteboard panels of the ceiling. One of them is broken; she can see wires above them.

"This is something you should really talk about with Catherine. I can tell you on broad terms, but she's your lawyer and she'll give you the best advice. I say you don't want to go to trial because you never know who might get picked for the jury. There are some very stupid, narrow-minded, and racist people in Louisiana."

Esperanza plays with an old manila envelope that someone has left on the table, perhaps the last attorney who had a meeting with a client. The maneuver is made slightly more complex because she is wearing handcuffs. All prisoners are cuffed during legal visits, a measure recently instituted by the Plaquegoula Parish Jail's authorities, since an inmate attacked a guard not long ago. Richard continues: "And you cannot get chosen for a jury in a case where the outcome could be the death penalty unless you swear beforehand that you believe in the death penalty."

"What do you mean?"

"This is a little complicated. If there's a case where they are trying someone for dealing drugs, and you get called up for jury duty, the attorneys might ask you whether you know anyone who has gone to jail for drug crimes, or you know anyone who uses drugs, or if you think drugs should be legal. If you say that you do, he will probably ask if, nevertheless, you can still judge the case on its merits, and follow the laws as they are written, despite your beliefs. And you might even get picked for the jury anyway."

Esperanza nods. This is abstract to her; they don't have juries in Mexico. There are no trials as such. Court cases are decided by judges after they read massive briefs delivered by lawyers from both sides.

"But in a death-penalty case, you can't get picked for the jury unless you swear to the lawyers that you believe in the death penalty. The only people who get picked are the ones who are ready to kill you—the ones who are almost looking for an excuse to kill you. Already, they're not going to like you because you're Mexican. It's like you're walking into the trial with one strike against you. Or maybe two strikes. That's why you want to negotiate for a plea bargain with the prosecutor."

Esperanza puts down the envelope, fingers a sleeve of her orange jumpsuit. "Do you believe in God?" she asks.

Richard pauses before answering. "I consider myself a religious person."

"I believe in God," says Esperanza. "My belief in Him protects me. No matter what happens to me. Do you understand? I will get what He wants for me, and I'll be all right. My fate is in His hands."

"I think it's great that you're a believer, Esperanza. I know that faith can help us enormously through the most difficult passages of our lives. But belief is not just a passive experience. It's not like your life is some lottery ticket you got handed from heaven. You can help Catherine and me with your defense, and try to make the best of this situation here on earth, and still be sustained by your belief."

"Jesus didn't feel he had to defend himself."

"Yeah," says Richard, smirking out of the side of his mouth. "And look how well he did in his death-penalty trial."

Against her better judgment, she laughs. "You're an idiot," she says, and picks up the envelope again.

"What music did you listen to when you were a kid?" he asks out of the blue.

The question is a relief. At least he's not prying into her family or explaining the law again. She begins to hum "Media Naranja."

"I know that song," he says. Implausibly to her, he begins to hum along.

"Where do you know it from?"

"I spent the summer in Mexico when I was a senior in high school. And they were playing that song everywhere. No matter where I went. I was in a village in Oaxaca building latrines, and all the little kids were singing it. In Oaxaca City, a blind man played it on a pan flute. In Mexico City, the taxi driver had it on his radio. It blasted out of every record store. I could not escape from that song. What's it called?"

"'Media Naranja.' It was very popular when I was a little girl."

"Keep on singing it."

"No!"

"Come on, just a little."

He must be crazy, she thinks. And then she wonders if she isn't crazy too, when she finds herself singing, *"Tu, mi complemento, mi media naranja, ya te quiero, sin cruzar palabra...."* until she cuts herself off.

They sit there in silence until he says, "That brought back memories."

For Esperanza too. "You're an idiot," she says with a smile. For a moment she forgets she is a prisoner in jail; she almost feels she is on a date with him. And she leans toward him, knowing that she is crossing some kind of boundary, almost flirting with him.

"You know what I really want?" she says. "So bad that I wouldn't care if they gave me the death penalty for it?"

"What?" he asks.

"A Coca-Cola," she says. "I haven't had one since I was arrested."

He smiles. "That's all?" he asks. "You know we're not allowed to bring anything to drink or eat in here to legal visits."

"I heard another girl say that her lawyer brings her a Coke every time he visits," she says. She can see his mind working behind the eyebrows. She knows he doesn't want to disappoint her.

"Let me see what I can do," he says. He looks at the door to see if anyone is peering into the Plexiglas window. "Next time I visit."

"Okay." She smiles and gives him a kick under the table. "Then at least you'll be good for something."

WHAT A DIFFERENCE
A DAY MADE

One of the stupidest sayings I have ever heard is that it is just as easy to fall in love with a rich girl as a poor one. What's love got to do with it? The crucial point is that there are so many more millions of poor girls than rich ones.

Having said that, falling in love with Carla was one of the easiest things I've ever accomplished. It happened in a dive called Dan's near my parents' apartment (which I inherited after their deaths, and where I was still living in Brooklyn—in Prospect Heights, before any hipsters arrived). I was putting some dollar bills into the jukebox when I felt pheromones waft over me, as if they had been sprayed at the back of my neck with an atomizer.

"What songs have you picked?" a woman asked.

I turned to her, prepared to make a caustic remark. Despite the darkness of the bar, I inventoried dark eyes with implausibly long lashes, cascading curly black hair, a pouty mouth with ruby lips. It was freezing outside, and she wore a long cloth coat, black with the collar turned up.

"James Brown," I said. "Archie Bell and the Drells." I looked into her eyes. "'Stardust.'" I moved so she could take her place beside me. "Feel free to cut in."

As she leaned toward the light of the jukebox I got a better look at her smooth skin and long neck, the attractive way her eyes narrowed as she squinted to read the titles. In high-heeled boots she was almost my height. From a coat pocket she pulled out a pair of glasses with black rectangular frames. She moved aside the coat and put a hand on her waist, revealing a slim figure, a shiny cream blouse, and the strap of a black bra at her clavicle. She chose a tune by Dinah

Washington. I told her that "What a Difference a Day Made" was one of my favorites.

She asked, "Did you know it was a Mexican song?"

I raised an eyebrow. "Really?"

"Really," she said. "'Cuando Vuelva a Tu Lado.' Written by María Grever in 1934. Look it up."

"Okay," I said. "I will." She had led me to a theme of conversation. "Have you ever been to Mexico?" I asked.

"You could say so," she said. "Nearly my whole life. I'm Mexican."

"Get out of here," I said. "How can you be Mexican? You speak English with no accent."

"When I was a girl I watched a lot of *Sesame Street*," she said, and left it at that. She spoke in a mocking tone that sounded as if it had been a clandestine, forbidden activity, accomplished behind closed doors and in dark alleys, like belonging to the French Resistance.

I said I'd published a book of short stories about Mexicans on Long Island. She hadn't read it but said she was aware of it—she'd seen a review somewhere, or had heard someone mention it. I wondered whether she was lying to be polite.

I decided that sharing Mexico was a license to dance. Although I was truly terrible on my feet, the Mexicans are not precisely famous for their terpsichorean skills either. Cubans and Colombians pity them. To the strains of "What a Difference a Day Made," I took her in my arms and we swayed for a few minutes, belly to belly, cheek to cheek. When the song was over, I whispered into her ear that I lived around the corner.

"Can I buy you another drink?" she asked.

"You don't have to ask twice."

The idea of proceeding with caution made perfect sense, but in my heart I most admired women who went to bed with me just after we met. I was grateful for the reckless gamble, placing an extravagant bet on a square marked "complicity." I appreciated the rebelliousness of immediately smashing the ice with a pickaxe to see if there was any reason for us to make a sculpture together. I liked the idea that sex was part of quotidian life and not a bargaining chip to be strategically proffered or withheld. Of course intimacy, like a garden, has to be planted and nurtured before it is cultivated and pruned. But all gardens have to start somewhere, in a patch of raw dirt.

I never had high expectations the first time. In fact, I had an idea that to find out if you are actually compatible with someone, you had to have sex with her every day for a month. (If you are skeptical of that suggestion, then we probably would not have been compatible.) By the time we got to my place, it was late, and Carla and I'd had plenty to drink. Under the circumstances, the sex was as good as it possibly could have been. There was a lot of promise in the abandon with which she gave herself to the encounter, the way she grasped my shoulders, the strangled grunts of her climax. What most excited me was hearing the language of love in another tongue—*mi vida, mi amor, Dios mío, me vengo*—panted words of passion, new or made new, in my ear.

I fell in love the following morning. In bed she wore nothing but my wrinkled shirt from the night before, with only a couple of the buttons fastened. I brought her coffee in a yellow cup and placed it on the bedside table. I told her I had nothing to do and if she stuck around I would give her breakfast.

"Well, it's Saturday," she said. "I don't have to go to the bank."

"You work in a bank? Which?" She named one downtown that had famously acquired one of Mexico's biggest banks. This was after a bunch of them crashed and had to be bailed out by a government that showed no similar generosity when it came to feeding fifty million poor people. I imagined her handing out bills at a cashier's window and asked, "How long have you been there?"

"About two years," she said. "Since I got my MBA."

An MBA was as exotic to me as any foreign country. "What do you do?"

She picked up the yellow cup and warmed her palms with it. After sipping the coffee, she wore the same smug smile with which she'd told me that "What a Difference a Day Made" was a Mexican song and that she learned English from *Sesame Street*. She took a deep breath and patiently tried to explain to me what derivatives were, how calls and puts work. Casually she mentioned Ito's lemma and the Black-Scholes equation, as if they were as simple as the alphabet or the times table. Later she would turn on my computer to show me a mathematical formula that might as well have been in Chinese. I also had a master's degree, but I felt like a child next to her. Indeed, I have never felt so stupid in my life. It was her intelligence that dazzled me. I undid the two buttons that held together her shirt—my shirt—hoping for further promise that we were compatible.

FREE TRADE

Esperanza and Hilda wake just before dawn. Their alarm is the belching caw of roosters that strut outside in the dirt. Arising from the mattress they share on the cracked cement floor, Hilda heats water for Nescafé on the hot plate, while Esperanza flicks a switch and a bare bulb lights the tiny bathroom. It's back to the basics: when she's finished on the toilet, she will go outside and, using a hose, fill a bucket with water so she can "flush." Next to the humming refrigerator, Hilda has hung a picture of the Virgin of Guadalupe in a heart-shaped frame and another of the mother and child she left behind in Cucaramácara.

Before setting off for work, their faces will be scrubbed, teeth brushed, clothes chosen from "shelves" of blue plastic milk crates. Hair will be combed, tightly pinned, and pulled back in ponytails. Breakfast will wait until they get to the factory. The cinder block shack where they live is an add-on behind a house where distant cousins of Hilda's live. The relatives don't ask the girls for much rent—they know how little people earn in factories here.

After waiting, huddled in the wind for ten minutes, Hilda and Esperanza encase themselves into a minivan alongside twelve other women. Their upper arms and thighs meld into those of the ones sitting next to them. It will take the women an hour to get to work. Most of them will sleep along the way, but the insomniacs can watch the dawn break over Rancho Amargo, one of the furthermost neighborhoods in the sprawling outskirts of Ciudad Juárez, one of many communities in the endless horizontal spread of the city. These shantytowns were constructed in a makeshift improvisation to accommodate the tens of thousands who poured into Juárez after the Free Trade Agreement was passed with the gringos, and the *maquilas*—

assembly and piecework factories—opened up or expanded their business.

Rancho Amargo has an unconstructed, do-it-yourself appearance. No matter how long its residents live there, there is an air of the temporary. There are no sidewalks or paved streets, just steep hills and dirt paths, where unpainted one-story cinder block shacks with rebar popping out of the roofs have been ground into the terrain and feebly assembled. The houses are interspersed with piles of rocks and rubble, and empty lots overgrown with weeds. It is a landscape of discarded tires, abandoned mattresses, upturned plastic buckets, empty bags that once contained potato chips. Cracks in the windows are covered with masking tape. Discarded grocery bags flap in the breeze.

Whole families of drained plastic bottles are embedded or impaled in fences of clapboard, chicken wire, razor wire, barbed wire—all of it sagging, somehow unable to contain the wilt of the populace. Graffiti, odd combinations of letters and numbers, decorates most available wall space. Raggedy clothes slump everywhere—drying on a line, hung outside a house in a hopeless jumble sale, mysteriously forsaken atop a clump of earth. It doesn't rain for most of the year in Juárez, but burst sewer pipes and water mains leave vast, soupy mud puddles in the middle of the road. When the rains finally come, many houses in Rancho Amargo are flooded up to their tenants' belly buttons. In the dry season, on a windy day the dust permeates hair and clothing, insists its way into squinting eyes and slack mouths.

To get to the factory, Hilda and Esperanza will pass the periphery of downtown. Next to the Rio Grande, cargo containers are piled one atop another behind chain-link fences: Hanjin, Hapag-Lloyd, Hamburg Süd. Who knows how many toasters or blenders, assembled in Juárez, can fit into each container? Or how many cars or computers? Or guns, or methamphetamines, or men from the Fujian Province whose fondest hope is to work off the debt to their smuggler in the kitchen of a restaurant at the end of a subway line in New York?

In this part of town, smirking day-trippers used to traipse across the International Bridge and wander the streets in search of a taste of the cargo they couldn't get at home: bargain-basement booze; cheap narcotics clandestine and over the counter; bodies built to endure, encased in tight skirts, flashing gold-capped smiles. But there are no more tourists in the downtown of rat-infested alleys, crumbling architecture, and prostitutes with bodies shaped like dinner rolls. Only a colony of ghostly presences that exists on the margin of piracy and contraband, counting out cash and splitting it behind closed doors, the proceeds of powders and pills, guns stashed in the trunks of cars, bodies in corners of abandoned buildings, all sexes and ages, dead and alive.

It had been Hilda's idea to try their luck in Juárez. Almost as soon as they met in Morelia, she suggested the plan to Esperanza. Wouldn't it be better to work in a *maquila* and make four thousand pesos a month—twice as much as they earned as domestics? Did Esperanza want to be a slave for the rest of her life, saying *"sí, señora"* and *"no, señora,"* taking orders no matter how capricious from some crazy lady who had nothing better to do than transfer her misery to the *muchacha*? Wouldn't she prefer to live independently, come and go as she pleased, without anyone snooping around in her room, in her life?

Esperanza didn't take the idea seriously until after Leonardo robbed the house and she was fired. It took her weeks to find another job, weeks where she uncomfortably slept on the lumpy couch in her sister María Concepción's house. When she finally found work, it was several steps down from her previous position. She was given a tiny cell on the roof of a house; it was fall and she shivered each night as she tried to sleep. The señora who employed her was meaner than the previous one: she made Esperanza work day and night, and paid her 1,500 pesos a month instead of the going rate of 2,000.

Juárez. Esperanza was wary. She asked Hilda, "Isn't that where they go around killing women?"

Hilda laughed. "They haven't killed any of my cousins yet," she said. "And you don't think they kill any women here in Morelia?"

What frightened Esperanza most about the plan wasn't the prospect of getting murdered, but the thousand miles that would separate her from her family. At the same time, she considered how detached her life already was from theirs. After she started her new job, she knew that María Concepción's husband, Juan Pablo, was glad to be rid of her, and she seldom visited. She went to Puroaire to see her mother only every couple of months. When she got there, Mamá was often too exhausted to even maintain much of a conversation. If she earned twice as much money, she could send more home.

Esperanza felt she could count on Hilda, even more than her own sisters. She had been especially sympathetic after Esperanza was betrayed by Leonardo. There were so many Sundays when Hilda had patiently listened while she cried her heart out, and tried to cheer her up with a walk in the plaza and a shared *torta*. Esperanza believed they could take care of each other just as well as if they were truly sisters. If Hilda was willing to leave behind her baby son with her mother in Cucaramácara, then she, who had no children yet, could also throw caution to the winds and embark on the adventure.

When she imagined the prospects of going to another city and beginning a new life, a kind of elation overtook Esperanza. She couldn't have precisely defined what might be different. She didn't dream of being rich. She never pictured herself living in a home as opulent as the señora's. But in her mind's eye she could halfway envision a house marginally better than the place in which she grew up. She could imagine living in or near the center of a city. She could picture living somewhere where the toilet flushed without the intervention of a bucket of water. She could imagine a table with a clean cloth beside a window. Against her better judgment, after her experience with Leonardo, she could still imagine a husband. She could imagine children. She could imagine love.

They finally arrive at the industrial park where the *maquilas* are located. Beyond enormous steel doors painted an industrial gray is the universe of Border Textiles & Sewing Internacional, SA. They cross a parking lot, from which huge trailer trucks move Border Textiles' products across the International Bridge, and enter the building, removing their coats and putting on blue smocks. In the company cafeteria, women disguised in shower caps and surgical masks dole out with ladles and spoons the subsidized breakfast of scrambled eggs, *chilaquiles en salsa roja*, a glass of milk, and a plastic basket of flour tortillas. Quickly swallowed, it will cost them each only ten pesos.

Border Textiles is five stories tall, and on each floor there is an immense fluorescent-lit work space the size of a football field. Any number of products is manufactured here. That cute little yellow onesie with the words WHAT I SAY GOES that Aunt Minnie found for the baby at the Family Dollar on the outskirts of Pine Bluff? It was made at Border Textiles. At the end of October, when the winds get vicious in Kenosha, it breaks Cousin Fannie's heart to watch Princeling quiver when she takes him out for his walk. So she bought him that darling sweater with the leopard print through which she can pass his little paws. Once he's got that thing on, he can stroll with his maw held high. She found the garment at the Pleasant Prairie Premium Outlets, but it was *hecho en México*, right there at Border Textiles. Remember when Uncle Carl swallowed the cap to the beer bottle last spring and had to be taken to the emergency room at Fresno Surgical? And that ER orderly with the maternal smile and unnaturally white teeth who held Carl's hand through the worst of it? Who later slapped him across the face after he couldn't resist pinching her on the heinie? Her scrubs, the color of lime Jell-O, were made at Border Textiles.

Along with a woman named Minerva, twenty-two years old and from Torreón, Hilda and Esmeralda take their places at a workstation where they will spend the next twelve hours. They are in the stitching section. At each three-girl workstation, a huge basket of blue straps emblazoned with WALMART is waiting for them as they sit down. There are also boxes of plastic buckles—some with three prongs sticking out of them, the others with a hollow into which the prongs fit and fasten. The girls loop one end of each ribbon through a slot in the buckle with the prongs, fold it and line it up at a rickety stitching contraption, then step on a pedal on the floor that activates the motor and sews the ribbon to the buckle in a lock stitch. They will repeat the operation at the other end of the strap, with the buckle that swallows and engulfs the prongs.

After sewing on the two pieces of plastic, each girl will have completed the first unit of the day—one of those ribbons with which babies are encased in supermarket carts so their mothers can shop undisturbed. The ribbons will be affixed to shopping carts in Walmarts from Brownsville to Bismarck, from Nashua to Beaverton, across Canada and in the new stores that are opening in Mexico. There is relief during two fifteen-minute breaks during which they're allowed to use the bathroom. They also have a half hour to wolf down a subsidized lunch back in the cafeteria.

Hilda, Esmeralda, and Minerva have a quota of a thousand straps per diem each. If they sew a greater number there is no reward, but if they produce fewer after the twelve-hour shift, they can be sure that they will be reprimanded the following day by Raul, the manager of their section. As long as they make their quota, he treats them with courtesy and respect.

Raul is well into his forties, with a widow's peak and a thousand-yard stare. Since Border Textiles opened a couple of decades earlier, he has supported a wife and three children through his employment with the enterprise, working his way up from the assembly line to transportation dispatcher to floor manager. His job is not easy. Two hundred people have been thrust upon him from a human resources department that believes there are only two criteria for new hires—that they be both living and breathing. Most of his charges are young women, with the attendant complications of their existence: bankruptcy as the calendar approaches payday; flu, fever, colitis, or eczema; drunken fathers, intransigent mothers, brothers who are both proprietary and unemployed.

The greatest complication of managing women is that so many of them have small children, so many cannot administer their medical, financial, or temperamental emergencies by themselves. Many of the two hundred come to Raul with their troubles. He will pretend to listen while counting silently to ten or twenty, by rote nodding in sympathy. Half the girls simply disappear after a few months; he cannot get involved. He just needs to be sure that they arrive reasonably close to the appointed hour when work begins (if they don't they receive a brief but stern lecture with a warning); that they fulfill their quotas (ditto); and that they don't leave before their shifts are done. He turns a blind eye to the fact that plenty of the girls are

clearly underage and have been hired with identification that probably belongs to an older relative. He also ignores the rumors of the
drugs he hears are bought and sold in the restrooms among employees: How else are they going to stay awake in front of the skeleton of
a sewing machine for twelve hours? The bad apples have a way of
weeding themselves out. Under Raul's watch, they can slack off or
show up late only three times. After that, they're out—no explana-
tions, no complaints. The hordes spill into HR every day to fill out
applications. There is a long line of available talent from wherever
it is they came.

Whatever his strengths and weaknesses of character, Hilda and
Esperanza have no complaints about Raul. As far as they are concerned, Border Textiles is a paradise, at least compared with their
previous place of employment, Servicios de Fabricantes, SA, where
they stood on an assembly line and with a razor removed loose bits
of plastic that hung off handles—handles that would ultimately be
attached to coffeemakers, irons, and blenders. Once the appliances
were assembled, they'd be boxed, shipped, and sold in superstores
across the U.S.

Servicios was a free-for-all, and Miguel, the manager, a terror. He
arrived to work unshaven and with tequila on his breath. He would
"joke" that the girls should kiss him when they arrived, or not bother to show up unless they wore miniskirts. He was not above un-
wanted pats, pinches, and squeezes—even while the assembly line
was moving. More than one girl threatened to use her razor against
Miguel, and was fired for opening her mouth. Unfortunately, the
owner of Servicios not only tolerated but encouraged Miguel. One
employee came back to the assembly line in tears after being sum-
moned to the owner's office—he had locked the door, tossed pencils
on the floor, and told her to bend over and pick them up one by one.
There were rumors that far worse incidents had occurred in his lair.
Hilda and Esmeralda lasted less than a year at Servicios, but quit
after two of their colleagues got into a razor fight while on the job
and sent each other to the hospital.

Border Textiles, on the other hand, is kept clean, brightly lit, and
run as methodically as a U-boat. The cheap meals in the cafeteria

are plentiful and reasonably tasty. If there are any problems with the functionality of the sinks and toilets in the employee bathrooms, they're fixed in a heartbeat. When Minerva accidentally stitched two of her fingers together, they sent her straight to the infirmary and she was back at her workstation the next day. Sure, the shifts are endless, but they go home twice a month with two thousand pesos cash in their purses. The factory is the opposite of everything else Esperanza has experienced of the world: orderly, sterile, systematic, predictable.

The monotony is broken up several times a day by Gerardo the Chinaman, who comes with a huge gray plastic basket and fills it with the Walmart ribbons, once the girls have attached the buckles. He will bring them to his own workstation and tie them into bundles of a hundred. Gerardo is stocky with short hair greased forward into a Caesar, and has small, ovular eyes and a thin Fu Manchu moustache, which is why everyone calls him El Chino. (He is actually from Nuevo Casas Grandes, three and a half hours southwest across the endless Chihuahua desert.) Once in a while he balances the bucket on his shoulders and executes a little breakdance, which is when Hilda calls him Hip-Hop Gerardo. If Raul catches him, he gives the young man a look that could kill, but Gerardo has proven to be a trustworthy employee over a couple of years, so it never goes beyond the nasty gaze.

Esperanza wonders what kind of moves he would be capable of if she and Hilda took him to Vaqueritos, where they sometimes dance on Saturday nights. They work only half a day on Saturday and have all of Sunday off. Going out on Saturday night is crucial to Hilda, who says, "I'm not going to waste the only night of the week when I don't have to get up the next day while it's still dark." Vaqueritos is an enormous hall, on the weekend bursting with men and women who work in the *maquilas*, the girls in their tightest jeans and the boys in straw hats and sharp cowboy shirts with snap buttons. They tend to dance *el pasito duranguense*, moves and music recently immigrated back to Mexico by people from Durango who live in Chicago. To a bouncy beat in which the saxophones and trumpets keep oompah time, the guys try to entwine their legs with Esperanza's but are generally cooperative if she prefers to dance a little less close.

There are always more men than women at Vaqueritos, so you can dance all night if you want, and most of the time a guy will volunteer to buy a girl a beer if she's thirsty. There is a big TV set over the bar that usually broadcasts soccer games so the guys can be entertained while they wait to be served.

Hilda and Esperanza have found a few temporary romances at Vaqueritos. There was one guy, Daniel, who said he wanted to marry Hilda, but then he snuck across the river to *el gabacho* and was never heard from again. A few months earlier one fellow took Esperanza out on a couple of dates, but he disappeared after the first time they had a furtive and sloppy coitus in the cab of his pickup. Someone told her he had joined the U.S. Army in exchange for a green card. It's been two years since they came to Juárez, and Esperanza feels more or less fulfilled: she and Hilda are independent and solvent. There is the satisfaction that they made something happen and that, more or less, it has worked. If she has no major complaints, she is also aware that none of what she fantasized about has come to pass. She is nowhere near the center of any city. She can't flush the toilet without a bucket of water. There is no tablecloth, and the only table is made from upturned milk crates. The shack where they live is a cinder block box with no windows. There is no husband. There are no children. She hasn't given up hope, but there is no love.

THE ROAD TO MEXICO

What I liked best about being married was the sprawling expanse of time it implied. Previous to marriage, when I dated, if I had trouble with a girlfriend, I immediately asked myself why I didn't dump her and start looking for someone better. Matrimony brought out the romantic in me. It was meant to last forever, and if a problem came up, it didn't have to be resolved that day or even the next. We had till death do us part to work it out.

Was this a healthy attitude, or merely ingenuous? There were issues and perhaps I didn't want to face their magnitude. Soon after we tied the knot, sex became less frequent and, on Carla's part, less enthusiastic. Gone were the gasps, the passionate panting, the abandon. When we made love, she would often bring herself to climax, which seemed splendidly self-reliant, but also made me feel excluded. I sensed she was hurrying to get it over with. When I brought this up, she confessed to a condition that I interpreted as the Catholic imperative. Before marriage sex had been about adventure and intrigue, secrecy and sin. She revealed, for instance, an affair she'd had with the boyfriend of her best friend, and another with her married supervisor at a previous job. Marriage was like leaving the corps of a loose-limbed modern dance company with an infinite number of possible partners, and being consigned to the strictest ballet, to eternally execute a strenuous pas de deux *en pointe* with the same colleague forever. She'd been unprepared.

"Have patience," she pleaded.

I was unsettled, but said, *"No hay problema."*

If you come from a severely dysfunctional family, as you make your own way, you follow one of two instincts. Either you run as far as you can from the possibility of your own family, or you create

one as soon as viable, as a form of repairing the damage. I wanted children immediately. I could imagine the joy of watching them
take their first steps, the happiness of looking at them lick ice-cream
cones with delighted concentration, the patience with which I'd
help them learn to read. Carla didn't want them, at least not yet.
What are we waiting for? "I want to make some money first." She'd
alluded to this many times; finally I asked her how much. "Five
million," she said, as if it were twenty-five cents. "Then we can do
whatever we want." *Five million pesos?* "No, dollars." *How are you
going to make five million dollars?* Carla was a junior banker—a glo-
rified assistant to the high-stakes players—earning a straight salary
of a hundred thousand dollars, which was far more than I'd ever
made and seemed like a fortune at the time. But you could live
for centuries and never save five million from it. She had hoped
to inherit accounts from private bankers who left to work for other institutions and as such build a fortune. Three years after being
hired, she had made no progress. She complained bitterly about
her bosses for not promoting her, and that her father's filthy-rich
friends in Mexico wouldn't entrust her to invest their millions.
Carla saved none of her salary. We didn't pay rent; our apartment
in an Upper West Side high-rise was her father's wedding gift. But
she had to keep up appearances, so we went out a couple of times
a week to the same over-the-top restaurants as her colleagues. To
imply to her cohorts that I had money, she asked me to pay for the
meals on my credit card and reimbursed me later. (It was my money
that paid for the more modest dinners that I cooked at home the rest
of the week.)

Carla wore clothes and jewelry the brands of which would be
immediately recognized by her associates as expensive. She didn't
ask me for pearls or Prada; she knew I was husbanding the modest proceeds from the sale of my parents' apartment and what I
earned from part-time teaching gigs and the occasional magazine
assignment.

They say men are resentful when their wives earn more than they
do. I had no such problem; I liked being married to a banker. Some
days I even let myself share her daydream of the five million she'd

one day have in the bank, and the freedom it would buy. In any case, her salary and the free apartment were a relief, given the vagaries of my income.

I enjoyed going to Fairway and choosing what we'd have for dinner. Most nights, as she ate, Carla complained about her work. "It's all politics," she'd say. "I'm no one's servant and they know it." Or else, "I'm too smart for the job. You have to be stupid to be satisfied with catering to the client's every whim." When I suggested that if she was so unhappy, she should perhaps think of doing something else, she dismissed me. She just wanted to blow off steam. I learned to keep my mouth shut.

Three or four years after the wedding, when my novel tanked and Carla failed to become a significant earner for the bank, married life lost all traces of the carefree. She was unhappy but stopped talking about it. When Bear Stearns ramped up its business in mortgage-backed securities and put Victor, a Mexican friend of hers, in charge, he was able to offer her a job. She went running to him with high hopes. Then she got pregnant, which I thought was a miracle. I remember the night she told me, and how happy she seemed as I fed her the olives from the Martini I mixed. Although she didn't drink Martinis, she so loved the taste of olives that had been marinating in gin that I always gave them to her from my glass.

Still, she worked many nights and sometimes weekends, and I felt very much abandoned when she traveled on business. I had become estranged from most of the friends I'd made in grad school and publishing. I told myself they hid from me because they were afraid my failure would rub off on them. In truth it was I who was ashamed and stopped calling. I consoled myself, remembering how Carla used to say she liked being married to a writer. But she'd liked being married to one whose work appeared on the *New York Times* list of Notable Books, not to a flameout.

Without family or friends, I believe I put too much pressure on the marriage. Carla must have sensed my neediness and felt suffocated. When we went for dinners with her colleagues, I knew I had little in common with them, but felt flattered that they accepted me—inasmuch as they spoke Spanish in my presence and felt free to criticize the U.S. around me. They may have seen me as a gringo, but I was *their* gringo, one who could be tolerated, even trusted. Later I would realize that they hardly saw me at all, except as an appendage to Carla.

In any case, by the time she got pregnant, I had a plan B. I'd been hired on my first case as a mitigation specialist—Roberto the cop killer. I went from town to town in Zacatecas and found the nun who gave him Bible classes, the brothers who bitterly remembered their father's beatings, the doctor who had treated his head wound when he fell out a window sixteen years earlier. The lawyers on the case made it clear that my work was exceptional. I had a future in mitigation. It was a job that gave me some perspective about all my previous petty worries over who and how many had read my books. It took me out of myself and into a much wider world.

For that first case I earned $65 an hour—more than I'd ever made before—and that was only because I'd just begun. In this line of work, people made up to $100 an hour, some even more. If I worked hard on enough cases, I'd be the one earning a hundred thousand, and saving lives in the bargain. A hundred thousand dollars may not have been a fortune in New York, but it would be pretty sweet in Mexico City. I could carry the weight while the baby was an infant and Carla figured out what she might do next.

When I proposed the plan to her, I thought she'd be as elated as I was. But she said nothing, just curled up on the sofa and cried. I took her in my arms, moved the curls from her face, wiped away her tears with my thumb. "What's the matter?" I asked. She just shook her head and said, "I'm sorry." That was when I knew I'd lost her.

She went on a business trip and didn't come back. I got her on the cell phone and she said, "We have to talk." *Okay, let's talk.* "Not now, when I get home." *When are you coming back?* "In a few days." *Carla, where are you?* She hung up.

ONE LIFE

A note came by messenger. She said she lost the baby. She needed to cool off. More than anything, she needed her own space. She admitted it was a terrible thing to ask, but could I please disappear for a little while? Just a few days, until she thought things through. If I didn't, then she wasn't sure when she'd come back, or if she would at all. Again, she said she was sorry.

Of course I was shocked. She wouldn't answer her phone. What was I supposed to do? A day stretched into a week. Knowing that she didn't want me there, I couldn't stay in the apartment. Another defense lawyer asked me to work for a new Mexican client, so I bought an exquisitely liberating one-way ticket to Mexico City. How American was I, anyway? My mother had been Lithuanian and I'd barely met my father's relatives in Mississippi. I was born and raised in New York City, a geographical and cultural extremity. I was only American inasmuch as I believed in my ability to pick up and reinvent myself wherever I wanted.

I let Carla know where she could reach me. A couple of weeks later, when the divorce papers arrived, I holed up in a hotel in the *centro histórico* for a couple of days, and moved between my room and the cantina off the lobby, which had the Los Panchos and Eydie Gormé cover of "Cuando Vuelva a Tu Lado"—the Spanish-language original of "What a Difference a Day Made"—on the jukebox. I listened to it over and over. Whenever Eydie sang, *"Une tu labio al mío y estréchame en tus brazos,"* I wept. I hadn't cried so deeply since I was a child. Luckily, a grown man sobbing was perfectly normal behavior in a Mexico City cantina. After a while I took a deep breath, signed the papers and mailed them back. I always thought that Carla was smarter than me. She realized she'd made a mistake, was adult enough to admit it and move on. I followed her example.

It took some time to get those five years with her out of my system. I wondered if Carla might have aborted rather than miscarried. I would never know. What was clear was that I could add our baby to my accumulating list of the dead. Within a year I found out that Victor, Carla's boss, had ditched his wife and that he and Carla had married. A child soon followed.

161

I like to think that Carla did me a favor. She set me free to take a giant step. If we'd stayed married in New York, I might have ended up one of those embittered old men you see drinking out of a cardboard cup in Starbucks, saying to myself, "If only I'd gone to Mexico."

INVESTIGATION

Inspector Rodríguez is small framed and round shouldered, and wears dark glasses. The lenses are so large that he looks like a house-fly. They are not precisely sunglasses—covering his eyes are black plastic slabs with minuscule holes that allow only a tiny bit of light to penetrate. After waiting around for a couple of hours in the gray lobby of the police station on Sunday morning, Esperanza and Gerardo are escorted into his office and asked to sit on chairs in front of his desk. When they speak, he lifts his chin at a space in between them, although never precisely at their faces. He thanks them for coming and asks when they last saw *la señorita* Helga.

"Hilda," says Esperanza.

The inspector pauses and then smiles. "Correct," he says.

"Last night," says Esperanza. Gerardo squirms uncomfortably. He tried to convince Esperanza that there was no point in going to the police station to file a missing-persons report. "They don't care," he said, "and won't do anything to find her." When Esperanza said she would go whether he accompanied her or not, he sighed and said he wouldn't let her go alone.

Inspector Rodríguez writes something on a sheet of paper. "Do you have a photo of her?" he asks. Rodríguez's thick hair is black as charcoal, but white at the roots.

Esperanza recalls a picture that María Concepción took of the two of them on her cell phone back in Morelia. They were standing in the Plaza de Armas, outside the cathedral with the famous pipe organ. Both she and Hilda were so tiny in the photo that she doubts it would do any good. In any case, she doesn't have it.

"No," she says.

"What does she look like?"

"Short." Esperanza stands and puts a hand at her clavicle. "About this high. Thin. Brown. With curly brown hair." As she returns to her chair, she realizes she has just described who knows how many millions of Mexican women.

"Any birthmarks? Moles? Scars?"

"None that I can remember."

"Where did you last see her?" asks the inspector, the smile still on his face.

"At Vaqueritos," she says. "It's a nightclub near Rancho Amargo."

"Oh yes," he says. "I know it well."

Esperanza can't imagine he has ever gone dancing at Vaqueritos. Does he know it "well" because other girls who went there have disappeared? Gerardo reaches under his baseball cap and scratches his hair.

"Tell me what happened," says the inspector.

"We were at the club. Hilda was dancing with a guy, and then when I looked for her a little later, I didn't see her. It was as if she disappeared into thin air."

"Interesting," says the inspector, still smiling. "Into thin air. So you and Señorita Helga work at Vaqueritos?"

Where did he get that idea? "Hilda," says Esperanza. "No. We work at Border Textiles."

"Correct," says the inspector. "Border Textiles." He scribbles on the sheet of paper. "Do you go to Vaqueritos frequently?"

"No. Maybe once or twice a month."

"And Señorita Helga?"

"*Hilda.*"

"Yes." He writes again.

"The same. Once or twice a month."

"So she danced with her boyfriend...."

"He wasn't her boyfriend."

A look of concern crosses Rodríguez's face. "He was a stranger?"

"Yes. I think so."

The inspector nods and writes. Gravely, he says, "So she danced with men she had never met before."

Esperanza absorbs the implicit accusation. "As far as I know."

"Did she do this often?"

"Do what?"

"Dance with strangers? Did she enjoy dancing with strange men?"

"Well, Vaqueritos is a club."

The inspector looks toward a spot on the wall, nodding.

"People go there to dance. Men and women."

After a pause, he says, "Yes, of course. Tell me about the men with whom Helga danced."

Gerardo sneaks a look at Esperanza and then up at the ceiling. He stifles a yawn. They were up all night looking for Hilda in and around the club. Then they stopped by the house and went on to the police station without sleep. Esperanza wonders about the inspector's insistence on giving Hilda a different name, and if there is any point in continuing to correct him.

"Last night," he goes on. "How many men did she 'dance' with?"

"I don't know...."

"Five? Ten? Twenty?"

"I don't know. Maybe three or four." *What in the world is he writing?*

"What were their names?"

Esperanza shrugs. "I don't know. She didn't tell me."

"She didn't know their names, and you don't know their names either?" He nods his head, his lips pursed.

"Well, I didn't dance with them, Helga did. I mean Hilda."

Rodríguez smiles, as if he had caught her in a lie. "Do you also dance with men without asking their names?"

"No. They tell me their names when we dance."

"What were the names of the men you danced with last night?"

In her mind's eye she sees an ocean of men wearing straw hats and cowboy shirts. They are crowded inside Vaqueritos almost to the point of bursting through its walls. Hundreds of them, thousands, smiling and stomping *el pasito duranguense* in place. She remembers Juan Carlos, with whom she went to a hotel almost as soon as he introduced himself, and Pablito, who turns up at the club nearly every time she's there. Neither was in Vaqueritos last night. In any case, she is not going to air out her personal life before the detective and Gerardo, who came to the club for the first time the night before.

Hilda and she had mentioned the place so often that curiosity finally got the better of him. And now look at the mess she's got him into. He looks to the floor, his eyebrows raised. *What did I tell you?*

"I don't remember," she says.

"Did your friend have 'relations' with the men that she danced with? I mean later, outside of the club," asks Rodríguez.

"Not really. She had dates once in a while. There was a guy named Daniel....they went out a few times."

"Daniel. Do you know his last name?"

"No."

"Do you have his telephone number?"

"No. He went to *el gabacho* more than a year ago."

"Ah. And what is your relation to Señorita Helga?"

"Inspector," says Esperanza. "Her name is Hilda, not Helga."

"Correct," he says, scribbling. "Are you family?"

"No. We're friends. We live in the same house."

"Correct. Where are her parents?"

"Her mother and her son are in Michoacán. In Cucaramácara."

"I see. Does she have family here?"

"Yes, cousins. We live with them."

"Ah. What are their names?"

Hilda's cousins adamantly refused to accompany Esperanza to the police station and strongly urged her not to go. *You don't want to get involved with the cops. You don't know what they're like around here. They're worse than the criminals.* But how could you do nothing after your best friend—a girl who has been a sister to you—goes missing? She feels she is betraying the cousins by mentioning their names and address to Rodríguez. She wonders what he will do with the information and immediately regrets divulging it. She is certain that her days are numbered in the cinder block shack in back of their house.

"And you, señorita. Where are you from?"

"Puroaire."

"And you and the other girl came to Juárez together."

"Yes."

"To seek your fortunes," he says, again smiling, again scribbling.

"To get jobs in the *maquilas*."

"Señorita," says the inspector, and puts his pen down. "I have to ask you some sensitive questions, and I promise that what you tell me will not go further than this room. Did Señorita Helga sell drugs?"

"No!"

"Did she use drugs?"

"No, never."

"She didn't use any drugs at all?"

"No, señor."

"Are you sure?"

"Yes, I live with her. I work with her."

"Were any of her boyfriends involved in the drug trade?"

"No!"

"What about all those strangers with whom she danced?"

How would she know? "The men who come to dance at Vaqueritos also work at the *maquilas*, inspector." That's what they tell Esperanza, in any case.

The inspector makes a brief notation and asks, "How long have you worked at Vaqueritos?"

Tears of frustration well in her eyes. "I don't work at Vaqueritos, inspector. I told you. I work at Border Textiles."

"Correct. How long have you worked there?"

"Two years. Two and a half."

"Inspector," says Gerardo. "We just wanted to let you know that Hilda is missing. So that maybe you can go looking for her. Or if she turns up...." He doesn't finish the sentence.

"Yes." Rodríguez turns his head at a point perhaps a foot from Gerardo's face. "Young man," he says. "Who are you?"

Without hesitation, he says, "I'm Esperanza's husband." She feels goose bumps on her upper arms.

"Ah," says the inspector. He writes something down and then says, "Well, I wouldn't worry about the young lady. Yet. Ninety-four percent of people who go missing turn up within twenty-four hours."

"And if she doesn't come back by tonight? Or tomorrow?" asks Esperanza. *From where did he get the number ninety-four?*

"Then we will look for her," says Rodríguez. Gerardo and Esperanza exchange glances. No one says anything until the inspector adds, "Young man, I have a piece of advice for you."

"Yes?" asks Gerardo.

The inspector purses his lips. "Don't let your wife dance with strangers."

Rodríguez asks no more questions. After a few moments of silence, Esperanza realizes the interview is over. She and Gerardo stand. The inspector doesn't attempt to shake hands or say good-bye. She realizes he has not even asked whether she has a telephone. Glancing at the sheet of paper on his desk, she sees he has not even made any notes. He has been playing tic-tac-toe with himself.

I'm going back to Michoacán. I'll go see my family in Puroaire, and I'll probably look for work in Morelia again. Maybe I'll be a muchacha *in another señora's house. Or maybe I can find something better. Who knows? I'll see what happens when I get there. I haven't seen anyone in my family for more than three years. I don't even know who's there anymore, except for my mother and father. Most of my brothers and sisters have moved away.*

In truth, Esperanza wonders what will be waiting for her in Michoacán. Can she live with her parents again? She could help her mother, cook for her, keep the house clean. But there are no jobs in Puroaire and she would be another mouth to feed. What happened to her family, to all those bodies that slept on the flattened boxes when she was a child? They've spread out to so many places that she doesn't even know where they all are.

I can't stay here. How can I go back to the maquila *without Hilda? How can I go to live with her cousins? They won't want me there anymore. I don't think they ever liked me. I was just there because I was Hilda's friend. If I stay, every time they look at me they'll think of her. They'll want to rent out the shack to someone else who can pay them more money. I'm afraid here. The same thing that happened to her can happen to me. This is no place to be on your own. I don't know anyone. I'm too far from home. We crossed half the country to get here.*

Her thoughts keep running around in the same track. Where is home? Puroaire? Morelia? Here, God help her? Does she have a home? Does a place become home just because you move there, find a job and a place to live? She supposes that home is where your family is, but her mother is getting older and weaker all the time. Her father? Who knows? When she talks to her mother, she says he's "fine." He never comes to the phone to say hello. Throughout her life, Esperanza treated him with respect but kept her distance. She was afraid of him. *The blood on María Concepción's fingers, her gory hands in her hair.* She considers what it means to have a family in the same way she wonders what it means to have a home. Can you lose your family in the pursuit of a home? The possibility that she has neither frightens her.

"Why don't you think about it for a little while before you make up your mind?" asks Gerardo. "You don't have to go anywhere today."

She was thinking about going to the bus station that very afternoon. It cost more than a thousand pesos to get to Juárez from Morelia, but she doesn't remember how much more. She isn't even sure she has saved enough money. She is soothed by Gerardo's suggestion, by his voice. "You're just tired. You didn't get any sleep last night."

"Neither did you," she says.

"Maybe things aren't as bad as they seem," he adds.

They sit in a little plaza downtown, outside the Capilla de Nuestra Señora de la Fe Perpétua. They drink the Coca-Colas that Gerardo bought them in the 7-Eleven. She imagines herself going home, getting a good night's sleep (alone? in the shack?), going to work the following morning. What will she say to Hilda's cousins? She imagines they will want her to leave, the sooner the better.

As if he had been reading her mind, Gerardo says, "If you want, while you think about what you want to do, you can stay with me and my brothers. Our house is nothing special, but it's got a roof and four walls."

Can she accept the invitation to stay in the home of a man she hardly knows? He's not exactly a stranger. They've worked together for two and a half years. He stayed up all night and looked for Hilda with her, and even accompanied her to the police station. Would she have her own room? Would she sleep in the kitchen on the floor? Would he expect that they would sleep together? She can't help but wonder: Does the toilet flush without having to dump a bucket of water in it?

"My mother's in *el gabacho* with my sister and her kids," says Gerardo. "I haven't seen her for three years either. She has no papers, and she's afraid that if she comes to visit us, *la migra* will catch her on the way back. So I sort of know what you're going through." He takes her hand. "Life is funny, in a way. Sometimes you don't know what to do. You feel like you don't have any choices. But if you have a little faith, something always comes up."

He reaches into his pocket and removes a round ball of transparent plastic, one of those orbs that contain prizes that you buy for a coin in a chewing-gum machine. He opens it and removes from inside the paper band from a cigar. He slips it onto Esperanza's little finger. "I don't have money for a real ring right now, but I'll get you one. One of these days. I've always liked you, Esperanza."

Those goose bumps that Esperanza felt on her upper arms when Gerardo told Inspector Rodríguez that he was her husband? Now she feels them through her entire body. She holds up her hand with the paper ring and asks, "You got this for me?"

"No," he answers, a smile on his face. "I've had it for a while. It took a long time for you to come along."

WELCOME TO THE CLUB

My mother was dead. My father was dead. I had no brothers or sisters. The child I had so hoped for, who would have been a corrective to the sadness of my own upbringing, was also dead before being born. My ex-wife may have been out there somewhere in a *ménage* with a millionaire, but she had made it clear she wanted no further contact. She erased herself from my existence. That may not have been a death, but it had hurt as much as one.

Those who have lived through the deaths of the people closest to us belong to an exclusive club. The rest of you may feel sorry for us and we appreciate your good wishes. But your supposedly reassuring utterances do not mean you become an honorary member. You cannot join the club until you step over and around the lifeless corpses of those who have been crucial to you. Until you bury them and stare into the empty space they once occupied. Sooner or later a membership card may await you—green, gold, platinum, or black, depending on how many bodies pile up. Maybe you'll be lucky enough to drop dead yourself before your application is processed. If anyone were going to mitigate my life, I believe the most salient detail would be that I was a member of that club.

Once you have survived all that death, it becomes how you define yourself. Everything is related to mortality. Life is lived more intensely. Each day, which brings you that much closer to the end, is a little gift. Any luscious meal may be your last. The sunshine that warms your face, a kiss, a caress, an endearment, the explosion of color from a florist's window—they are one less of those you will enjoy until you meet oblivion. While this is true for all of us, we members of the club always have it in the backs of our minds. We cover ourselves in this awareness, as if it were a shroud.

If you are the last one standing in your family, there is but one certainty: you will be the next to go. Maybe not today and maybe not tomorrow, but wherever you walk, the Reaper is somewhere behind you. She ambles along with her scythe balanced jauntily on her shoulder; once in a while you could almost swear you felt her sisterly tentacle touch you on the neck.

There could hardly be a better place for members of the club than the country I chose to live. Mexico City is our clubhouse. Perhaps because life is so cheap, death consciousness pervades. In the sugar skulls and laughing skeletons that crowd the market stalls and store windows before the Day of the Dead. In the altars and emblems of Santa Muerte—a saint known as Holy Death—pictured on votive candles, hanging on rosaries from taxi drivers' rearview mirrors, on chains around the necks of the guys who deliver gas and water. In the smells of putrefaction on the streets. In the corpses on the front pages of the newspapers—bloody, decomposing, mutilated, burned alive.

On those streets where more than twenty million gasp for air, and many wear surgical masks on the way to work. In the noxious fumes billowing from the exhaust pipes of the buses, in the microbes simmering and sizzling along with the hot fat and beef maws and tripe in stalls on the sidewalk, in the limp bodies of helpless drunks, their arms embracing lampposts after the cantinas close. In the immense, sprawling, choking-with-dust shantytowns on the outskirts. In the accumulating corpses of accident victims, people run over by drunk drivers, by unlicensed cabbies, by bus drivers temporarily insane at the wheel.

Being surrounded by all that death makes you feel more alive.

When I got to Mexico City, while looking for an apartment, I rented a couple of furnished rooms in the Colonia Roma Norte, near the Chapultepec metro station. One Friday night after both of the nearby cantinas closed, I walked around looking for someplace that would serve me another drink. I found a joint called La Cueva, a stone's throw from where throngs of minivans collected outside the metro to take the masses to farther destinations.

La Cueva, like its name suggests, was a cavelike place, hot and dark and loud, with white plastic tables decorated with the logo for Corona beer. The tables were set around a dance floor, empty while a group of musicians set up on a small platform. It was packed with people of both sexes who looked like minivan drivers—short, round, and brown, from the struggling classes. Plump waitresses in tight skirts trawled about taking orders. Most people, even singles and couples, ordered *cubetazos*—buckets containing six bottles of beer, which were cheaper than buying one at a time.

As soon as the band began to play a *cumbia*, the couples galloped to the dance floor, while several men stood up and held out their hands to the unattached women, enough to get most of them to their feet. The dance floor became as crowded as the minivans at rush hour—a collection of sweating bodies so dense, sharing such tight space so intimately, that it looked just short of an orgy.

Two stocky women in T-shirts didn't wait for men to choose them and danced together. Another woman, her arms in the air, had long wavy hair and wore a black blouse with a scoop neck that gave a teasing display of her bountiful breasts. A cell phone with a flashing red light was clipped to her cleavage. A delicious overstatement, that red light: as if it were an arrow pointing to her bosom, as if anyone might otherwise have overlooked it.

Two women sat at the next table. There had been six or seven only moments before, but Prince Charmings in sneakers and baseball caps had whisked their companions to the dance floor. The music was so loud that the two girls talked directly into each other's ears, moving aside the other's hair with her fingertips. One had a boiler-shaped body, a bulbous nose, and hair that needed cutting. Her friend was a diamond in the rough, what is known in Mexico as a *gordibuena*: heavy but curvy, pretty eyes, a mischievous smile. I turned around to get a better look at them. The one who needed the haircut peeked at me briefly and averted her eyes, but the diamond returned my gaze for a long moment of luxurious scrutiny, a stare just short of a challenge. My skin tingled. After all those years in New York, where people scrupulously avoid eye contact, I'd almost forgotten what it felt like to be looked at.

I wondered if I should approach her. And then I thought it would be criminal not to. Each of us had arrived to La Cueva hoping for only one end to the evening. I walked to their table. I warned her that I had two left feet, but wondered whether she'd be willing to dance anyway.

In the coming months I came to realize that Mexico City is one of the sexiest places in the world. Not in the most obvious sense; you wouldn't even notice unless you were looking for it. Its residents are not particularly prepossessing, and few of them go out in stylish, let alone provocative, dress. But a city's population doesn't grow past twenty million unless there's a lot of sex going on. There is a vibe if you have the nose for it.

Every time I walked through a park, I would see couples making out—sitting on benches, their arms crawling around each other like octopus tentacles, or sprawled on the grass, or standing with one of their backs against a tree. Having grown up in a culture more diffident than demonstrative, sometimes their exhibitionism raised my eyebrows. I saw a couple smooch against the plate glass window of a McDonald's, another all but make a baby on the metro at rush hour, yet another in a clutch under the art nouveau staircase at the National Museum of Art. The streets were loaded with cut-rate hot-sheet hotels, each with a garage so that entry could be anonymous.

In a Mexico City drugstore, the display of French ticklers and KY Jelly was in the front counter, or on display behind the cash register, never hidden discreetly. There were red-lit bars around the corner from Alameda Park, where you could pay a woman a few pesos to dance with you, then buy her a drink and make a deal for whatever extracurricular activity you had in mind.

It wasn't just that night in La Cueva. In restaurants, on the street, and in public transportation, women, under eyelids painted with multicolored shadow, not only welcomed my gaze but returned it.

I had an unfair advantage over the local talent. I wasn't terrible to look at, but more to the point I stood six feet in my socks, I was white, and I spoke their language with an endearing foreign accent. I was "exotic." Women may not have imagined taking me home to mother, but some of them could envision waking up in my arms. I would be an adventure, a notch in their belt, an anecdote they could tell their girlfriends. I was also at a magical age—thirty-five—in which I could have had an affair with a twenty-three-year-old, or with her mother, without too many creepy connotations at either end.

I had been enthusiastic about sex before moving to Mexico City. Of course it felt good, but beyond that, giving pleasure to a woman was a signal that there was something at which I was effective in the world, that I was useful, that there was something I knew how to do that could positively affect another person. After I got to Mexico, let's just say I became more single-minded in its pursuit. The best thing I can say about sex—and there are a lot of good things I can say about it—is that it takes your mind off death for a while.

BONES IN THE DESERT

Most Mondays, the headline story in the morning papers was about how many people had been murdered in the city over the weekend, particularly if there was a holiday on Friday and the body count exceeded its normal parameters. This Monday, the papers announced that forty-two people had been slaughtered in Juárez in the three preceding days. Among the victims were seven waitresses getting ready for the evening shift at Ponchis-Ponchis, a popular discotheque. They had been lined up against a wall and shot to death, in a fashion reminiscent of the Saint Valentine's Day Massacre.

Also similar to Capone's Chicago, but unreported in the news, was an arrangement that had been imposed upon the disco's owner by a local gang. In exchange for a weekly payment of thirty thousand pesos, they allowed him to operate the club without interference. However, when he fell behind in his disbursements, the gang members had to make it clear to him who the proprietors of his establishment truly were. They needed to make their point compellingly, but without harming him—he was, after all, the Goose with the Golden Eggs. There were so many waitresses in Ciudad Juárez. Seven more, seven fewer—what difference would it make? They were only bodies. As if by magic, seven more would appear the next day to replace the dead ones.

After the carnage, the owner got the picture. He never missed another payment, until one night, just before dawn, he padlocked the doors of the disco, got in his car with a suitcase full of cash, and drove off, never to be heard from again.

The police told the reporters that the waitresses had been beaten, sodomized, tied up, and shot in the back of the head, a modus operandi that suggested they were murdered as an act of revenge by drug traffickers. Off the record, they indicated that they were investigating whether a prostitution ring had been operating at Ponchis-Ponchis. None of this was true, but by disseminating these stories, they made it clear to the journalists that the girls had more or less brought their fate upon themselves after engaging in criminal activity. Some people still believed that the murders of Ciudad Juárez were a cops-and-robbers story, and the casualties were criminals killing each other: good riddance to bad rubbish. It would make matters more complicated if it were widely understood how many innocents were caught in the crossfire.

On the same weekend, among the forty-two dead were three men who worked at Ta-K-Brón, a taco stand on Paseo Triunfo de la Revolución. Before being gunned down in broad daylight, one of them had been frying a mass of onions on the grill, which was meant to be a garnish for beef and sausage tacos. Another had been arranging bottles of Boing and Coca-Cola in the cooler, and the third was putting on a new pair of plastic gloves, the better to collect money from customers. The owner of the taco stand had been similarly delinquent in his extortion payments. The police told the reporters that they were investigating information that the taco guys had been selling cocaine and methamphetamine at the stand. This was another fiction. Indeed, the employees barely survived on their minimum-wage salaries and the few meager tips left by diners similarly cash-strapped.

That Friday afternoon, in a dusty vacant lot in a landscape of gray earth and clumps of weedy bushes, three ten-year-old boys, in an improvised soccer game, were kicking around an empty plastic bottle that had been squashed flat. The discovery of a corpse—decapitated and also bereft of hands and feet—took their breaths away. It was as if they had entered a world of wonder and instantly become characters in a movie. However, they weren't sure whether the script should include a declaration to the police, which would have meant a confession that they were playing hooky from primary school. While making their decision, the vision of the naked body minus appendages made a permanent imprint in their imaginations. The victim was a woman and marked by multiple welts and bruises.

Later, an autopsy would attest that before being murdered, she had been tortured, beaten, and raped. The police would once again go to work, murmuring to reporters, *Another prostitute. You go around fucking gang members and this is how you end up. A dysfunctional family. A crazy boyfriend. One of those sick bitches who lure underaged girls into lives of whoring and dope dealing.* Around the corpse, they would spin almost as many tales as Scheherazade, some of which found their way into a paragraph in Monday morning's summary of the weekend's murders. The girl's identity remained a mystery. Hilda would never again have a name.

EXHIBIT A

"My Way" or the Highway?
In Ciudad Juárez karaoke bars, Sinatra song still knocks 'em dead—literally

By Masayuki Watanabe
Pan-American News Service

O ctober 10, 2009—It was the last song of his life, but Héctor González never got to the final refrain.

On Friday night, in Melodías, a karaoke bar in the Leyes de Reforma section of Ciudad Juárez, the 29-year-old man patiently waited his turn to step up to the microphone and serenade the tipsy crowd. He got his chance a little before midnight. He chose the song "A Mi Manera," the Spanish-language version of Frank Sinatra's popular hit "My Way."

He didn't finish the second verse before another patron of Melodías sprayed González with bullets from a semiautomic pistol. Police sources say eight cartridges were retrieved from the scene, and that the weapon was a Beretta 925, probably slipped across the border from the United States. Rumors that González was involved in a dispute between the Gulf and Sinaloa drug cartels are being investigated.

"Mexico is a free country," says Edgar Escobar, the proprietor of Melodías. "Here, the sovereign rights of all citizens are protected. Mexicans can do whatever we want, as long as we don't break the law. That's why it pains me to make decisions that will interfere with those rights. But I felt I had no choice." After last week's shooting, Escobar removed "A Mi Manera" from his bar's playlist.

"I'd never seen the man before in my life," says Escobar of González. "Was he a drug dealer? Who knows? As far as I'm concerned, the only thing he was guilty of was singing out of tune."

Few would consider Escobar overly cautious for eliminating "My Way" from his bar. By unofficial count, eight people in Ciudad Juárez have been murdered in karaoke bars in the last two years while singing the same tune. No matter how poorly they croon, patrons of the same places have not been murdered while warbling their way through other numbers, say Juárez police.

"It's that particular song," says Inspector Mario Ramírez. "It's so arrogant. *Puedo seguir hasta el final, a mi manera.*" The Juárez detective quoted some of the Spanish lyrics, which mean "I can go on until the end, my way." He adds, "So proud, so self-important. You hear someone sing that and you just feel like shooting them between the eyes. I mean that as a figure of speech, of course."

The detective also points out that the "My Way" shootings may have become a self-fulfilling prophecy. "Getting up to sing it becomes a badge of honor," he explains. "These guys know that people are getting killed for it. If someone gets up and sings it despite the risk, it shows he's got big ones."

Some sources say that the actual number of "A Mi Manera" murders may be higher than the official count, as Juárez fast becomes the most violent city in the world outside of a declared war zone. Last year there were about 130 murders per 100,000 inhabitants in Ciudad Juárez, and the city is on the road to surpassing its own record this year. With numbers like these, it's possible that karaoke murders have gone unreported and some would-be Sinatras have fallen through the investigative cracks, according to police.

To offer some perspective, according to FBI statistics, the most dangerous cities in the U.S. have far lower homicide rates than Ciudad Juárez. Washington, D.C., has 21.9 murders per 100,000 residents, while New Orleans weighs in at 49.1 and Baltimore at 34.8. New York City has only 6.4 homicides per 100,000 habitants and Los Angeles has 7.6.

Most of the news coming out of Ciudad Juárez in the last fifteen years has been about murder. Between 1993 and 2003, about 600 women, most of them factory workers, were killed here, and another thousand or so went missing, presumably murdered. All but a handful of these crimes remain unsolved, despite the international outcry at the ineffective response of police, as well as local, state and federal governments.

However, the numbers of those earlier murders—known as "femicides"—pale in comparison to the amount of people who have been killed in recent years. Much of Mexico is engulfed in the escalating violence related to turf wars between gangs of drug traffickers.

Previous to the "My Way" massacre in Ciudad Juárez, the song represented only a metaphorical killing, with "A Mi Manera" a huge success for such Spanish-language pop stars as Raphael, Vicente Fernández and the Gipsy Kings. Many Mexicans realize that the song was an American hit before the version with Spanish lyrics came out. But outside of France, few anywhere remember that, before Frank Sinatra recorded the song with new lyrics by Paul Anka in 1969, it was a huge success for Claude François, a Gallic pop idol, in its original 1967 version called "Comme d'Habitude."

François died in 1978 after he accidentally electrocuted himself while standing in a bathtub full of water, trying to straighten an electric sconce on the wall. He was only 39 years old. To date, 70 million of his records have been sold. It has been said that, in 1968, David Bowie wrote lyrics for an English version of the song called "Even a Fool Learns to Love." Bits of a studio recording exist but the Bowie rendering was never released.

Proprietors of other karaoke bars in Ciudad Juárez could not be reached for comment about whether they would allow patrons to sing "A Mi Manera" in their establishments. Meanwhile, Escobar says he will hold fast to his rule prohibiting the song in Melodías. What will he do if a customer insists on singing it? "It's my bar," he says. "We'll do it my way."

PART THREE

I'll Fly Away

KING OF HOPELESS CASES

I can't remember when it began. But at a certain point, I would wake up in the morning, and the first thing I saw was her face. At night, unless I drank myself into oblivion—sometimes even when I did—I thought of her face again as I went to sleep. I seldom remembered my dreams, but during waking hours I thought of her constantly.

Before Esperanza, I'd had no trouble keeping an emotional distance from my clients. Even the oldest of them was boyish, not quite a man—males who'd assumed the roles of men, like actors who'd been cast in a movie. They had gone out in the world to do the work of men, and some had united with women as if they were men. But they'd never been sufficiently prepared or parented to take the requisite emotional steps into manhood.

I felt sorry for them, and especially sad for their mothers, whose hearts were broken by their sons' prosecution thousands of miles away in a country that would not even give them a visa to visit (if they'd had the money for a ticket). However, I looked at the situation with a level head. Some of the boys were murderers. And even when they were not—if they hadn't actually pulled the trigger and put a bullet through someone's head—they were complicit. They were part of a stickup crew that ended in a shootout, or they'd guarded the door or driven the car.

And as Mexicans stuck in the U.S. criminal justice system, they had to pay a steep price. Had they been white, they might have got a better deal. Being Mexican in the U.S. in the 2000s was like being black in the 1950s. At least in the states where I worked, it was perfectly acceptable for the white populace to express out loud that *they*—those people with brown skin hiding in the shadows of their cities, who "didn't speak good English"—were savages, somehow less than human. (Of course most of them still thought the same about blacks, but many refrained from saying so out loud.) If lynching was no longer socially permissible, then judges, juries, and prosecutors had carte blanche to throw death or Draconian sentences at them.

I visited my clients in jail as often as possible and tried to commiserate with them, to answer all their questions, to listen to their anxieties and complaints. As long as I worked on their cases, I did what I could. I held the hands of the most emotional relatives. Even after the cases were settled, and I was no longer being paid, I told the families they should feel free to call me whenever they liked. I was their only conduit to the terrible system in which their sons, their brothers, their husbands, had found themselves. But in fact they almost never phoned. After I was done with a case, I was really finished. I seldom thought of the clients once I was through, except as war stories from a safe distance.

While working for Esperanza, I found myself swimming in uncharted waters. Although her life may have been no harder than that of any other client, the hardships and dangers she had passed touched me like never before. I would imagine her sleeping on the floor on a flattened box in Puroaire, shivering on the roof in Morelia, suffering the grinding monotony of the factory in Juárez. I began to fantasize about what I could do to improve things for her, if only in a small way.

I started by trying to reassure her that Catherine was working hard on her case. That was inconsequential; I'm not sure it made any difference to her. Then I tried to make her smile or laugh when I visited. If I succeeded, I felt like Heracles or Sir Galahad. If I didn't, I was a shameful failure. When she told me she wanted a Coca-Cola, I vowed to smuggle one in for her, even though it was not allowed. Although I could probably hide it from the authorities in the Plaquegoula Parish Jail, who had more serious things to watch out for, there was at least a slight chance that I could get myself censured for it.

Of course I could be of much greater help if Esperanza were out of jail. As little as it may have made sense, I began to fantasize about what a shared life might be like with her outside.

If she were somehow sprung, what sort of an existence would she want? I thought of all the things I took for granted that she'd never had, things that would have constituted luxury for her: a clean, sunny apartment like I had in Mexico City, the rent paid, sheets fresh out of the laundry, a firm mattress, a refrigerator full of food. A closet stuffed with choices of what she could put on in the morning. A weekend at the beach. A little money in the bank.

Had anyone ever brought her a cup of coffee in bed? Given her flowers, an unusual pair of earrings, something silken to set against her skin? It wasn't difficult to imagine all that she'd never had: security, both emotional and economic. A day of life that hadn't been a struggle. Love. Devotion. If she wanted a baby, I would be thrilled: I'd wanted children since marriage with Carla, and believed that parenthood was the only important endeavor on which I'd never embarked. What if Esperanza wanted to go back to school, or get a job? I could help her achieve those things. I imagined giving her reasons to trust me and then spending the rest of my life living up to that trust.

I could picture waking up by her side, kissing her, and telling her I loved her every morning. I imagined a life dedicated to honoring that love. A life of nurturing her, looking after her, giving her the care she'd never had before. Getting out of bed in the morning to serve another person seemed like the very definition of love. Particularly for someone like me, who had no one else to serve (outside of my professional life): no parents, no brothers or sisters, no children. I'd never experienced love like that. Carla and I were planets orbiting the same sun, but at the end of the day it was a little ridiculous to imagine we made sense together.

In Mexico City, I had lost my way in the search for love. I'd contented myself with a series of skirmishes, showdowns, and face-offs with women, but nothing close to a relationship that might stick. After my divorce, I took refuge in the pleasures of sex, and skepticism about love, but scratch any cynic and you'll find a hidden romantic. It was not uncharacteristic of me to fantasize about having a life with the women I knew, but if I truly wanted one, I had made some preposterous choices. I'd been with married women, women who were only passing through Mexico, women who had no interest in an enduring relationship. I was the King of Hopeless Cases. But at least, with them, the possibility existed: they were not in jail cells facing the death penalty.

When I studied to be a writer in Maryland, in a class discussion about Chekhov's "The Lady with the Dog," a professor told us that all love stories were tales of bad timing. Now I understood what he meant. I was pegging way too much hope on the slim possibility that Catherine could convince the prosecutor it had all been an accident. Criminally negligent homicide—what you get if you inadvertently run someone over, or if you are unmindful of your pit bull and it bites to death Grandma next door—carries a penalty of two to five in Louisiana, if the victim is a child. But it would be almost impossible to sell that kind of a story. The pictures of Yesenia's brutalized corpse were devastating.

Still, I had been a writer, and I couldn't help but ask myself, *What if?*

"Not guilty" wasn't much of a possibility; I had worked only one case where I believed the client was innocent, and he spent a decade in jail before we got him out on appeal. He was mentally disabled, and had been convicted of killing two men in the parking lot outside of a bar in Texas. Even after another man, who had also been in the bar that night, confessed to the killings, my guy had to plead to a lesser charge before they finally released him.

But there might be other ways to get Esperanza out before she spent decades in jail.

There was the question of forensics. I'd been reading a lot about medical examiner's reports in cases where babies and infants had died, and they were often careless and shoddy, not the result of serious scientific investigation, but simply documents that aped the conclusions of the police. A lot would be riding on whether Catherine's forensic expert could find inconsistencies, incongruities, or outright untruths in the ME's findings.

There was also the possibility of a lucky break. How badly did the district attorney's office want to put away Esperanza? And for how long? Were they hell-bent on killing her? In a case I'd worked on in Arkansas, the client went home after just four years in jail. But in truth, he'd played only a minor role in the killings, and the real murderer had copped a plea for thirty years. In Louisiana, a notoriously vengeful state, something like that would have been a miracle along the lines of transforming water into wine.

I knew that if I was going to get anywhere toward bringing Esperanza to justice—and possibly seeing her somewhere other than prison—I'd have to find out what really happened the night that Yesenia died. Precisely what Esperanza claimed she couldn't remember.

GETTING THERE
IS HALF THE FUN

Eleven people gather at sundown, twenty miles out of town in the desert. Nine men and a woman will be shepherded by El Moco, a sinewy man with a sparse beard and a mournful expression. Before beginning the journey, he removes a small figurine from his knapsack. It is a skeleton clad in a purple hooded robe. He asks that the others form a circle around the plastic statuette.

"You have led your people across the wilderness," he says to the figure. "You parted the Red Sea for the Israelites and led them through another desert for forty years. Our journey is humble in comparison, but please protect us from the heat, the wind, the rain." The ten companions are silent as El Moco speaks. "Flaquita, protect us from the thorns that might prick us, the bees that might sting us, the scorpions, snakes, and tarantulas, whose deadly poisons could kill us. Protect us from bandits and thieves who may try to steal what little we have and prevent us from completing our journey. And protect us from *la migra*, who would put us in jail and send us back across the border."

Purposefully, El Moco lights an unfiltered cigarette from a squashed pack and blows the smoke around the purple figurine. From his back pocket he produces a half-pint plastic bottle, fills his mouth with the liquid it contains and spits it out over the skeleton. He swallows a small sip and then hands the bottle to one of his ten charges. They pass around the liquor, most of the men wincing after drinking a bit. Esperanza only has to smell its astringent contents to know she will forgo her sample, and passes it to Gerardo.

"If we arrive at our destination, Flaquita," says El Moco, continuing to address the statuette, "it will not be due to me or my efforts.

It will be because of you, because you chose to bless us and show us the way."

Later, Esperanza will remember the first steps of the journey: her belongings, sneakers, and socks in plastic garbage bags as she wades in murky water up to her belly button. She will recall the discomfort of trying to keep her balance with the slippery mud under her bare feet and, once reaching the other side of the river, beginning an endless walk in wet pants and underwear. She was terrified that as soon as they made it across they would be caught by *la migra*. It almost seemed miraculous that they crossed the river without incident. At sunset, they began to follow a trail, their path lit by stars. In hindsight it would seem like a moment of calm.

The slow walk across the desert. Each evening, a couple of hours before dusk, the group begins to move and continues until after sunrise, only resting occasionally. Esperanza carries a gallon jug of water in each hand and her knapsack on her back. Later, she will not be able to remember how many hours, days, or sunsets she endured. It is said that we have no memory for pain, but she will recall tears dripping down her cheeks from the aches lacerating her back, legs, and especially her feet, grotesquely swollen in the sneakers. She wanted to drink all the water so that she would no longer have to carry it, but El Moco warned them to consume their rations slowly, as people died of thirst on the journey. He made it clear that he had lost people on previous trips, and if anyone dropped dead there was nothing to do but leave the corpse for the vultures. "When you drink," he said, "have a real drink. If you just take tiny sips you will get dehydrated. But don't take a drink until you really need it. Alternate from the two bottles so you are carrying the same weight in each hand."

In daylight they see evidence of *compañeros* on the same journey. Squashed plastic bottles. Empty cigarette packs. Discarded cans and cellophane bags. An abandoned pair of sneakers. Esperanza imagines that someone's feet hurt so much that he had given them up and decided to try his luck barefoot. She is haunted by this figure. Who is he and where is he from? Wherever he is going, how can he possibly expect to get there with no shoes? They come upon a tattered denim shirt. El Moco goes through the pockets and finds a slip of paper with an address and a telephone number in San Antonio. What will the man who wore the shirt do once he gets there and realizes he no longer knows where to turn?

She remembers the hope and exhilaration with which she began a new life in Juárez. She feels nothing of the kind on this journey, only apprehension, fear, even dread about going farther away from everything and everyone she has ever known. They can't turn back. In her mind's eye she is haunted by the solemn faces of Alfredo and Antonio, Gerardo's older brothers, with whom she shared a ramshackle construction in Rancho Amargo. The three siblings and Esperanza had pooled their savings and handed over $1,000 to El Moco. Esperanza and Gerardo will have to earn close to $2,000 more along the journey or El Moco will have Antonio and Alfredo killed. It isn't personal, he said. It's just the way it goes.

Antonio's hair is gray, although he isn't even forty. He seethes in silence, as if he wants to hit someone. He made the same trip with El Moco and lasted two years in Texas. But he was caught driving without a license and, after a couple of days in jail, was sent back to Mexico. Now he's worked his way up to manager in one of the *maquilas*. Alfredo has strangely sleepy eyes and doesn't seem quite right in the head. She felt like an intruder in their gloomy little house. It wasn't what they said or did; it was that they hardly said or did anything at all. After twelve-hour shifts in the *maquila*, they walked around like zombies or zoned out in front of the television, mumbling only a word here and there to each other.

Women did not seem to be a part of the brothers' lives. Alfredo's wife left him for another man and Antonio never married. Their mother and sister were in *el gabacho*, somewhere in a place called Waco.

Esperanza and Gerardo slept on a mattress in the living room. Once in a while Gerardo would touch her and they'd couple joylessly for a few minutes. At first she was surprised at the perfunctory nature of their encounters. She tried to indicate her ardor by breathing into his ear, or grasping his back, or thrusting into him with slower and then more agitated movement. But her passion made him embarrassed or uneasy, and caused him to finish even more quickly. She wouldn't dream of actually saying anything to him directly about sex—if she were to open her mouth, she knows he would wonder about the source of her knowledge and ultimately consider her a whore. In any case, as time passed, their encounters became less frequent. They made her so uncomfortable that ultimately she was relieved they ended so speedily.

No one asks questions on the journey. She doesn't know where they are; all that El Moco has said is that it is "Texas." Esperanza understands that Texas is one of the states across the border from home and that many Mexicans, including some of her own brothers, have gone there to find work. Otherwise the place, even the word, is meaningless. She has never eaten barbecue or watched a John Wayne movie. She's never seen a head of longhorn cattle, or heard anyone say "howdy," "y'all," or "this ain't my first rodeo." To her, it's an endless flat dirt path, bordered by brush and weeds and punctuated by barbed wire fences that they crawl under, on their bellies, like worms.

She is constantly hungry but she and Gerardo eat only once a day, in twilight before setting off to walk. The meal is raisins, peanuts, and packaged bread going stale. Every other day as a treat they share a small can of sausages.

It's not easy to sleep in the heat of the day. There is hardly any shade in the desert among the overgrowth. Everyone wears long-sleeved shirts and pants, and most of them have caps on their heads to protect themselves from the elements and the insects. Still, as they sleep, the flies buzz endlessly and annoyingly around their faces. One man had both eyes stung shut by mosquitoes. The lids swelled monstrously and one of the others had to lead him by the hand.

She goes to sleep inside Gerardo's embrace, spoon fashion, and dreams she is attacked by him and his brothers. When she awakens in a cold sweat, her body is apart from his. Held by him, she feels familiarity but not comfort. While in his arms, they have never been alone. His brothers were on the other side of the walls when they slept on the living room sofa in Rancho Amargo, and now the couple is surrounded by companions—people who are hardly enemies but not precisely friends. She cannot get out of her mind El Moco's comment about losing people on previous journeys. If she were to die, the others—including Gerardo—would leave her body behind. She cannot imagine a more horrible fate than being picked at by predators so far from home.

M-I-C-K-E-Y M-O-U-S-E

Burt wrapped his fingers around half a loaf of French bread. It was stuffed with pulled pork, dripping with plum-colored sauce. He had draped a pink necktie over his shoulder to spare it from the threat of gravy stains. As he moved the sodden sandwich to his maw, I waited for its juice to squirt over his white shirt.

"New Orleans isn't much of a barbecue town," he said, a lump of po'boy lodged in his left cheek. "But this place is pretty good." It was called the Pig Pen, a half hour's drive from downtown. A joint where you picked your poison at the counter and a sad sack in a hairnet handed it over on a paper plate. You carried it to your table on a brown plastic tray, and before the meal was over, you'd used half the napkins in the dispenser wiping your lips and fingers. Burt's pink tie, ruddy skin, and thick orange hair all seemed to fit in with the garish venue. Despite his appetite, he was painfully skinny and had bulging green eyes; I wondered whether he had a thyroid condition. If that gob of dressing had dripped onto his white shirt, it would have looked like he'd been shot in the belly.

"If I could eat pork every day I'd be a happy man," he said. With a plastic spoon, he shoveled some potato salad into his mouth. "But my wife has other ideas about the family diet."

Most of the time, court-appointed defense lawyers do not choose their co-counsel. You're pretty much stuck with whichever second chair the judge appoints for you. In this case, Catherine would give Burt specific instructions and cross her fingers that he wouldn't fuck up.

"Have you figured out what you're going to do while you're here?" asked Burt.

"Yes," I said. "I'm going to that housing complex where she lived. I'm hoping I might find a neighbor who knew her, even if I have to knock on every door. And I'm going to look for that guy who hired her to work on the cleanup crew."

I'd gone to Burt's office downtown and he drove us to the Pig Pen for lunch. We talked little about Esperanza and the case. Mostly, he gave me pieces of his autobiography. He was somewhere in his fifties. Twenty years as a social worker for the welfare department in Memphis, early retirement and a pension, a move to New Orleans, where his wife's people were from, and law school. Apart from the bulwark who monitored his pork intake, there were three children, the youngest of whom had just turned twenty-one. Every year—sometimes several times a year—Burt took his holidays in Walt Disney World.

Sometimes he would make the trip with one of his children, the eldest of whom was twenty-nine. Or else he would go alone with the pork policewoman, or sometimes with the whole family, grandkids included. The idea of his eldest daughter—a childless woman about to turn thirty—accompanying her father to an amusement park in Florida appalled me. Could the trip still amuse her? Or did she simply not have the heart to tell her dad that she was too old to lick ice cream with him and get her picture taken shaking Dumbo's hand?

"You've been there, right?" asked Burt, after slurping some coleslaw.

"Actually, not yet," I said. "I'm saving it up for when I have children of my own." This was my standard crack about Disney theme parks. Burt didn't even smile.

"I remember a trip I made when our eldest, Charlene, was eleven, and the youngest, J.R., was three." He puckered his lips around a straw and sucked sweetened tea from a Styrofoam bucket. "At first, when J.R. saw Mickey, he was scared witless—he was just a little bitty thing and Mickey must have seemed like a giant. But as the day went on, he became more and more curious. He kept wanting to get closer to him. By the end of that day, J.R. was kissing Mickey on the nose," said Burt. He spoke in an affectionate tone, a benevolent smile on his face. It was as if the incident had occurred hours before.

Finished with his meal, Burt reclined in his chair. "Do you know why Disney World is such an enchanting place, Richard?" he asked. He didn't wait for me to answer. "Because deep inside all of us—I don't care how old we are—are the same people we were when we were little boys and girls. You really ought to go one of these days."

The implication of Burt's declaration was that he believed we were more or less the same. We'd had similar boyhoods and he was well aware of who I was.

"I heard the most terrible stories from my clients in Memphis," he said. "You can imagine. Thugs on street corners blowing each other's heads off over five dollars' worth of crack. Teenage girls, pregnant and battered to a pulp. You know? The same kind of stuff you must see day after day when you do your investigations.

"But Disney World is an oasis of happiness and serenity. For me it's therapy. My trips over there are what I do instead of having my head examined by a shrink." As if to acknowledge the head that needed no shrinking, he ran long, slender fingers through his carrot-colored hair. "They make a hell of a pecan pie here, if you have any room left."

I nodded and smiled. Inside I was thinking, *Moron. Baby. Mickey Mouse.* The difference between Burt and me was that I accepted, even embraced, the fact that the world was a tough and unjust place. And I lived in it accordingly. He wanted to hide from the truth in Disney World.

It was only later, around four thirty in the morning, that I realized how much we were alike. Awakened from a troubled sleep, no matter how much I rolled around in bed, no matter to how high a number I counted my inhalations, I could not empty my mind of Esperanza. Staring at the shadows on the ceiling of the hotel room, I scolded myself for judging Burt so harshly. We all needed some kind of relief. I had gone to Disney World that evening; indeed I went there nearly every day after dark. All it took was three shots of whiskey and two beers. Whatever gets you through the night, however fitfully.

PIECEWORK

The white sheet unfolding, wafting over the mattress. The scent of freshly washed fabric, recently released from an automatic dryer with her own hands. The bottom sheet is fitted, the top one combined with a blanket and tucked tight as a straitjacket before Esperanza lays out the bedspread above and sets the pillows next to the white wooden headboard. She dusts the desk, the chairs, the bedside tables; vacuums the carpeting; scours the sink, bathtub, and toilet; polishes the TV screen and the mirror; and replaces spent towels with fresh ones. Fourteen more rooms and her day will be done.

Her shift at Maddy's Motor Inn lasts ten hours. It's on the east side of the expressway, surrounded by gas stations, fast-food outlets, a used-car lot, and a drug store. When Esperanza arrives at six she launders sheets and towels, and then begins to clean the rooms of whichever guests have stolen off early. At ten minutes past ten she and Mariana, the other Mexican chambermaid, go to a small salon off the lobby and break down the continental breakfast bar—a bowl of mealy apples, a tray of cinnamon buns, a pitcher of orange juice, and coffee with powdered "creamer"—that is included in the price of the room. Although breakfast is supposed to end at ten, sometimes they find baggy-eyed guests lingering over coffee in a Styrofoam cup, unable to stir from their morning stupor. Mariana and Esperanza are allowed to partake of the inevitable leftovers. Purchased at the Dollar General, the cloyingly sweet bread, stuffed with gooey nuts and raisins, covered in hardened white syrup, has enough sugar to give them the requisite buzz to complete the morning's work.

At one o'clock Mariana and Esperanza are allowed a half-hour break. They go to the nearby Capon Coop and buy sandwiches wrapped in orange tissue paper, and eat them at a Formica table out-side while the traffic hurtles by. The meal, served between soft buns, is made with corn derivatives, sugars, leavening agents, a smattering of dimethylpolysiloxane, a spoonful of tertiary butylhydroquinone, and a mess of MSP—mechanically separated poultry—that has been smashed, pulverized, and pressed through a sieve, soaked in ammo-nia, and rewired with artificial flavoring and coloring before being formed into a patty, covered with bread crumbs, and deep-fried.

When they return from lunch, they nod their heads and exchange greetings—among the few English words they have learned—with "Maddy," the hotel's nominal owner, whose name is actually Mad-humalati. She has a red bindi on her forehead and wears a sari be-hind the front desk. Checkout time was two hours ago; Esperanza and Mariana can begin to clean the remaining rooms.

On the other side of town, Gerardo works at another hotel, a shut-tered Comfort Inn, soon to be remodeled into a Homewood Suites. Unlike the modest Maddy's, there are more than two hundred rooms in the hostelry, and in each of them, Gerardo uses the beveled edge of the carbon steel blade of a putty knife to scrape the paint off the walls. He begins by finding an area in the wall or ceiling, however tiny, where the paint has already loosened and works outward from there, pushing under the paint bit by bit. He works with a partner, Martín, who happens to be Mariana's husband.

Esperanza earns $7.50 an hour while Gerardo earns a princely $8.50. A chunk of their money will be deducted for taxes, thanks to clandestine Social Security numbers obtained through a network of Mexicans that trades in them. The cards cost them $125 for the priv-ilege of paying taxes in their adopted country.

They have to pay $100 each for rent in the trailer park where they are staying. Every week, they send $100 each to El Moco via Western Union, a process for which the wire-transfer company charges them $10. They will have to settle their debt before they are permitted to move on. In two or three months, they will be free.

In the late afternoon the four of them come home to the trailer at more or less the same time. It is about seven miles from Maddy's and eleven from where Gerardo and Martín are renovating. They are chauffeured in the bed of a pickup truck and taken to the trailer park by other Mexicans who live in the area—not out of the kindness of their hearts but as a business venture (they charge a dollar per head each way to take Mexicans without wheels to and from work). Esperanza and Gerardo hold on to the fifty or sixty remaining dollars for personal expenses—primarily food, but also a few changes of clothes bought at a Walmart outside the town limits.

The trailer has holes in the floor and duct tape over the cracks in the windows. The other residents of the trailer park are also undocumented Mexicans and Central Americans, with the exception of a couple of trailers full of doughy Caucasians who are either down on their luck or never had any in the first place. The white people have tethered dogs to their trailers. Strangling at the yoke, they bark and whine incessantly.

In the trailer where Esperanza lives, apart from a few lumpy mattresses, a table, and a couple of chairs in the kitchen, there is hardly any furniture. At night, after the men shower—wearing rubber flip-flops, because no matter how the women have scrubbed the bathroom, there are brown spots that won't go away—the four Mexicans share dinner. Usually it's a pot of beans prepared by Esperanza or Mariana, with hot dogs cooked in a frying pan. The tortillas come from a package and the salsa from a can. The flavors are further reminders of how far they are from home.

There is no privacy in the trailer. Martín and Mariana sleep in one bedroom, while a family from El Salvador, with three small children, huddle together in the other. Gerardo and Esperanza sleep on the living room floor. Esperanza is haunted by having seen one of the Salvadoran children—she is not sure if the creature, still wearing diapers, is a boy or a girl—sitting on the patchy sun-scorched lawn outside the trailer, playing with what she thought was a cat. Her heart practically stopped when she saw that in fact it was a gray rat, burrowing inside a bag of potato chips that had no doubt been left there by one of the toddler's siblings. As she approached the animal tore away, and she brought the infant inside.

After everyone has gone to bed, lying atop the mattress, Esperanza and Gerardo have whispered conversations. They speak as quietly as possible; the thinnest of walls separate them from the Mexican couple and the Salvadoran dynasty.

"Chino," Esperanza murmurs in the darkness, "after we pay off the debt, why don't we just stay here?" Neither of them has ever earned anywhere close to what they're making in Texas. "We'd have more than an extra two hundred dollars a week. I'm sure we could find a better place to live than this. After a while, maybe we could even get jobs that pay more."

It isn't the first time they've had this conversation. Gerardo will not budge. He doesn't say so out loud, but he doesn't want Esperanza to work at all. He will spring this on her only when he's making enough money to support them both. "This isn't bad. But over there it's better. They say that anyone with two arms and two legs can make double what we're making here. We'll make as much money as fast as we can and then we can decide what we want to do. We can stay in *el gabacho* or go back to Mexico with what we've saved."

"I don't know, Chino." Her opinion holds no currency with him; it is almost as if she doesn't exist.

"We came here to make money, and the money's over there."

It's hard to believe, but people are saying that, although the hurricane touched land and the levees broke over a year ago, they still haven't cleaned the garbage from the streets or picked up the rubble where the houses collapsed. Once that's done, they'll have to build all over again. To the rest of the world it might look like a heap of trash, but if you're a Mexican, the streets of south Louisiana are paved with gold.

DINNER PARTY

On the way to Louisiana, I met Susan at the next stool at Wingnuts, a bar in the Houston airport—I'd had another delay thanks to American Airlines. She wore a royal-blue dress, black high heels, and a black hat with a wide brim, and drank Gibsons straight up with Bombay gin. It was as if she had been transported to the bar via time-tunnel from the 1950s. I ordered what she was drinking, and she told me that either I had no imagination or extremely good taste. I suggested that perhaps I had both; the long and short of it was that she invited me to dinner at her house in New Orleans three nights hence. I imagined it would be just the two of us. I hadn't counted on there being several other guests involved. They were all, to say the least, opinionated.

"Willie Mae's has the best damn fried chicken in the world. Bar none," said Louanne, in a voice loud enough to be heard on the other side of the Mississippi.

"I don't know," drawled Varnel, sitting across the table next to Susan. He had an unkempt beard, greasy hair, and black-framed glasses that tilted sideways. "It's all right, I guess, but seriously oily. You could drain a pint of grease from every thigh."

"That's the whole point of fried chicken, knucklehead!" screamed Louanne. "If you want it dry, Shake'N Bake it."

Dirk, dressed in a seersucker suit with an ascot around his neck, tittered. He had been introduced as a dealer in antiques on Magazine Street. "I haven't had Shake'N Bake since my mother was alive," he said.

"I'm not the biggest fan of Willie Mae's either," said Deanna, the woman who had come to Susan's house uptown with the unkempt Varnel. She also wore glasses but seemed to have washed her chestnut hair before she arrived. "I don't think the seasoning's anything to write home about. And they served me my red beans cold."

I took a bite of some kind of fish in a tomato sauce. Susan sat there smiling, but had hardly said a word all evening as she ran back and forth from the kitchen. She had spent who knows how long preparing this meal, only to listen to her guests talk throughout about foods they'd eaten in other places.

"Red beans!" cried Louanne. "No one gets the red beans at Willie Mae's!" She laughed out loud. "You get the butter beans." Louanne was inordinately tall and rangy, and wore a tank top, baggy cargo pants, and a battered straw hat. Instead of a hatband, she'd strung it with green and purple Mardi Gras beads.

"And the service is slow as all get-out," said the disheveled Varnel. "It takes them forever to rustle up that damn bird."

"And so it goes," Louanne said, and sighed. "Some of our brown brothers are in no hurry to serve the white man in this not-so-fair city." There was a slight pause, but none of my fellow Americans batted an eyelash, either in agreement or disapproval. "But there's something about the crunch when you bite into that chicken that makes it worth the wait."

"I'm sorry but I have to disagree," said Deanna of the apparently clean hair, draining most of a glass of red wine in one gulp. "Have you ever had the chicken at Li'l Dizzy's?"

"Li'l Dizzy's?" said Louanne. "That ain't nothing but shit on a steam table."

This comment merited another titter from Dirk. "Personally," he said, "I'd just as soon go to Popeyes."

"May I have some more wine, please?" asked Deanna.

"Richard, do the honors," said Susan, handing me a fresh bottle and a corkscrew.

The walls of Susan's parlor were painted a peach tone, and both the sofa and the lampshades were covered with gauzy scarves, giving the room a bordello glow. Her friends continued the fried chicken discussion.

I'd worked a case on the outskirts of New Orleans a couple of years earlier. Three Mexicans walked into a bar where the locals knew that the owners cashed checks every Wednesday. The Mexicans had guns and demanded the money. The owner, by all appearances a milquetoast, calmly said he was going to his office behind the bar to open the safe. Instead he decided to play John Wayne. He grabbed a gun, started shooting, and a bloodbath ensued. Six people were killed, including one of the Mexicans, four of the customers, and the owner's seventy-six-year-old mother, who'd dropped in to share some pecan pralines that she'd made the previous afternoon.

Ballistic evidence showed that the owner's bullets were responsible for the deaths of two customers and his own mother. Despite his recklessness, prosecutors drove abysmally hard bargains in Louisiana. My guy, Javier, hadn't even been inside the restaurant. He was the driver, waiting in the car outside, unarmed. Louisiana's laws of complicity made him eligible for the death penalty. All we could negotiate was a downgrade to second-degree murder, which in that swampy backwater means mandatory life without parole, no matter how long he hangs on. The relatives of the dead customers sued the owner. In my dreams he went down and shared a cell with Javier, but I never followed up to see what happened to him. Before the bargain was reached, I conducted a long investigation and became friendly with the lawyers and some other locals. I like to eat as much as the next guy, but I was kind of amazed at how people in New Orleans talked about food incessantly. It was as if there were no other topics of conversation.

"I was on the Magazine Street bus the other day," said Dirk. "The driver pulled over at a Popeyes and kept us all waiting while he ate his dinner."

I poured the wine while the other guests continued the fried chicken debate. "So what do you do for a living?" asked Louanne.

"I'm a driving instructor," I said.

"No, you're not," she said.

"Okay," I said. I'd had enough wine to play along. "Then what I am I?"

Louanne pushed back her straw hat, revealing tight brown curls. "Susan told me. You're some kind of a do-gooder, right?"

"If she says so."

"A regular little Dudley Do-Right. You help people in jail get back out on the street or something."

"Or something."

"What is it?" she said. "It's like the Innocence Project, right?"

"Sort of," I said. "There's just one little difference."

"What's that?"

"The clients I work with tend to be guilty." I gulped some wine, pausing for effect. "*Way* guilty."

"While you're in town helping out the murderers, I hope you're packing," she said. "Where I live, down in the Bywater, the animals will shoot you in the head just to get your shoes."

"Is that right?"

"I got a neighbor. He's a pediatrician, Doctor Peters. He was drinking an Old Fashioned on his porch in broad daylight and one of *them* pointed a gun at his nose. Doc Peters hands over his wallet, but the kid knocked out a couple of Doc's teeth with the butt of the pistol anyway. Just for the fun of it."

"That's terrible," I said.

"And then there's Miss Mindy. She's a dwarf. Couple months ago she was on her way home from making groceries and a gang of *them* beat the last drop of the living crap out of her. Six weeks in the ICU. They broke half the bones in her little body. Took the groceries too. She can barely get around with a walker."

"I'm sorry about your friends," I said.

"Animals is what they are. Gorillas. No consideration for human life."

I knew where she was going. Many people would tell me their favorite horror stories about urban crime after they found out what I did for a living. The implication was that, since I tried to save people from the death penalty, I was complicit in every homicide, beating, rape, armed robbery, and perhaps a few tsunamis and famines the world over.

"It must make you feel impotent to live in a city with such a high crime rate," I said.

"Ha!" she cackled. "Impotent my ovaries." She pushed back her chair and lifted the left leg of her cargo pants. A concealed-carry holster was fitted tightly around her calf, held in place with a wide Velcro strip. A .38 Special fit snugly into its pouch.

"You don't ever worry that thing could be used against you?"

"Let them try," she said. "If they rassle it from me, it won't be until after I've had the satisfaction of taking a couple down on the way."

"I'll drink to that," I said, looking across the table for the wine.

"I know this makes me a plebeian," said Dirk, "but I can't get enough of Popeyes' dirty rice. After I eat there I feel like I should go to confession."

"I used to be against the death penalty too," said Louanne. "Believe it or not, I was part of the feel-sorry-for-the-animals pity party."

Where was that bottle of wine? "What made you change your mind?"

"The danger to society. If you're not prepared to give them the gas, those guys will just get out and do it all over again."

"If it makes you feel any better, it's not likely that they will," I said. "Most of my cases boil down to two choices: the death penalty or life without the possibility of parole. That means they could live to be a thousand years old and they'll never get out of jail."

"But what about the ones that do?"

After a sigh, I said, "There are studies. By professors at reputable universities. Almost all violent crime is committed by men between the ages of fifteen and twenty-five. Once they get to thirty, they pretty much know the consequences. They're old enough to grow a conscience, or at least to get scared, and they stop. By the time they reach forty, the curve is steeper than the drop in a roller coaster. If they get out of jail at that age, they just don't commit violent crimes again."

"What about the serial killers? What about Jeffrey Dahmer?"

"How many serial killers have you ever met? There are way more of them on TV than in real life. And anyone who's a serial killer has got to be crazy. Look at Dahmer. How can you kill umpteen kids and cook them and eat them and still be in your right mind?"

"They're not crazy-crazy. You can't be nuts and go around planning murders and then committing them in cold blood."

"Not every person who's mentally ill is sitting on the floor drooling in a corner. I'd say a guy who plans multiple murders has got to be out of his mind."

"You don't really believe that. You know they're malingering. They're pretending to be crazy so they don't get fried. Some people are just bad to the bone."

The reason I tended to tell people I was a driving instructor was to avoid this kind of conversation. It was a waste of time: people who believe in the death penalty will keep their faith in it no matter what evidence is laid out for them to the contrary. Just as those of us who are against it cannot be turned around, no matter the argument.

"More than half of the people in prison are mentally impaired," I said. "Back in the eighties, they closed down a lot of the mental hospitals in the U.S. The people who were in them ended up on the street, homeless. Now many of the crazy people are warehoused in jails all over the country. And it's against the law to give the death penalty to a crazy person."

She ignored me. "America's got to have a death penalty. It's irresponsible not to. If they know they can get killed for it, people will think twice before they go and murder someone."

On the one hand, it was probably a good idea for me to have this kind of chitchat once in a while—to keep in mind what the juries were thinking and to make sure I remembered the arguments. On the other hand, it was a bad idea to spar a few rounds with an aggressive woman after I'd had too much wine. My tone got sharper. "The death penalty is not a deterrent. The more people that Texas puts to death, the more murders get committed there."

"When I think about how my tax dollars are paying to keep these creeps alive in jail, it burns my butt to a crisp," Louanne said.

"If the bottom line is money," I said, "it's actually cheaper to give someone life imprisonment than for the state to pay for a death-penalty prosecution and ten years of appeals. Leave them in general population, even for fifty years, and you're actually saving money."

"What a racket," she said.

By now the rest of the guests were aware that Louanne and I were in the midst of an altercation, but they pretended not to notice.

Across the table Susan was saying to Dirk, "I'm not much of a fried chicken person, but if you want to talk catfish, that's another story."

"Bode's in Mid-City," said Varnel. "They get my vote."

"Middendorf's at Pass Manchac," said Deanna. "Those thin crispy slices. It's like eating big old fish chips. Mmm—better than sex."

"I would imagine that would depend upon with whom," said Susan. She stole a glance at Louanne, not me.

"If you don't feel like driving for forty-five minutes, there's Joey K's," said Dirk, "down the street from my store."

"Don't they have an all-you-can-eat deal over there?" Susan asked Dirk. "Not a good idea for my figure." She looked at Louanne and winked.

"I got you. Keep them in jail for the rest of their lives so they can shank the guards, right?" said Louanne. She was screaming now, so loudly that the rest of the gang looked up from their catfish think tank. "Or the other prisoners in there for smoking dope and drunk in public. Or so they can escape and then go on a field trip to kill a few more sons of bitches. What a scam! Have you ever thought about the victims' families?" A little bit of spittle had appeared in a corner of her mouth. "What about the victims' families?"

"What about them?" I asked. "You know what? They're not my problem." I picked up the blue cloth napkin from my lap and threw it across the plate. I thought of Esperanza, festering in her cell in Plaquegoula Parish, and wondered what had been dished out for her dinner that night. What if her fate were ultimately in the hands of a passel of people like Louanne? "You're my problem, at least tonight. And yeah, you're right. You got me. I've been wrong about this all along. There's not enough death penalty. They should give it across the board, not just to murderers but to rapists and tax cheats and kids who shoplift Hershey's Kisses. Especially the kids. Set an example early on. Scare the shit out of them before they're toilet trained, if that's not redundant." They were all looking at me as if I'd defaced a church, or perhaps raped a nun. I stood up and said good night. Luckily, there was no death penalty for stupidity, or I would have bought it that night.

GO GREYHOUND

Esperanza and Gerardo board the bus a little before five in the morning. She takes the window seat. Too nervous to sleep, she watches a strip of pink light that marks the rise of dawn on the horizon, somewhere between San Antonio, where they boarded, and Houston, where they would change for another bus. The air-conditioning chills her to the bone during the three-hour ride.

The driver has an Alabama drawl and a deviated septum. Through the tinny microphone, his nasal voice is incomprehensible as he announces in English that Houston is the last stop, thanks the passengers profusely for going Greyhound, and suggests they make sure they have all their belongings. Surrounded by the downtown skyscrapers, it surprises Esperanza to see Spanish in huge block lettering outside the station: *CENTRAL DE AUTOBUSES*.

Groggy and restless, they sit on a wooden bench in the station while waiting for the bus to New Orleans. They do their best to assume the affect of casual travelers, she leaning into his shoulder and closing her eyes, their backpacks at their feet. He doesn't show it, but the uniformed men in the station put Gerardo in a panic. What if they come over and ask questions in English? The game would be over, and the two of them would land in jail.

They make sure to buy tickets for seats 29 and 30, two rows from the back, according to El Moco's instructions. It would be at least nine hours from Houston to New Orleans, so Esperanza tries to relax and even dozes for the first couple of hours of the journey, dreaming of wheels running over mice in the desert, until the bus abruptly lurches into Port Arthur, whirling her awake.

Within moments of getting up, Esperanza urgently has to use the bathroom. She steps over Gerardo and totters to the little cubicle in the back. It is a mistake to open the door. The stench from the latrine is worse than what emanated from the broken toilet in back of the house in Puroaire. She slams the door shut and makes her way back to her seat, struggling to contain her bladder until a half hour later, when they make it to the border—the one between Texas and Louisiana, at the Beaumont Vidor station. She hastily finds the toilet inside the terminal, and as she sits she feels dizzy. Her eyes cross with relief.

They have barely arrived in Louisiana when the bus stops and admits two muscular figures dressed in camouflage, patches at their shoulders and gold stars pinned to their chests. They wear green caps and mirrored sunglasses, their pants legs tucked into jackboots. Sidearms are holstered at their hips. In primitive, heavily accented Spanish, they select passengers randomly and ask for identification. Several rows ahead of Esperanza, a traveler in a white T-shirt and a baseball cap engages one of the soldiers in conversation, but they are too far away for her to hear. She watches the uniformed man escort the traveler outside and, through the window, sees him put his wrists in handcuffs. The other soldier approaches the back of the bus, his white teeth glistening, his Adam's apple jutting from his throat. By the time he reaches her, Esperanza thinks she will spit out her heart onto the floor.

But when he gets to where Gerardo and she are seated, he merely glances toward the numbers above their heads, then ambles his way to the front of the bus and out the door. As they take off again, Gerardo clasps her hand in his.

Did El Moco pay the soldiers? If not, why did he insist they sit in seats 29 and 30? Or was the soldier's disregard of them completely arbitrary? Gerardo begins to snore.

BACK AT THE RANCH

Mugrero was like a lot of places I visited in the post-crash U.S.: barely there. An ACE Cash Express, a Walgreens, a Family Dollar, a store called Ernest's Get-'Em and Hit-'Em Package Liquors. A bail bondsman with a sign that read 1-888-NOT-GUILTY. A mall with four stores, two of which were shuttered. The gastronomic offerings included Burger King, Popeyes, and Subway. There was also a taco truck parked along the widest street with *LA BONITA* painted across its side.

As the GPS sent me farther away from this excuse for a downtown, the houses got shabbier. I passed the odd secondhand store and boxy churches of diverse denominations. The voice of the GPS sounded vaguely British and slightly scolding: *Recalculating*. I imagined a purse-lipped Tilda Swinton under the hood appalled at my nonexistent sense of direction. A wide street of unkempt wooden houses, all patchy lawns and paint peeling off the walls. I drove around the block looking for signs of life, but it was deserted. I parked the car.

When I got out of the air-conditioned vehicle it became obvious why everyone was inside: the damp heat was like stepping into a vegetable steamer. The temperate climate of Mexico City had spoiled me. I wondered how people lived in this weather. Louisiana was fit for barnyard animals, not humans. A skinny adolescent in basketball shorts and a wife beater, a stocking covering his hair, stood on the sidewalk, eyeing me suspiciously.

"Hi," I said. He nodded, almost imperceptibly. "I'm looking for 729 Delachaise. Do you know where that is?"

He shrugged his shoulders perhaps an inch. I couldn't blame him for the unsociable reception. What could anyone standing on the sidewalk in this heat be doing besides dealing? A white stranger was nothing but trouble.

I moved along the broken concrete, under patches of shade offered by the few sickly shingle oaks and their spotted leaves. On the other side of a broad empty lot full of rubble and patchy earth there were more buildings, two-story slabs divided into tiny square apartments. Four doors on top and four on the bottom, the same on the other side—sixteen diminutive dwellings in each slab. Creaky outdoor staircases led to the top floors. The doors were ill fitted into their frames and many were missing the numbers that identified the apartments. Some of the windows were broken and the roofs were buckling. The buildings had been painted mint green and the staircases white, I guessed around the time that I was born.

I heard the tinny murmur of a *cumbia*. It was a song you could find on any jukebox in Mexico, to which couples swayed at every dingy nightclub, cantina, and house party from Matamoros to Mérida. *If every time I kiss the cross you're there, if every time I say a prayer you're there, how can I forget you?* Evidently, the empty lot that I had crossed separated the blacks from the Latinos.

I knew what I would find inside these apartments. A few sticks of furniture acquired on layaway, the fabric already frayed and tearing. Some dented implements of tin and Teflon with which to cook, bought at the Family Dollar. A stove, a refrigerator, the almighty television set, as large as the tenants could afford. On the parquet floor a plastic bowl of cereal, upended by a mewling infant. One or two bedrooms, so tiny that if you got out of bed quickly, you'd smash into the wall.

A man busied himself under the hood of a car. It was like most of the vehicular fleet in the area, the detritus of people born in the U.S., what they left behind after trading up: a heap of paint and rust, floorboards with bald spots, flat tires, spent shocks, transmissions with tuberculosis. Held together with dental floss, Scotch tape, and Krazy Glue. The *cumbia*, in fact, emanated from its radio.

"Pardon me," I said in Spanish.

He emerged with a rag in his hand that had once been part of a checked shirt. Beads of moisture dripped from his face and his bare upper body was caked with perspiration and grease. Honey-skinned, with close-cropped light brown hair and green eyes. A Honduran? There were more of them in south Louisiana than anywhere in the world except Honduras. *"Sí,"* he said, only a little less mistrustfully than the teenager down the street.

"Sorry to interrupt your work. Do you know which of these buildings is 729 Delachaise?"

His face seemed to relax. I probably wasn't *la migra.* "I don't know but it's one of these." He pointed to the various slabs lining the street.

"Thanks," I said. That much I could have figured out by myself, but those were probably as specific as instructions got back in Tegucigalpa. "Listen, by any chance, do you know a woman who used to live in one of these buildings, called Esperanza Morales?"

He thought about it for a moment and then shook his head. "No."

"A Mexican? From Michoacán? Tall, brown, with wavy hair down to her shoulders?"

His expression indicated a search into the recesses of memory. "No," he said.

"Did you hear about a woman who got arrested around here? The cops said she killed her baby?"

That rang a bell. "I think someone might have said something about that."

"I'm working for her lawyers, señor. Louisiana wants to give her the death penalty and we're trying to save her from that."

"Oh," he said.

"So I would be grateful for any information you could give me about her."

"I just moved here a couple of months ago," he said. "Like I told you, I don't know her."

"Can you tell me who said something to you about her?"

Again he reached into those dark caverns and came up with nothing. "I don't know. It was just something somebody said."

I gave him a card and asked him to call me if he remembered anything. I began to search for other signs of life among the slabs. From the muck a cockroach took wing. I ducked as it flew toward my face.

Who would choose to live around here, so far from anything resembling civilization? In my mind's eye I saw Esperanza again. Her hometown, Puroaire, was something out of *National Geographic*. When she got here, did she feel she had traded up? Around here, people earned $7.50 an hour—or $8.50 or $9.50, maybe a little more if they could operate heavy machinery. They washed their clothes in a machine instead of a sink. There were groceries in the refrigerator, instead of the rotting fruit discarded in the market at the end of the day. They had roofs over their heads that seldom leaked. Perhaps the paint in the bathroom peeled, but the toilet would reliably flush and there was hot and cold running water.

In a patch of dust in the shade of one of the buildings, two women chatted in Spanish while sitting on plastic lawn chairs. Brown, squat, and chunky, they wore tank tops, shorts, plastic flip-flops. One fanned her face with an old section of newspaper and the other patted the curlers in her hair.

"Buenas tardes," I said. I gave them a card and explained why I was there. Did they know Esperanza? They exchanged a glance. Was each checking whether the other remembered, or were they communicating something else, like *Should we be talking to this gringo*?

"I don't know her," said the woman with the newspaper fan, rotating her ankle and the flip-flop. Her toenails were painted blue.

"Me neither," said Curlers, crossing her arms around her ample bosom.

"She's been in the Plaquegoula Parish Jail for more than a year. They say she killed her baby."

"Ay, sí," said Blue Toenails. "There are people around here who talked about her."

"Who?"

She looked at me quizzically. "Who what?" she asked.

"Who are the people who talked about her?"

"I don't know," she said. "Just people."

I nodded. "You don't remember who?"

"It was a long time ago," she said. This is one of the problems with the glacial pace of the justice system in the U.S. I often did not begin an investigation until six months or a year—or sometimes more—

after the arrest. The Mexicans I was trying to reach frequently disappeared into the shadows, and if I could find them at all, it was a miracle if they remembered anything.

I asked them to call if they thought of anything, and began to search the slab for an open door, the sound of another radio, of voices, of laughter. I had been to microcommunities such as this in various parts of the country. The Mexicans lived in the farthest forgotten outskirts of big cities like Houston and San Antonio, as well as smaller ones such as Birmingham and Jackson. And in trailer parks and shantytowns outside agricultural hubs in east Texas, central Georgia, the saddest parts of Florida nowhere near the ocean. In all these places they'd re-created their *ranchos* in shabby, ill-constructed dwellings.

Up the termite-ridden staircase, on the second-floor landing. Salsa blared inside an apartment. I knocked. Nothing. I banged on the door more loudly. Still, no response. I knocked as hard as I could without breaking down the door, and a woman opened it, clasping a robe around her breasts. She glared at me in rage and slammed it shut before I had the chance to open my mouth.

If around here Esperanza earned a salary that would have been considered handsome in Mexico, I scanned the balance sheet and considered what she had lost by coming to the United States. Her family. Her community. The sense of connection to the place in which she lived, a feeling of belonging. The ability to walk, as they would say, *con la frente en alto*—without the terror that with every step she took she might be picked up by a man in uniform and thrown in jail. In the papers in the U.S., Mexico was painted as the Wild West crossed with Beirut, an impossible badland with combat rifles, rocket launchers, and M249s. Yet back at home Esperanza knew her neighbors by name, had relatives all over town, and in a pinch could probably get a pound of beans or a dozen eggs on credit. For what it was worth, the church where her parents and grandparents had prayed was in walking distance. According to my math, she'd lost more than she'd gained.

Downstairs I went to the other side of the building. One of the doors had been left ajar. I knocked and peered inside, but it was too dark to make anything out. All I heard was a radio playing "Midnight Train to Georgia." I knocked again and then heard footsteps.

A black man appeared. About sixty, he had gray hair, bloodshot eyes, a not-so-trim moustache, and a kindly smile. What was he doing here? Didn't he recognize as clearly as I the Maginot Line that divided his people from the Latinos? And how likely was he to have known Esperanza? I considered saying that I'd knocked on the wrong door, but there I was and so was he, with that smile on his face, so I explained who I was and what I did for a living.

"I knew the girl," the man said, "just a little bit. Nothing much, just to say hello."

"You did?" I asked.

"Yeah, but I knew her husband a little bit better. He was my buddy." His smile grew wider with the memory. "What was his name again?"

"You mean Gerardo?"

"That's right, Gerardo. He was my boy."

"Could I trouble you for a few minutes of your time?"

"Sure," he said, and opened the door wide. "Make yourself at home."

LAND OF DREAMS

"Now you and me can have us a little old Mexican standoff right here," says the gringo, standing behind his desk. "Right now. Do you want that?" He is built like a one-story building, squat, square, solid. His blond hair, parted on the side, falls over his forehead. His bulbous nose is red from the sun. "FEMA don't pay me, I don't pay you. That's all there is to it. The minute I squeeze my money out of them, you siphon out your share. I ain't got mine, I ain't got nothing to give you neither. It's just simple math is what it is, son. Comprendamundo?" He looks Rogelio in the eyes, challenging him to answer back.

Rogelio stares at the gringo, then at the floor. He doesn't think the math is all that straightforward. In his estimation, it's a complicated calculus with the following variables. He could take a swing at the man and, if he has great luck, knock him out. If his fortune is spectacular there will be a thick stack of bills in the gringo's wallet, although it would probably be short of what the three of them—Rogelio, Gerardo, and Esperanza—are owed. He might not have any cash at all, in which case Rogelio will merely have the satisfaction of putting the guy on the ground. But they'd be just as broke.

The gringo is at least thirty pounds heavier than sinewy Rogelio—maybe forty, maybe more. He's heavy but he's not soft. Looking into the red rims of the man's blue eyes, Rogelio actually doubts whether he could knock him to the floor. The alternate picture that he conjures is himself with his ass kicked outside the office, a mouthful of sidewalk, a couple of cracked ribs, his face pummeled into pulp. Not just penniless but beaten into hamburger.

If Rogelio accepts his lot, then maybe, sometime down the line, he and his *compañeros* will be able to collect their money. This would mean going back to the gringo—a week, a month, half a year later—and squaring off again, hoping that he will remember the debt and honor it. Wouldn't that be a little miracle? Ever since they got to Louisiana, all the Mexicans and Central Americans have tales of getting ripped off by cunning, unscrupulous gringos. Everyone knows that the government is paying the contractors way more than the contractors are paying the Mexicans to clean up the city. The rest goes straight into the gringos' pockets. You even have to watch out for the Mexicans, many of whom are stealing from one another.

Rogelio gives the man a dirty look so timidly that it passes unnoticed, and leaves the trailer that serves as the gringo's office. He walks outside to where Esperanza and El Chino are waiting for him, sitting on the sidewalk in the boiling sun. The overgrowth of weeds behind them is taller than a grown man and thick with insects—swarms of mosquitoes, fat flying German cockroaches, brown widow spiders, and almost invisible midges that can slither inside clothes and make mincemeat out of a human leg. He sits beside them.

"The gringo says he gets paid by the government. They haven't given him the money yet and until he gets it he can't pay us." Rogelio doesn't have to add that this is after they worked for several weeks without getting paid at all, and when they were finally given their wages, the cash in the envelopes amounted not to the fifteen dollars an hour they were promised but something closer to nine. The gringo explained that the rest had been withheld for taxes. Again, said with an expression that begged them to make his day by opening their mouths.

Because he speaks better English than they do, Rogelio knows that Gerardo and Esperanza might believe that he is conspiring against them with the gringo. It isn't true. But if he were to blurt out, "I'm not cheating you, *compadre*," the first thing they would think is that he is cheating them. So he sits with them on the broken sidewalk in silent solidarity.

They look at the house across the street, whose roof has caved in the center, collapsing the entire second story. It is as if King Kong had emerged from the overgrowth, sat on top of the residence and crushed it. There are no people in the neighborhood, just block after block of abandoned, destroyed houses, from which seep the stench of decay, destruction, and death. More than a hundred thousand houses have been abandoned in the city. Day after day, the Mexicans have come here to move debris from the street to the sidewalk and eventually into dumpsters.

On the front wall of the house across the street, a large X has been scrawled in red paint, with a hieroglyph on each quadrant of the letter. On the left TX has been painted with a 9-6 on top, an NE on the right and a 0 on the bottom. These scribbles are all over the doors and walls of the city. No one has explained to the Mexicans what the symbols mean. Only Rogelio, with his limited English, understands the other message scrawled across the wall of the house: I AM HERE I HAVE A GUN.

As dawn breaks over the city the air is still and clammy. By the time the sun rises Gerardo will have broken a sweat. He squats on his haunches on a platform that supports a Doric column, on top of which, sixty feet in the sky, a bronze rendering of General Robert E. Lee presides over the surrounding traffic circle and the Mexican minions gathered there. Were he alive, the general might more or less approve of the immigrants, a newly arrived workforce a mere step or two above slave labor.

Close to a hundred brown men are congregated, competing for the privilege of doing a day's work. They wait for the gringos to arrive in pickup trucks. Each will select two or three, or however many Mexicans can squeeze in the cabs of their vehicles. They will be driven to neighborhoods equally abandoned as the one where Esperanza, Rogelio, and Gerardo worked, but with larger and more well-appointed houses that are already being rebuilt. The Mexicans are chosen to nail the plywood that will frame a home, spackle the holes in a wall, lay a cement floor, or climb up on a roof, risking their necks to save someone's habitat. All Gerardo's colleagues are dressed alike: ratty jeans, threadbare T-shirts, baseball caps, sneakers or work boots. He realizes that for his employers, he and his *compañeros* are backs and biceps, bodies without faces or names.

Gerardo is often among the first to be chosen because of his muscular build. But sometimes he is overlooked, and some days only a couple of gringos come by, offering work to just a handful of men. He misses the nine dollars an hour he earned on the cleanup crew—if it wasn't what he was promised, at least it was steady. After a year in Louisiana, Gerardo senses that the work is drying up and the adventure has been a failure.

He can imagine his mother sighing when she receives the meager MoneyGram he is able to send to her every so often in Waco. This on top of the pennies she gets from his brothers in Juárez and whatever she earns cleaning other people's homes. He remembers the night so many years ago when she gathered him and the rest of his siblings and left Nuevo Casas Grandes in a second-class bus, stealing away to Ciudad Juárez while her husband was passed out in a stupor. Gerardo was only six years old and has not seen his father since. His older brothers have told him that she left because he screamed, broke the dishes, and even beat her, but there is a pit in his stomach when he thinks of his snoozing dad abandoned on the kitchen floor. She raised all of them by herself, cooking in the industrial kitchen of a supermarket, the food she prepared served and sold at an immense steam table.

Gerardo quit school when he was eleven and went to work bagging groceries at the market so he could be closer to her. After his sister, Belinda, and her husband went to live in Waco, his mother sneaked across the border too. Gerardo hasn't seen her since. Occasionally they exchange awkward syllables on the phone. She lives around the corner from Belinda, who isn't much relief; her husband earns little and they have four kids.

In his mind's eye he pictures Esperanza, who sometimes cleans houses and occasionally still works on garbage crews, the muscles in her arms and back growing as she lifts smashed roof tiles, two-by-fours, and waterlogged wooden planks to the sidewalk. Sometimes she bakes pound cakes and sells them to the neighbors. It pains him to see her work so hard. Gerardo has never said out loud that he wishes she would stay home. It's better not to say anything. He knows she would answer back that they need the money. He dreads returning home to her, for she has seen him in a weakened state, cheated and robbed by gringos, unable to financially support her. She makes him feel like less of a human because she, a woman, is out there operating in a world of men. He's been told that his father had the same complaint about his mother. What was never made clear to him is that if the family had tried to survive on what he earned unloading trucks they would have starved to death.

If his father is a ghostly presence, there is another phantom in Gerardo's life, a baby named Eduardo, left behind after a sojourn working in a factory in Ciudad Cuauhtémoc. When the baby was born, Gerardo was sixteen, and Evelyn, Eduardo's mother, fifteen. Gerardo left because Evelyn didn't listen to him—she would go off with the baby to her mother's every day, sometimes all day, and not come back until well into the night. If he complained, she would raise her voice and tell him that Eduardo was the baby and he, Gerardo, could take care of himself. He knew no one in Cuauhtémoc except for Evelyn. So he went back to his brothers in Juárez.

The first of the pickup trucks pulls up. A gringo gets out and barks something unintelligible to the assembly of Mexicans. Gerardo stands and looks at the spot between the gringo's eyes. He is erupting with rage for how the gringos have cheated him out of the money that is rightly his, the money that was signaled to him as a whispered promise all the way from *el gabacho* to Mexico. He has contempt for those of his colleagues who smile with eager-puppy eyes at the white man. There is no one to whom he can say it, but it is a point of pride that he bends his head before no man. What he does not realize is that, if not bowing, he is breaking.

Esperanza knocks on Lourdes's door, on the second and highest floor of a creaking, sagging, termite-infested building that has been subdivided into tiny rooms, under the overpass where the police are said to have shot some *negritos* after the flood. The cops in Louisiana, they say, are even worse than in Mexico. If you cross their path you avert your eyes and try to blend in with the walls.

The tenants are all Mexicans or Hondurans, living two, three, four, or more to a room. Lourdes's door is so crooked in its frame that a school of squirrels could climb through the triangle that separates it from the upper wall. No one answers so she knocks again. "Lourdes?" she calls.

Finally Rogelio opens the door, barefoot, clad in low-slung jeans and an untucked threadbare T-shirt that barely fits over his wide shoulders. Across its front the garment says:

FIND

EVERY

MEXICAN

AVAILABLE

There is a cleft from where his cheek was mashed into a pillow. He looks at her with rheumy eyes and smiles. She wonders when he will go back to the gringo to try to retrieve their money. Weeks have passed since he sent them home penniless.

"Sorry if I woke you," she says. "Lourdes said she wanted two of my *panqués*." Esperanza makes them from a cake mix, adds cinnamon and raisins, and sells them for three dollars apiece. If she can move all ten that she baked in a morning, it's a good day.

"I wasn't asleep," says Rogelio, running his fingers through the hair on his stomach. Unlike Gerardo, he has no belly. "Lourdes isn't here."

"When will she be back?" says Esperanza, nodding.

"I don't know," he says, a tiny insinuation in his smile. "Maybe three. You want to come in?" He opens the door a little wider.

Sure, she thinks. *Cabrón.* As if she had nothing else to do but spend the afternoon in bed with him. She regrets their two encounters: Men cannot keep their mouths shut; will he be able to resist telling Gerardo? She wonders why he is at home on a sunny afternoon and not out working with Gerardo and the crews. Why isn't he trying to get their money from the fat gringo? Probably he's sponging off Lourdes, who is scavenging used clothes that she sells in a flea market on the weekends.

Still, she wonders what it would be like to return to bed with him and not to have to think about work, even for a day or two. She wonders: Since they arrived in Louisiana has she had even a single day off? The best-paying job was the cleanup crew: nine dollars an hour take-home. She will never forget the cars upended on front lawns or crashed through walls, their windows shattered, their innards gutted like a fish. The foreman said that three hundred thousand of these rudderless wrecks had been abandoned in the city.

Mostly she worked moving the wooden skin of demolished houses, but some objects had floated through doors and windows onto the street. She handled the sodden, moldy remnants of what had once been the fluffy cushions of plush sofas, television sets with their skeletons exposed, lamps disengaged from their shades, parts of pianos that would never again make a sound. The smell of the rot was enough to turn her stomach. The first time she uncovered a cat, dead for over a year, she wanted to run crying into Gerardo's arms, but he barely acknowledged what she had in her hands, as if it were just another piece of rubble. She still has nightmares about the cats and dogs. Even though she wore rubber gloves, it was as if her skin caressed their matted fur, their bones, their desiccated entrails.

"I can't," she says. "I have to deliver these *panqués*." In a half hour, he pleasured her as Gerardo hasn't in a year. He was such a good lover, she thinks, that maybe that is why he is at home and Lourdes is out working.

"Come inside and sit down for a minute," says Rogelio through his smirk. A thumb looped inside the front pocket of his jeans pulls them down to reveal a bit more of his torso. "We can have a cup of coffee. Or a beer."

"Thanks, Rogelio, but I have to go. Just tell Lourdes that I was looking for her, okay?" She feels terrible for betraying Lourdes. Rogelio doesn't even blink when he's around his wife or Gerardo.

After she has sold her *panqués*, she will wander through the city, half of which still has no electricity, water, or plumbing, and pilfer the trash bins for empty soda cans, and if she collects enough of them, she'll walk three miles to the only supermarket that has reopened in the vicinity. She will feed the cans into the machine and exchange them for nickels. On Fridays she will help Lourdes sort and clean the bags of used clothing, and on Saturday they will sell them at the flea market in Saint Flocellus Parish.

Esperanza found these other ways to earn a little income after the gringo stopped paying them to work on the cleanup crew. Gerardo now leaves before dawn to take his place at Lee Circle to find day labor. He comes home in the late afternoon, sometimes after dark. He opens a quart of beer and drinks it out of the bottle, saying nothing, staring into the middle distance.

They hardly ever speak; he only grunts when they have sex. In the mornings before going to work, while he sips a mug of Nescafé, he also gazes into space. What is he looking at? What is he thinking of? She gazes at him from the tiny bedroom off the kitchenette, unable to sleep in the excruciating heat. When they share the mattress, he watches the ceiling as if it contains the answer to an important riddle. Sometimes she will say something and he won't respond, as if he hasn't heard. One night, wishing to stun him into a response, she said, "I told you we should have stayed in Texas." He didn't say a word. Texas is almost as far away, geographically and emotionally, as Ciudad Juárez.

South Louisiana is another planet, sparsely populated around the wreckage of a disaster. There are so few people in the expanse they have colonized. The white foremen, the scowling black colleagues who look at the Mexicans with hostility and distrust, the enormous woman with the pale pimply skin who works at the grocery store and rings up Esperanza's purchases without so much as a smile. The one-house ghetto of Mexicans and Hondurans, who populate the tiny rooms along with the roaches. Through the drywall she can hear her neighbors argue, the squall of a baby, the occasional cry of pain or ardor. She can smell pork frying in cheap oil, a pot of rice, an unflushed toilet. In Mexico, she found herself periodically on the precipice of despair, but somewhere, if you scraped around the edges of life, there was also aspiration, faith, possibility. In Louisiana, Esperanza finds only darkness.

Still, even here, existence is not without its miracles. After missing two periods, she realizes there is another life within her body.

LEAN ON ME

"He was my boy," said Clarence in a relaxed drawl. "We worked together over here."

"Over here where?"

"Right here. In these apartments."

"What did you do?"

"Whatever needed to get done. Painting. Plastering. Cleaning. Fixing up the toilets. Patching up the roof. Lot of people come and go round here. Any time one of these apartments come empty we fixed it up so Rolando could rent it to somebody new."

"Rolando?"

"Boss man. The manager round here."

I wrote the name in capital letters and would ask Clarence to introduce us when we finished talking.

"Was Gerardo a hard worker?"

"Yeah. He showed up on time, did what had to get done, worked as late as he had to work. Didn't complain about it."

I had a good feeling about Clarence. A straight shooter, convincing, believable. Easygoing, not at all defensive, mistrustful, or threatening. Did he know Esperanza at all? If he had positive things to say about her, he might do us some good on the witness stand in a penalty phase. Many Louisiana jurors, of course, would not like the fact that he was black. Could Catherine pick people for whom his credibility would be more decisive than his color?

He smiled, a nostalgic glow in his bloodshot eyes. "Yeah, we used to sit here and get high every night after work."

"Get high?"

"Yeah, smoke us a little weed. You ain't no cop now, right?" He laughed.

There goes my witness, I thought. "Are you kidding? Like I said, I'm working for Esperanza's lawyers, just trying to save her from the death penalty."

"All right then. We'd smoke up a little weed most nights after work. Just sit here and chill." He laughed again. "Sometimes before work too." I wondered whether he was high then and there. The apartment didn't smell of pot.

My memo would be confidential, but what if the prosecution found out that Clarence was a smoker? Even recreational drug use would compromise his integrity with a jury. In the Bayou State, if you're caught with a little grass and it's a first offense, it's a misdemeanor good for six months and a $500 fine. Second time, it's a felony worth a nickel in state prison. Third strike means a mandatory minimum of ten years, but if the judge is a sweetheart, she'll slam you with twenty.

"Did you do anything else?"

"What do you mean?"

"Other drugs."

"No." He stopped to consider. "*I* didn't."

"Gerardo?"

"Don't know about that." He said this decisively enough to tip me off that the answer was yes. "He was friends with some of the Honduran dudes up around here and I don't really know what they was into."

What were the Hondurans' names? He didn't know. "What about Esperanza? Did you know her at all?"

"Mostly to say hello to, you know? She was okay. Good old gal. I can't see why they'd want to execute her."

"They say she killed the baby."

"Yeah," said Clarence, his lips stretched, shaking his head. "I don't know about that."

"*What* don't you know?"

He paused. "I don't believe in no death penalty. That's like a man's trying to do what's up to God, you know what I'm saying? Only God supposed to decide when you going to die."

"That's right," I said. How I wished he could say that while look-ing at the jurors straight in the eyes.

Clarence leaned back in the sofa. "And you know that baby wasn't right, you know what I'm saying?"

"Wasn't right? How?"

"She was sick all the time. If it wasn't one thing it was something else. She was always sick. She had a hard time breathing."

"Did Gerardo talk to you about that?"

"Not much. But you could see it. You could hear it when she was trying to breathe."

"Did she have asthma?"

"Maybe. Probably. I don't know. I ain't no doctor. But she wasn't right."

"And Gerardo never said anything about it?"

"We didn't talk all that much. Like I said, mostly he'd come over here after work and just chill out with a little reefer."

"Wait a minute," I said. I wondered: How the hell would he and Gerardo have spoken to each other? "*¿Hablas español?*" I asked.

"*Po-co,*" he said, and added, in wildly broken Spanish with an even worse accent than mine, "I've been working with these guys for so long that a little bit of their talk rubbed off on me."

"So how long did you and Gerardo work together?"

"I don't know. Year or two?"

"Until he split?"

"Nah. Up until he broke his back."

"How did he do that?"

"He fucked it up when he fell off the roof. Something got broken up there."

"Tell me about that."

"He was fixing a drainpipe over by 735. Lucky it wasn't any high-er or he would have killed himself."

"And after that he couldn't work anymore?"

"He tried. Rolando kept him on as an assistant for a while. That's mostly what I do, assistanting. I'm sixty-two. But even that's still physical work, you dig? Mixing up the plaster, putting it up on the wall, moving tools and buckets and bricks and shit around. The pain was too much for him."

"And did you guys keep hanging out after that?"

"Just once in a while he'd stop by."

"Like how often?"

"Not much. That's when he started hanging with the Hondurans."

"Did he come to say good-bye before he split?"

"No. He just disappeared after the baby died."

"*After* the baby died?" This was not Esperanza's version. She said he left a month or two before.

"Yeah, right around when the baby died."

I tried to play it as cool as possible. "After, Clarence? Or before?"

"Man, I didn't write nothing down on no calendar."

"Yeah. But you think it was around the time the baby died."

"I know I didn't see him no more after that."

"Do you know where he went?"

Clarence nodded. "He went back to Mexico."

"He told you that?"

"No, he didn't tell me nothing. But after he got hurt he was saying he couldn't make it around here no more. And that he missed his kid."

"But she was right here."

"Not the baby. The other kid. His son."

"Gerardo had a son?"

"Yeah. Over by where he comes from, where they kill the women."

"Juárez?"

"Yeah."

"And this was before the baby died, right?"

"Yeah. No. I don't know. I mean I told you already, I didn't look at no calendar. But I know I didn't see him no more after she died."

I just nodded. I was off to the races.

It was pretty much out of the realm of possibility that a prosecutor would ever get Clarence on the witness stand and ask, "Have you ever done drugs with anyone on the defense team?" Nevertheless, it was imprudent to smoke dope with a witness. But he offered, and I thought, *What the hell*. My justification was that, between being black and a pot smoker, he wasn't going to make it to the witness stand in any case.

I could count on the fingers of one hand the number of times I'd smoked dope in the previous couple of decades. One summer during high school I smoked it every day, only to come to the conclusion that it wasn't my thing. It made me paranoid and depressed; while under the influence, I'd focus on how tragic life was.

I guess I had graduated to another zone. I felt completely peaceful, listening to Clarence's music from the 1960s and 1970s. Was he the only man left in the U.S. who had held on to his cassette tapes? He asked me some questions about my job, and I got a little motormouthed, telling him about traveling between Mexico and the United States, trying to put together the pieces of a story that could save someone from the death penalty.

"Don't you get all stressed out with that? Having someone's life in your hands?"

I had halfway melted into Clarence's couch. "It's moments like this, when I'm really relaxed, that I realize that, yeah, my job is a little bit out there. But I never think that their life is in my hands. I can't save anyone myself. I'm part of a team. If we all do our jobs then maybe we'll be lucky and save them. And everyone's life is stressful, no? I mean, you can't avoid stress. It's all about the way you handle it. You can let it get to you or try to go with the flow."

"But that's heavy, going to jail and getting all up in their family shit."

"You get used to it. And it makes me appreciate how sweet the rest of my life is."

Then we kind of stopped talking and just listened to the music. I imagined this was what it had been like between him and Gerardo.

He had a quizzical smile on his face. After a while he asked, "Who's got your back, Richard?"

The pot had slowed me down. "What?"

"Who's got your back?"

The response that occurred to me—"What makes you think I can't take care of myself?"—sounded defensive, even truculent. I wasn't fast enough to come up with another one.

"You got a wife?" Clarence asked.

"I'm divorced."

"You got kids?"

"No, we didn't have any. When I was married, we tried, but my ex couldn't have any." This was a fiction I invented for those occasions when people asked me about my childlessness. It struck me as less complex and more acceptable than the truth.

Clarence's smile broadened. "Where your parents at?"

"The sweet hereafter."

"So who's got your back, man?" he said. I was going to say something about all the friends I had, but it sounded hollow even in my own ears. "I mean, you up here in the middle of nowhere. You telling me you going all over the world saving people's life like you the Lone Ranger or some shit. What about you? Where's Tonto? Shit, you ain't even got no *Silver*?" He laughed out loud. "Who's going to save your life?"

"Well, I'm not in jail, Clarence. I think they need me more than I need someone to watch my back right now."

"Motherfucker, *please*," he said. He began to clap his hands, then sing along with the music. *"We all need somebody to lean on...."* As he continued to croon I felt completely exposed. He had my number. I was so accustomed to taking care of myself that I didn't even know what it meant for someone to have my back.

The stakes had grown fairly high. I was forty-two, a failed novelist alone in a foreign country. I'd managed to save a little money since I began to do mitigation, but emotionally, I was flying without a net. I'd never really had anyone I could count on, or who would be able to count on me. How sweet that could be. Would I ever find her? I pictured Esperanza's long lashes, those eyes, black like a deer's; the mouth that reflected a history of hurt.

And I realized why I fantasized about a life with her. Somewhere along the line, I had lost my way. I was an exile, an orphan, adrift without a sail. Some lawyers appreciated the work I did, and some writers liked to get drunk with me. A few women might have vague memories of moments we'd shared together. But I belonged to no one. I didn't matter.

I imagined she would be my connection to the world, she and any children we might have. Together, we could have staked a claim in the universe. We would have fit in somewhere on the planet. My life could have changed with her. But did that possibility truly exist? She was in jail. When Clarence sang the part about *"For it won't be long, till I'm gonna need somebody to lean on,"* I burst into tears.

He didn't say anything. We just sat there for a couple of minutes until I pulled myself together. By the time the tape played "Papa Was a Rolling Stone," I was singing along with him.

Had I taken his words to heart, would I still be alive?

HOME REMEDIES

Although it can happen at any time, it is usually after nightfall when Yesenia begins to exhale with a gasping whistle. Her lips dry, her eyes shut tightly, her nostrils flared as she inhales, she looks like an old lady with a world of worries. Sometimes she gets a coughing fit, and cavernous sounds emerge from her tiny shallow chest. So Esperanza gathers earth from the patchy lawns around the building, mixes it with water to make a thick mud, and boils it on top of the stove. Once the sludge has cooled a little, she rubs it over the baby's chest. Yesenia gurgles at her mother's touch, and Esperanza could swear that the infant is able to inhale more deeply afterward.

She knows how to execute this treatment because she saw her own mother perform it on one of her cousins' babies back in Puroaire. When Yesenia has relaxed, Esperanza washes the mud off with warm water and then holds the baby against her own breast, rocking her slowly until their hearts beat in unison. Soon Yesenia is asleep and she lays her down on the foam mattress next to the bed.

Then Esperanza discovers the tender red rash on the infant's back and chest. Yesenia often cries from the itching, and soon develops a fever. Opaque blisters appear on her skin. Esperanza pops the blemishes, although knowing how much it hurts the baby causes her pain too. She rubs alcohol into Yesenia's inflamed skin. At a Mexican neighbor's suggestion, she pours cider vinegar into the infant's bath water, which seems to relieve the itching, at least temporarily. So does an oatmeal compress, which the same neighbor recommended.

Remembering a treatment that María Concepción used when one of her children had some kind of a rash, Esperanza is inspired to parboil a potato and, while it is still warm, slice it and place the slivers on Yesenia's popped blemishes, to absorb and lift up the pus. She continues to pop the boils intermittently for a few days until they harden into white crusts. Then she squeezes the scabs, which leave little holes that form into scars that Esperanza imagines—hopes—are temporary.

In Puroaire, no one went to a doctor, not unless he had broken a limb or was at death's door, and then it was to the emergency room at the hospital in Huetamo. Once, a firecracker exploded in her cousin Paulina's left hand, and she was taken away. Paulina lost her thumb and forefinger. Just before Uncle Oscar was to get married, something went wrong with his kidneys. He lost consciousness, foamed at the mouth, could not speak or walk. This warranted a trip to the hospital, in an ambulance no less. Oscar survived, but only as a shadow of the man he'd been before. Under such momentous circumstances, physicians and surgeons were tolerant about payments and let the impoverished compensate them over time.

One morning on her way to work in the kitchen at Biddy's, a breakfast-and-lunch cafeteria, Esperanza spotted a pediatric clinic. She has heard that doctors report their Mexican patients to the authorities and that they have been deported. Nevertheless, the next day she hauled Yesenia to the storefront doctor. But a security guard on the curb outside gave her the stink-eye before she could walk through the door. Too frightened to follow up, she took Yesenia to work with her that day and left her in a high chair in the corner of the kitchen. When the baby began to cry, the manager sent Esperanza home and told her he'd fire her if she brought Yesenia again.

To offset her daughter's constant and recurring illness, she continues to employ her mother's home remedies. When the baby has a fever she puts boiled water with sage, thyme, and honey in her bottle. When Yesenia vomits, Esperanza cuts an onion in half and rubs the split vegetable on the infant's underarms. When she has diarrhea, she boils a tablespoon of cider vinegar and a teaspoon of salt in water, and fills the baby's bottle with the mixture, again with a little honey to make it palatable.

She cannot count on Gerardo to support her in her efforts at Yesenia's wellness, although he has worked only sporadically since falling off the roof. When Esperanza gets home in the afternoon after her shift at the cafeteria, most often the house stinks because Gerardo hasn't taken the trouble to change the baby's diapers. For the subsequent rashes, Esperanza will rub an aloe vera cream she found at the drug store on Yesenia's thighs and bottom.

It is amazing how completely and quickly Gerardo has fallen apart. Esperanza prefers to avoid fighting with him, and has tried to patiently explain that Yesenia is too young to be given the aspirin that he has let dissolve into her bottle. They make special aspirin for babies. She also suggests that the infant's skin is too sensitive for him to leave her out on a blanket in the sun, which he seems to think will improve her blemishes. As if she were an idiot, Gerardo barks that he is doing what his mother did when his sister suffered from the same conditions. Gravely, Esperanza nods. It is a losing battle to argue with a man after he has invoked his mother.

Less than a month ago she came home to find the infant alone in the apartment, crying in a cardboard box. Gerardo arrived moments later and swore that he had been away for only fifteen minutes due to an emergency he left unnamed. And today she finds Yesenia alone again, sleeping soundly on the foam mattress, wrapped in a blanket so tightly that she could have suffocated. When Gerardo comes home she wants to break something over his head. Instead she asks him in as steady a voice as possible: *Doesn't he understand that you can't leave a baby alone? That she could seriously hurt herself? Or even die?*

Gerardo snorts and rubs the thumb of one hand against the fingers of the other. "It was only a few minutes," he says.

"A few minutes is enough," she says.

"Enough for *what*?"

"Enough for your daughter to die."

"So stay at home," he says, drinking from a can of beer he brought with him from outside.

"How am I supposed to stay at home if you don't work?" she shoots back. "Who's going to pay for food, for diapers?"

"How am I supposed to work if I'm a prisoner in here all day?"

"I didn't make this situation."

"Well, neither did I, *hija de la chingada!*" He throws the can against the wall, inches from her head, and walks out of the apartment, slamming the door behind him. The baby begins to cry.

There are only a couple of rickety chairs in the apartment, and the sofa with its flaccid cushions is uncomfortable. Esperanza sits on the floor, cradling Yesenia in her arms, and rocks back and forth until the baby is silent and sleeping. She tries to hold at bay a cavernous emptiness inside of her, tries not to think bitterly of her present situation. But she cannot push it away. In her mind, she turns over again and again a journey of fifteen hundred miles. What has she proven, alleviated, or achieved on this voyage? She is as undernourished, insecure, and unprotected as ever. The toilet, stove, and refrigerator may work, but she is more bereft than she was back in Mexico. Added to her burden is the responsibility of a sickly baby and a man who acts up like a sullen child, or else disappears entirely, even when he is right there. Along the journey she has met only one person she would qualify as a friend, and that woman disappeared and without a doubt is dead. She has lost touch with her parents, grandparents, brothers, and sisters. There is not a soul to whom she can turn. She imagines an abandoned boat in the middle of the sea. What can happen to that vessel but shipwreck, drowning, destruction? She cannot imagine how to stop it or change course. It is as if there is something inevitable about her destiny, and there is nothing she can do to change it.

If only she could turn back the clock and tell Hilda what will happen to them if they leave Morelia and go to Juárez. Then she is tormented because such time travel would mean that Yesenia would never have been born. Esperanza weeps desperately, but silently, so as not to wake the baby. Her mouth is agape as the tears stream from her eyes, but she does not make a sound.

I'LL FLY AWAY

Rolando wasn't around. It was Sunday so he wouldn't be back until the next day. I knocked on the door of every single apartment in that complex looking for Hondurans. Few people were home. I found a couple but they claimed not to know what I was talking about, to have never met Gerardo or Esperanza. I would try again the following day when I came back for Rolando.

The story was taking on the complexity of real life, rather than a prosecutor's black-and-white comic book. For a year and a half we'd been operating under Esperanza's version, that Gerardo had left months before Yesenia died, but now it looked like he left around the time the baby was killed. Did he have anything at all to do with it? And what about his son in Juárez? Yesenia had been sick. We'd looked all over for medical records, but there weren't any after her birth. Esperanza had explained they didn't take her to the doctor or hospitals because they were scared that *la migra* would deport them.

How did the baby die? The photographs were horrifying—it couldn't have happened without anyone's intervention. I would find out what I could while in Louisiana. I would visit Esperanza later that week, on the way out of town. And I would go to Juárez and find that broken-back boyfriend if it was the last thing I did. (Please refrain from the obvious remarks. Nobody likes a smart-ass.) I hoped against hope that there would be more to the story, and that I'd find out something that would change the game for her.

But that was it for the moment. It was early afternoon. I had a couple of hours to kill. It was time to steal a moment. Anything to take my mind off the job. Anything that didn't have to do with a dead baby, a woman in jail, and Mexicans trying to keep from starving to death.

I drove around, looking at trees and houses, listening to the radio. There was nothing to do in Mugrero. Should I go back to New Orleans? And then I saw it. A funny little one-story church that looked like it had been added on to someone's house. Wood siding, whitewashed, with the conical spire on top. The sign outside said GOOD NEWS HOLY ZION. Why not? It was Sunday. It would be cool in there compared with the Louisiana steam bath outside.

Services had already begun. There were maybe a hundred in the congregation and few empty seats. I snuck into a pew in the back, in between a couple of elderly people. Many of the men had neckties, jackets, or both, and the women were decked out in hats, jewels, and bright colors. Not only did I feel underdressed, but conspicuously, prominently, exceptionally white.

"Did y'all wake up this morning and find out you wasn't dead of a stroke?" intoned the preacher. I would have guessed he was in his sixties, with a short black Afro and a few days of graying stubble. He must have put on weight in recent times, for it had taken a mighty effort if not divine intervention to squeeze the button closed around his belly. If he was not a beautiful specimen, he had a lovely trilling voice. Many in the congregation answered: *Yes, indeed, that I did, amen.*

"Is that a reason for y'all to be thankful?" sang the preacher.

The murmurs of the appreciative: *Yes, indeed, yes, it is, amen.*

"Did y'all wake up this morning and find out you wasn't dead of a heart attack?"

Amen, yessir, yes, I did.

The woman to my left wore a dress that looked like it had been made out of the striped curtains in someone's front parlor, and a hat with a bow on top and a brim so wide it came close to poking me in the eye.

"Did y'all wake up this morning and find out you didn't have cancer?" he crooned.

"Amen, that I did," said the lady in the hat.

"And who we have to thank for another day of life?"

Thank you, Jesus! Amen! Thank you, Lord!

"Another splendid glorious day of life!"

Well, yes, it was. Why not? I was in fact grateful for the day. The encounter with Clarence had psyched me up about carrying on in Esperanza's defense. Could I be inspired by something in addition to professionalism and the love I felt for her? It might not have occurred to me that God or Jesus or the Virgin of Guadalupe had anything to do with it. But I wasn't going to be petulant at the Good News Holy Zion, not on a sunny Sunday afternoon. The organist began to play a quiet groove. "We have some visitors with us today," said the preacher. "Y'all sitting next to Ida Mae Collins. Stand up and say your name."

A balding man in a shiny pin-striped suit stood up. He had a pocket square that had been folded so four points emerged at his breast, like a crown. "My name is Hubert Henry Parker Junior," he said. "And this is my wife, Veronica."

"Where are you from and what is your church?"

"We're from Jonesville, Louisiana, and our church is the Saint Mark Baptist."

"Thank you, Mr. Parker. You are most welcome here. And what about you, young lady?"

The "young lady" was an ancient woman a few rows from the altar. She wore a blue-and-white wide-checked suit, a blond wig, and dark glasses although indoors. Her walker was parked in the aisle beside her. "I am Anne Grady Jordan," she said. "I'm visiting my people here from Albany, Georgia. My church is the Providence Church."

"Thank you for coming, Miz Anne," said the preacher.

The sun was coming through a stained-glass window with a western exposure. It depicted an angel blessing a couple of black pilgrims. I almost didn't realize that the preacher was talking to me.

"You there, young man," he said. "In the white shirt. What is your name, young man?"

My heart pounding, I stood. "My name is Richard, sir."

"Where are you from and what is your church?"

It came to me like the light shining through that window. "I'm from Mexico City," I said, "but this is my church."

At least a few people thought this was a good answer. I heard half a dozen *amens*. The organist picked up the beat and the choir—eight women dressed in black from head to toe, but without robes—began to sing "I'll Fly Away." There was a mammoth one with gold teeth banging a tambourine. *Some glad morning, when this life is over, I'll fly away.* Man, was she into that song. It was almost sexual, as if there were an electric current between God and her voice and my skin. *To a home on God's celestial shore, I'll fly away.* Oh, but the beautiful one next to her, the one with the wide hips and the slim waist, the horn rims and the cornrows. If it was possible for anything to make me believe, it was her voice. *Like a bird from these prison walls I'll fly, I'll fly away.*

I was happy. I knew I was happy and I didn't know how long it would last, so I tried to capture the happiness and hold on to it. The lyrics to the song were all about how glorious death would be. I could almost believe it would be a joyous occasion.

IT'S THE REAL THING

It disappoints Richard that Esperanza is even more sullen than usual, even after he produces the can of Coca-Cola from his knapsack. She resists his efforts at small talk, so he begins to go over some of the issues in the case. "The birth records say Yesenia was underweight," says Richard. "But you're telling me she was born healthy?" His elbows on the table, he is hunched over the open can. The guards in the Plaquegoula Parish lockup tend to leave inmates and their legal teams alone in contact rooms when they visit. But just in case one happens to walk by and peer inside, Esperanza also leans toward Richard, the soda hidden between their frames. Richard told Esperanza that if a guard busts them, she should keep her mouth shut. He will explain that he brought the soda for himself.

Her head inches from Richard's, she takes a furtive swallow of the drink, then leans back in her chair with her eyes closed, as if only in this position can she truly taste it. Her mouth opens slightly, her jaw slack. To Richard she looks as if she were waiting for a kiss. She ignores his question.

"I know we've already covered this ground," he says. "It's just that a neighbor told me Yesenia had asthma."

She opens her eyes. "Who?" she asks.

"One of the people on Delachaise. I don't remember who. I talked to a lot of people." Of course he remembers, but he makes it a practice to never tell one person what another has told him.

"She was a perfect baby," says Esperanza.

Richard smiles. "No one's perfect," he says. "All babies might seem that way to their parents. But they get sick."

"Do you have any children?"

"No. When I was married, we tried, but my ex couldn't have any." In Esperanza's expression Richard reads reproof, and an opinion that, since he has no children, his beliefs on the subject are illegitimate.

"My baby was perfect," she repeats. Her face looks carved in stone.

"You never took her to a doctor after she was born?"

Esperanza sighs with impatience. "I could take care of whatever problems she had."

"Tell me about those problems."

After leaning in toward Richard again and taking another sip of the Coke, she says, "Colds, sniffles. She had diarrhea once or twice. Same as any child." At his prodding, she describes some of the home remedies with which she took care of the baby. Richard takes scrupulous notes. Mexican folk cures are valuable information. They denote her inability to protect Yesenia, at least by the standards of the U.S. health-care system, however it may be deteriorating.

"Nothing more serious than that?"

"No."

He knows she is withholding. In mitigation, revelations often come slowly. Richard has tried to work around Esperanza, formulating her story based on other people's testimony.

"Tell me about Juárez again," he says.

"What do you want to know? That I haven't already told you?"

"A day in your life. What time did you wake up in the morning?"

"I got up to go to work at five," she says with a sigh. "I lived with a friend from Michoacán named Hilda, in a shack in back of her cousins' house. She disappeared. We worked at Border Textiles. I stitched together straps to hold babies in Walmart shopping carts. Nothing has changed since the last time you asked."

"What was the name of your boss at Border Textiles?"

"Raul, I think. It was a long time ago. It's already about four years."

"What are Hilda's cousins named?"

"I don't remember."

"But they live in Rancho Amargo?"

"Yes."

"On what street?"

Esperanza pauses for a long time and sips some soda. Richard wishes she wouldn't treat him as if he were a policeman interrogating her. "Avenida Revolución," she says finally. He wonders how many streets there are with that name in Juárez. In Mexico City there are more than a hundred.

"What house number?"

"I don't remember. It's almost at the end of the street, a few doors down from a little store that someone set up inside their house. They sold potato chips, soda, and cigarettes."

"And when you went to live with Gerardo, it was the same neighborhood?"

"Yes. We lived on Calle Aldama with his brothers, Antonio and Alfredo. Okay?"

"I just want to make sure I have all the information possible for when I go there."

She looks at him in disbelief. "You're going to Juárez?"

"*A güevo.*" He can always conjure a little smile from her when he uses Mexican slang.

"Are you crazy?" she asks. "Don't you know they kill people there?"

"Yes, but I have to do a complete investigation anyway."

"When are you going?"

"Tonight."

"Listen," she says. "Be careful."

It is the first time she has expressed any concern for him—one of those rare times, it feels to Richard, that she has recognized him as a human being. "Thank you," he says.

"A lot of people get killed in Juárez."

"I'll watch my back," he says with a smile.

"Take what I tell you seriously. Someone must have killed Hilda. That's what happens when people 'disappear.' She didn't just walk out of town without telling anybody."

He hopes he looks heroic in her eyes. He could have said no to the Juárez trip. Catherine could have filed a motion that, given the homicide rate, it was too dangerous to go there, and therefore Richard was unable to complete his investigation. The judge wouldn't have cared, but if they gave Esperanza the death penalty, it might have been a seed for an appeal. "I will," he says. "I'll be very cautious. Tell me about Gerardo's brothers."

"What do you want to know about them? Look, I don't know where you're going with all this. I've told you a hundred times. I don't care what happens to me. I am responsible for my baby's death."

"You're responsible or you actually killed her?"

"Stop trying to confuse me. There is nothing I can tell you that I didn't tell the police, nothing that I didn't tell you already. I don't remember the details. I blacked out. But there was no one else there. *I killed her.*"

"How do you know if you don't remember?"

She shakes her head but says with conviction, "I know."

"Where was Gerardo?"

"I have no idea. I told you he left us."

"When?"

"A month or two before Yesenia died."

"Esperanza, think hard about this. Please. Are you sure? Different people think that Gerardo was in Louisiana up to the time that Yesenia died. Are you sure he wasn't there?"

"Were those people with us in the apartment? They don't know what they're talking about," she says.

"I'm just saying, our memories get confused. You're only human."

"I'm not confusing anything." She grabs the Coca-Cola and gulps from it greedily, almost draining it. Immediately she wishes she had continued to sip slowly.

"Esperanza," Richard says, "you understand that I am not asking you all these questions to make your life miserable. I am doing what I can to try to make sure you don't end up sentenced to death."

"Who asked you to do that?"

It isn't the first time a client has wanted to know. "The state. Every time someone is charged with capital murder they're stuck with one of me. The idea of the kind of investigation I do is that the death penalty shouldn't be exercised without careful consideration. It's not a caprice."

•

"I've said everything I have to say. I've made peace with God. I am prepared for whatever happens to me."

"That's marvelous, Esperanza. But wouldn't you rather be at peace with God alive than dead?"

"It doesn't make a difference."

"Look, I know how you feel."

"No, you don't," she says sharply.

"I may not know exactly—"

"You're outside. I'm in here."

"That's true."

"Have you ever been to jail?"

"Only as a visitor."

"There you are. So you don't know how I feel."

"Okay. But look. Let's say you get a different sentence, anything besides the death penalty. If they give you a sentence with the possibility of parole, even if it's a long time, you'll get out eventually and be a free woman again. You could be out in twenty years."

"How do you know? Are you God? I could die in jail. I probably will."

"You're not God either, Esperanza. You're a young woman. You don't know when you're going to die."

"Neither do you."

"That's right. But even if they give you life without parole, there's still a chance that you will get out of jail somewhere down the line. Especially if the economy in the United States continues in such bad shape. One day Louisiana might decide that it no longer wants to support Mexican prisoners and send you back across the border." This is a carrot that legal teams who work with Mexicans have been encouraged to dangle before their clients.

Esperanza merely nods. "I'll be an old lady," she says.

"A free old lady. Out of jail. Back home."

She touches the can and takes a tiny sip because she is coming to the end of it. "Thanks for the Coke," she whispers. She looks at him with a smile so mischievous you'd think he'd snuck in a million dollars and passed it under the table.

"You're welcome," replies Richard, who sneaks the empty can into his backpack. He wants to say, "I wish I could fill your cell with cans of Coca-Cola." Instead he says, "You said that it doesn't make a difference to you if you're dead or alive. But it makes a big difference to other people."

"Who?"

"Your family. Your brothers and sisters, your mother and father, some of your cousins, nieces and nephews. They all miss you. There are many people out there who love you. They would prefer that you were alive than dead."

"What's the difference? They're all in Mexico. They have their own families. They will never be able to come here and visit me."

"You don't know that."

She looks at him with exasperation. "I know that," she says. "*You* don't know."

"Someone's fortunes can change. You don't have a crystal ball. And anyway, they still love you very much. They care what happens to you." She stares at a spot on the cinder block wall, evident impatience on her face. "And I care," he adds.

She looks at him sidewise. "You care about what?"

"I care about you," he blurts out. "It matters to me whether you live or die. I don't want you to get the death penalty." Richard is aware that he is crossing a professional boundary. "I'll come and visit you," he continues. He is telling her the truth. He cannot think of a single more pressing duty than to maintain contact with Esperanza, even after her case is closed. "If I visit you as a friend, instead of someone on your defense team, I'm allowed to buy you a Coke. I can continue to leave you a little money in your commissary so you can buy your own Cokes." If he has never previously maintained contact with a prisoner after finishing work on a case, Richard knows that if he did, he wouldn't be breaking any laws. He believes that because he is telling her the truth—he *will* come and visit her—he is absolved from any professional breach. "I can send you books in Spanish if you want," he says.

She remembers the weather-beaten comic book starring El Cholo that she used to read in the mornings when she boiled water for her mother's Nescafé. She read it so many times that she knew the dialogue by heart. What could have happened to that book? She had it in Morelia, but then lost track. No one has ever offered her a book before.

"What books would you get me?"

"Whatever you want to read. I'll make a list. Tell me."

She can't recall any titles except for the Bible. She hasn't read a book since El Cholo.

Scrutinizing Richard's face, she tries to fathom his motives. Can she believe what he's saying, or is he like any other man, who will say whatever occurs to him to get what he wants? Maybe he would come and visit her once in a while—maybe he is so lonely that he has nothing else to do. Then again, maybe he really does care whether she lives or dies.

He is telling her he is someone she could count on and imagining himself as someone who could count on her. And she realizes she's spent her whole life looking for someone who fits that description. Yet all the people she has ever been close to have been so wildly overextended with the exigencies of survival that they couldn't possibly have made that promise to one another. If they did, they couldn't have fulfilled it.

"When I was a kid, I liked love stories," she says.

"I'll find some for you, Esperanza. I'll send you a bunch of books here. Just leave it to me."

She wears a sad smile, remembering that her own mother was unable to do what this man is offering. "Thanks," she says.

He puts his notebook in his knapsack, the pen in the pocket of his jeans. "And Esperanza...."

"Yes?"

He is about to fall into an icy pool. But he can no longer stop himself. "You know that I told you your family loves you?"

"I know," she says.

"Well, I love you too," he says. *There.* What a relief. He sees a range of emotions play on her face at once, her mouth and eyes twitching. Will she laugh or cry? She is certainly confused. Is she angry? "I do."

"Richard," she says, after collecting herself.

"Yes?"

She leans toward him. "You really think it's possible that I could get out of jail one day?"

"It's always possible."

"Tell me how could that happen."

"I could give you a better answer if you tell me what really happened the day Yesenia died."

She rubs her temples and sighs. She looks in his face, trying to decide whether she can trust him. What would it feel like to finally tell someone the truth? He is the only one on the defense team who seems to have any feelings. He's the only one who has ever made her laugh. And he certainly is the only one who has told her he loves her. Could he be that person, the one that she could count on?

He remembers two men he saw in a cantina, years ago. One was standing up, trying to get his friend, who had melted in his chair blind drunk, to leave with him. Richard repeats what the standing one said to the man in the seat: *"Ándale, anímate."*

His mispronunciation of Mexican slang never fails to make her smile...."*Órale,*" she says.

IT IS WHAT IT IS

At first Gerardo couldn't believe how much better he felt. All it took was a line or two every couple of hours. He could spackle the walls of an apartment, move a load of bricks with a wheelbarrow, or crawl inside the cabinet under a kitchen sink to unclog a pipe as quickly and efficiently as he could before the accident. He had never tried cocaine before and believed it was nothing short of miraculous.

However, a few months down the line, the drug's effects, hardly exponential, were disappointing. At the end of a day, the pain was unbearable, and two or even four more lines were only sufficient to get him back to the apartment, under a hot shower, and on top of the mattress. From there, he listened to Yesenia cry, or else wheeze painfully, while Esperanza fretted endlessly over the baby's health. There was a tone of accusation to her voice. What did she expect him to do? He wasn't God; he couldn't wave a magic wand and make her ailments disappear. Tomorrow was another day. He hoped the kid would grow out of it.

So for the first time in his life, Gerardo began to lie down on the job. It would take him two or three days to spackle an apartment instead of one. He'd load fewer bricks into the wheelbarrow. Lowering his body to the floor and getting under the sink was so painful that he couldn't help but take two or three times as long to unblock the drain. Such lackluster performance was a matter of self-preservation over self-respect.

Even though Gerardo knew he couldn't function on the job, he was hurt and offended when Rolando let him go. He said Gerardo and Esperanza could have two months' free rent while they figured out their next step, but after that he'd have to charge them $600 monthly for the one-bedroom apartment, just like every other tenant. Gerardo felt that he had been demoted back to being a child. The insult was compounded when Rolando helped Esperanza find the job cooking in the cafeteria. Suddenly he was supposed to stay at home and change diapers. What did they think he was, a woman?

He desperately wanted to prove himself by finding work. A Honduran neighbor told him to go to Save-Your, the closest supermarket. They always needed extra people to stock shelves and unload delivery trucks. Gerardo didn't think that his back could handle carrying heavy boxes all day. If only he knew how to operate a forklift. Besides, he loathed supermarkets and did everything he could to avoid them. Each time he saw one, it was as if he were eleven years old again and bagging groceries in Ciudad Juárez. Bag boys earned no salary, only tips. There were so many people who accepted the sacks he'd loaded without even looking at him, let alone leaving him a peso. He still bubbled with anger when he thought of them.

It made him feel even worse to remember being so close yet so far from his mother. She was only a hundred yards from him in an industrial kitchen preparing take-out food for the steam tables. But during a shift of work, he saw so little of her that it was just as bad as being miles away at school. He recalled a woman who had an exceptionally large load of groceries. She was beautiful, with yellow hair and sunglasses. While he bagged several boxes of cookies, he watched her unsheathe a lollipop from its cellophane wrapper and put it into the mouth of her son, a boy only a few years younger than he. Gerardo wanted to cry but knew he had to be a man. After he loaded her shopping cart with over a dozen bags, she gave him five pesos (the biggest tip he ever earned) and a maternal smile. In his mind, her expression evoked pity and made him feel even worse.

The first day that Gerardo worked at the supermarket he earned more than a hundred pesos in tips. This was almost as much as his mother made and he worked only half a day. The money was all in half-, one-, and two-peso coins, but he changed them at the manager's register for two fifties. He went home alone on the microbus but waited up for his mother, who had to work until after the supermarket closed, cleaning the kitchen and wiping down the steam tables.

"I'm so tired, son," she said as she melted on the sofa without removing her windbreaker. "Why are you awake at this hour?" He handed her the money. "Oh, my son," she said tenderly, and took him in her arms. It was the first time in his life in which he felt useful, the first inkling that he was taking up space on earth for a reason. Impulsively, in a voice yet unbroken by adolescence, he began to croon to her a fantasy: the day when he would be earning so much that she wouldn't have to work at all. He promised.

But he has failed her. He is ashamed to even telephone her. All he has been able to do is send a few paltry dollars every once in a while.

Gerardo went looking for work making sandwiches at Subway, but didn't understand most of the English in the application form. Besides, he noticed that almost everyone working behind the counter was a woman. Nearly all jobs that involved food preparation were performed by women, except for fry cooking at McDonald's and KFC. Word was they were using some kind of computer thing to check whether your Social Security number really belonged to you. If it did, you got the job. If it didn't, second prize was deportation back to Mexico. Besides, being on his feet eight or ten hours in front of a grill would be hell on his back.

In his desperation, Gerardo considered telling Esperanza that he was going out for a quart of beer and disappearing forever. But imagining himself skulking off in the darkness brought back bitter memories. The first was of stealing away in the night with his mother and siblings while his father was passed out and boarding a bus to Ciudad Juárez, as if they were a gang of thieves. He has always been torn by that last image of his father, lying on the floor, snoring, spittle formed at the corner of his unshaven mouth. He doesn't even know if the man is dead or alive. The second image is of the similar fashion in which he fled Ciudad Cuauhtémoc, leaving behind Evelyn and little Eduardo.

He doesn't want to be too hard on himself—he was only seventeen. He'd originally left Juárez at fourteen because a cousin had found him work in a *maquila* in Cuauhtémoc. Gerardo thought that ipso facto he'd become a man. But at this point, he realizes that manhood is not so simple. He is confused. On the one hand, he wants to run away again, for he hates to see himself broken and diminished in Esperanza's eyes. On the other, he is considering the principle that a man doesn't run. Instead, he confronts life head-on.

Sometimes he dreams of making a lot of money and sending lump sums to Evelyn for the boy. How old would he be now? Seven? Eight? Gerardo wouldn't want anything to do with Evelyn at this point—she's had other men's *vergas* inside her. Who knows how many? But Eduardo will always be his son and he has not been a responsible father. The boy is young enough that he could still make it up to him, repair some of the damage he did by abandoning him.

What is a man supposed to do if all he has to offer the world is his back, once that back has been damaged? Gerardo never had any doubts that he could do whatever was needed to take care of himself, and others, with his body. Now he is in crisis. He cannot suddenly become one of those guys who sits at a desk for a living. What is the measure of a man with no money in his pocket? A man who allows a woman to support him? After the accident his body is worth no more than the loads inside Yesenia's diapers that Esperanza always hounds him to change.

"I'm never going back to Honduras," says Wilberto, cracking open another can of Corona. The six-pack is on the table in front of the creaky beige couch, a piece of furniture inherited after some tenants stole away into the night, beating Rolando out of two months' rent. "There's nothing for me there. It's off-the-charts *loco*. Of the guys I came up with, five are dead, four are in jail, and the rest—*¿quién sabe?* You want one of these?" he asks, pointing at the beer.

"No, I'm going to make some coffee," says Gerardo. "Don't you miss your family? Where's your mom?" He fills a pot with water, places it on the stove, and turns on the burner underneath. There is a vague scent of shit in the air—Yesenia must have pooped again.

"I don't know," says Wilberto. "I guess she's in La Ceiba. If she's still alive. I haven't been back in seven years."

"You don't even want to know what's up with her?" asks Gerardo.

Wilberto shrugs. "It is what it is," he says.

Gerardo can't imagine anyone being so cavalier about his mother, and silently frets about how long it's been since he's called his own. "You got brothers and sisters?" he asks.

"I used to," says Wilberto, running a hand along his close-cropped light brown hair. He tilts his caramel-hued face toward the window, his green eyes staring out, as if his siblings might be located among the shingle oaks along the broken sidewalk.

"You want some of this?" asks Wilberto. With someone's driver's license from a stolen wallet, he chops cocaine on top of the rickety coffee table. Gerardo rolls up the dollar bill that Wilberto placed on the table and snorts a line. His sinuses clear a little and he realizes how the reek of Yesenia's dirty diaper has imbued the living room. If he changes the baby in front of Wilberto, he will think he is less of a man and might even crack a joke at his expense. It's better to smell shit.

"Not for nothing, brother," says Wilberto, "but you know it stinks in here."

"It does?" says Gerardo, as if he just noticed. And then, as casually as possible: "Yeah, it must be the baby. Let me take care of the diapers." He brings Yesenia in from the bedroom and places her on the countertop next to the stove. She turns her head and stretches her arms. Her chest and back are covered with the red spots or crusts from where Esperanza has popped her pox. Deep in a sleepy reverie, she begins to suck on her fist. Although they are so little, Gerardo thinks it's remarkable how strong her hands and arms are—she's not even a year old. He makes a mental note to keep track of the water for his Nescafé, which will soon come to a boil.

As he opens the diaper the stench is like a boot to the head. It's been that way ever since she started to eat solids. *Híjole*, how much of a load can one little baby dump?

"You ought to get yourself one of these someday," cracks Gerardo. "There's nothing in the world like being a dad. She's already crawling around like she's late for work."

"What are you talking about?" says Wilberto. "I got four. Two of each."

"One more," says Gerardo, "and you got a hand of poker."

Wilberto laughs, and then says, "I want to talk to you about something." Gerardo helps himself to a little more coke.

Now Wilberto is a man to admire, a man who has calculated and figured out the ways of the world. Gerardo knows he is not as smart as Wilberto, but he has tried to prove to him that he is trustworthy and intrepid. To wherever Wilberto asks, he drives around that orange heap of paint and rust with holes in the floorboard, exchanging product for money while Yesenia rests at home in her cardboard box. (He's been busted by Esperanza only twice.) Wilberto gives him a little money and sometimes pays him in coke, but Gerardo hopes that when he proves himself to the Honduran, his responsibilities— and his pay—will increase.

"Five guys ripped off more than two hundred thousand dollars from some people I know," says Wilberto. "They asked me to come along to back them up. You understand? All I did was sit by the door. I didn't even take the gun out of my pocket, let alone kill anybody. But I would have done it if I had to."

"Sure," says Gerardo.

"My people hurt those guys bad before they killed them. They stuffed their mouths with newspaper and shut them with duct tape. They put bags over their heads so they couldn't breathe and then beat the shit out of them with pipes. They used an electric cattle prod. It was nasty, believe me." He sighs and looks at the threadbare carpeting on the floor. "You ever see anything like that?"

"Not really," says Gerardo. "A lot of people got killed in Juárez, though. You'd go down the street and they'd find their bodies in the trunks of cars. Or hanging from a bridge." Thinking of Hilda, Gerardo says, "People I knew."

Wilberto shakes his head. "It is what it is, man."

Gerardo has never heard anyone express anything resembling a philosophy before. *It is what it is.* The phrase makes Wilberto sound wise and experienced.

"Could you handle shit like that?" Wilberto asks.

"Like what you did to back up your friends?" And Gerardo realizes that this is the instant in which he may finally be catching his break. If he understands correctly, Wilberto is trying to find out what kind of a man he is. "Of course I could," he says, and snorts another line. Yesenia starts to whine. He ignores her.

"If you had to be the one doing the killing, could you handle that too?"

Gerardo looks him in the eye. "Just try me, man. Give me the chance."

"Right now I don't need you to kill anyone," says Wilberto with a laugh. "I'll tell you what I really need. That shit that I sell? You know it comes from Mexico. By the time I get it, it's been through so many middlemen, and cut with so much milk sugar and baby powder and who knows what the fuck else, there's hardly any money left to make. I need someone in Mexico, man. Someone who can go back and forth regular, get it pure and bring it back. It doesn't have to be that much. With half a pound, even a few ounces, we'd make a lot. The more trips you make, the more money we'd make."

Gerardo has never done anything in Juárez but work in the supermarket and the *maquilas*. His older brothers told him that if they ever caught him anywhere near drugs they'd kick the shit out of him. But how hard can it be to find coke in Juárez? The place is supposed to be crawling with drugs. He's got to know someone who knows someone.

"I can do that," he says. He also wonders how he'll go back and forth across the border time and again. It was difficult and costly enough to do it once. But with enough money you can buy anything. Yesenia whines more loudly. That's the part he hates most about being a father, even worse than the diapers. Why can't she just keep her mouth shut?

"You know people down there?"

"*¡A güevo!*" Gerardo says. He extends his hand to Wilberto. They shake hands and then share a firm, masculine embrace.

All at once: a clank, a thud, a splash, a cry. Gerardo runs to the kitchenette. Next to the stove, somehow Yesenia is on her back in the sink, almost submerged in boiling water, the pot on top of her stomach. Her eyes are wide and she is trying to breathe but only able to expel strangled gurgling exhalations.

By pure instinct Gerardo does everything he can. He lifts his daughter out of the sink and drains the hot water. He turns on the cold tap and lets it pour on her skin, now pale, waxy, and peeling from her stomach. After a while he realizes that Yesenia has stopped breathing and is turning purple. He lays her down on the counter and places his mouth on top of hers, blowing as hard as he can. He knows this will revive her—he saw someone do it on TV once. When mouth-to-mouth resuscitation proves useless, he presses his palms against her little chest, imagining it will cause her to suck in and puff out huge gusts of air. Nothing happens. He pushes harder.

Why is she doing this to him? At the very moment when things seem to be going his way. He has spent his whole life taking care of other people. No one has ever done a thing for him. They have just taken from him, anything he can possibly give and even things he doesn't have. It's unfair. What does he have to show for his twenty-four years but a broken back?

Wilberto watches him for what seems like forever as he shakes the baby. He calls Gerardo by name several times, but it is as if his *compadre* cannot hear and on some level has disappeared from the physical plane of existence. Finally Gerardo stops but Wilberto is not sure whether he has returned to earth. "Listen," he says. "I know it was an accident. But the cops won't understand. Pack a bag. I'll take you to the bus station."

It dawns on Gerardo that there are as many ways of being a man as there are men. Wilberto is the most solid example of manhood he has seen in Louisiana, and the only one who has offered any possibilities for the future. As much as he wanted to stick around, it is no longer an option. He will follow his mentor's instructions.

Her bones aching from being on her feet since six in the morning, walking home from work, Esperanza sees Gerardo, a bag in his hand, run with Wilberto toward the latter's car. The two drive off in a hurry. *What is the matter with him?* she asks herself, wondering if all men are as irresponsible with their babies as he is. She runs toward home and the unprotected Yesenia.

HAPPY HOUR IN THE HOMICIDE CAPITAL OF THE WORLD

One

I'd already passed through a lot of places that were supposed to be bad news. Misbegotten towns in Durango, Zacatecas, and Michoacán, where residents were reluctant to open the door when I knocked. People were suspicious, sometimes hysterically, and I couldn't blame them. Dead bodies were showing up on the outskirts of these burgs, and sometimes smack in the middle of downtown. Some were missing heads or limbs. Others hung from overpasses, their tongues stuffed in their breast pockets, with notes pinned to their shirts along the lines of "This is what happens to people who talk too much." Business owners who didn't pay their quotas to gangsters would go out for a pack of cigarettes and be found five miles from the city limits, shot through their skulls and stuffed in the trunks of their cars. In these towns, soldiers patrolled from the beds of pickup trucks, machine guns at the ready.

The designation of the most dangerous spot in Mexico is morbidly contested and fluctuates from year to year. But in 2010, when I was killed, Ciudad Juárez could boast that distinction handsdown. The homicide rate was off the charts, even greater than in Baghdad or Kabul. I had never seen so many police and soldiers trawling around anywhere in my life. In Juárez they wore black ski masks so you could never be sure who they actually were. There was nothing to stop an enterprising criminal from obtaining police uniforms, painting the proper insignia on the side of his truck, and doing dirty business in the drag of officialdom. (Not that anyone had ever accused the authentic cops and soldiers of being straight arrows.)

Downtown, the populace moved among decaying buildings with a scratched, discolored patina. The red-light district had been reduced to rubble, the stones and cement of demolished constructions piled in empty lots. Mud puddles of toxic liquid stretched for city blocks. Bars and restaurants that had once been brimming with insouciant locals and slap-happy day-trippers were now nearly derelict.

The dusty dry heat made me feel like a potato baking in an oven. My local guide was a droopy sixtyish character called Manolito, who drove a dented mummifying jalopy held together with Krazy Glue and dental floss. I wouldn't have had it any other way: you don't want to call attention to yourself in a place like Juárez. He took me to Border Textiles, where I spoke to Raul, Esperanza's boss. He remembered her well: the people who work in the *maquilas*, he explained, rarely stay in one place for more than a few months. She had hung on for more than two years. He gave me copies of her employment records, but didn't have much to say, except that she was a hard worker, showed up on time, and never caused him problems. If she had been difficult, he assured me, she would have been fired. He didn't know if she had any personal conflicts because he never got involved with his employees outside the professional realm. As long as they did their jobs he was satisfied. One day she didn't show up for work and, for Raul, that was the end of the story.

After Border Textiles, Manolito drove me to Rancho Amargo, crumbling shanties on the edge of town. Once on television in a strip-mall hotel room, I had seen a documentary about townships in South Africa. Compared with Rancho Amargo they looked like Park Avenue.

I canvassed the appropriate streets. Gerardo's brothers were not at home and, trying to find Hilda's cousins, none of the neighbors who might have oriented me answered their doors. In another town I would have returned to look for them after dark, when they presumably would have been home from work. That seemed like a lousy idea in Juárez. The next day was Saturday. I would come back early in the morning and try to catch them before they left. I hoped I wouldn't have to stick around until Sunday.

Manolito dropped me off at the hotel and we made arrangements for early the following day. I showered off the dust and sweat and wrote an elaborate e-mail to Catherine about what Esperanza had told me the previous day in Louisiana. Big surprise for a Mexican hotel: the internet wasn't working. The receptionist told me the server was down and would be fixed *ahorita*—an annoying word that could mean in five minutes, five days, or five years. I left a message on Catherine's answering machine to watch for an imminent e-mail; it would be a game-changer for Esperanza's case.

After seeing Esperanza in jail the previous day, I had to go directly to the airport for the night flights that would take me to Juárez. Once there, I began to work. I have thought thousands of times about my carelessness at not making sure that Catherine understood what Esperanza had told me—if not via e-mail, then in a detailed phone message. I know this isn't an excuse but it never occurred to me that I was going to die. It is the greatest regret of my entire life. I cannot stop thinking about how Esperanza's life might have turned out differently if I'd reached Catherine.

I didn't intend to make a big night of it. I just wanted a drink and a light dinner before turning in. In the lobby of the hotel there was a restaurant. It would be fine for a Caesar salad or some *enchiladas suizas*. But what about my whiskey? I felt I deserved one for braving Juárez. Off the lobby there was a bar. I stopped and looked, but it was deserted. I didn't want to be the only customer in a depressing cave. Should I give my liver a little rest? And then I thought, *Later*. I was sure I could find somewhere more lively without venturing too far.

A block away, tucked into a strip mall, I found it: La Rana Que Canta Karaoke Bar. A guy in a shiny shirt found me a table amid various customers, mostly men in boots and cowboy hats. Some skinny mama's boy in glasses was warbling "¿De Qué Manera Te Olvido?" It was a dive with a capital *D*, but good enough for a couple of drinks, I thought. I ordered a shot of tequila and a dark beer.

Two

When Gerardo finally reaches Juárez he feels like kissing the ground. He surveys the scene on the Mexico side of the International Bridge: the crippled newsie hawking papers to cars inching their way toward downtown, the sullen-faced spirits walking their bundled purchases across the bridge, and the pink cross with its multiple nails, a tribute to the countless women who have been murdered here. It's total chaos. People seem to be walking in circles amid the stench of diesel, tortillas, and pork sizzling in oil. What a relief to be home. He will go back to *el gabacho* only once he finds a way to import drugs to Wilberto.

It took him over a year to get back to Mexico. When he left Louisiana, he had only enough money for a bus ticket to Waco, where his mother found him a job washing dishes at Los Dos Compadres, a restaurant that issued a simulacrum of what its Mexican customers pined for from home. He slept on a foam mattress in the mildewed shack where she lived, in back of another Mexican's house. She asked him no questions about the years they had been separated or the woman and child he left behind. She only made sure his clothes were washed, that he was fed, and, during those first days before she found him the job, that he had a little pocket money. As she slept, he took solace looking into her face, which had set into a mask of permanent suffering.

The first months were the hardest. He would wake up screaming from dreams of bleeding babies, or of himself, naked and prostrate in the desert, his eyes and his sex plucked out by vultures. His palpitations were so riotous he thought his heart would explode.

"What's the matter, *hijo*?" his mother would ask.

"Nothing, Mamá," he would say. "Go back to sleep."

Every time he heard a baby cry he would feel sick to his stomach. Sometimes he thought of Esperanza and the price she was undoubtedly paying for the accident. It was an accident, he told himself, a constellation of occurrences that conspired against him. He understood there were no good decisions that could have been made that day, no right or wrong, only instinctive reactions to the threat to his survival. Sometimes he would remove from his wallet an *estampita*, a little card that bore the image of the Virgin of Guadalupe. He would pray to her, bring the card to his lips, and express thanks for her protection.

He knew he could never repair the damage he had caused to Esperanza and poor Yesenia. Everyone had moments in his life that he wished he could erase, or turn back time to correct. Of course that was impossible. You could only suffer from regret and do your best to carry on. *It is what it is,* he would say to himself with a sigh. After a while, it became easier to forgive himself. He began to sleep through the night without distressing dreams. He imagined a return to Ciudad Cuauhtémoc and a reunion with Eduardo, a fresh start that included resuming his responsibilities as a father. God was teaching him lessons. He dreamed of deliverance, even redemption. If somewhere in the sky there was a parchment that measured good and bad actions, at the very least he could try to redress the balance.

It was not meant to be. After receiving his mother's blessing, Gerardo took the little money he had saved in the past year and crossed the border. At Cuauhtémoc he found that Evelyn and Eduardo were no longer in the house where he'd left them. His former mother-in-law told him that Evelyn had married a man with whom she'd had three more children, and that in another city this man was raising Eduardo as if he were his own son. She added that Gerardo had a hell of a nerve to return after almost ten years as if it had been ten days. She refused to tell him where his son was and hissed at him to disappear. If she ever saw him again, she said, she would get her husband to shoot him in the balls. He returned to Juárez.

Three

"Never trust a gringo," says Gerardo. "They'll do anything they can to cheat you or steal from you."

"*Simón,*" says Little Luis in agreement. "They're a bunch of thieves."

"I worked for this son of a whore for three months in Louisiana," Gerardo continues, looking from Little Luis to the Monkey. "He promised us fifteen dollars an hour to clean up the trash after the hurricane. But when he paid us it was less than ten. He said the rest was for taxes."

"Son of his whore of a mother," says the Monkey, smiling bitterly and shaking his head.

"Me and a buddy of mine showed him what happens when you cross a Mexican," says Gerardo, rubbing the tips of his sparse Fu Manchu moustache. "We never got our money but we had the pleasure of busting his face in two." He makes a fist and thrusts it forward, to indicate what it would feel like to get fucked. It accentuates the muscles in his arm, mostly uncovered in a skintight plaid short-sleeved shirt.

"He deserved it," says Little Luis, who exceeds five feet only as a consequence of the heels on his boots.

The three of them are having a few beers at La Rana Que Canta, a karaoke bar in a strip mall. Little Luis worked with Gerardo years ago at Border Textiles but later left to join forces with the Monkey in a more lucrative profession.

"That country is going to pieces," says the Monkey, who earned his nickname for his girth and more or less simian features. "There are no rules over there. It's a free-for-all." He drains the rest of the bottle of Bohemia and looks around for the waiter.

"They're a bunch of hypocrites," says Little Luis. "The gringos put down Mexico for selling drugs to them but look who's buying them. Look who's using them."

"They're inconsistent," says the Monkey. "They don't make any sense. First they say we should have free trade between our countries. Then when you try to set up an honest business they pull out all the stops to keep you from selling your product."

"They play dirty," says Little Luis.

"They set up the rules and then they break them." The Monkey makes slurpy kissing noises to get the waiter's attention.

For the first time since hanging out with Wilberto in Louisiana, Gerardo feels he is in the presence of intelligent men who know more than he does about how the world works. What he desperately wants is to cut himself in for a piece of their action. All it will take, he knows, is to offer them a service that no one else has proposed.

"Bring us three more of these," says the Monkey. "And three shots of Tradicional."

After they have toasted Mexico and drained their tequila, Gerardo cannot contain himself any longer. He leans in toward the table, rubbing his palms along his thighs, sheathed in yellow jeans with a label that says VERSACHI. "I have a friend over there. A Honduran named Wilberto," he says. The Monkey and Little Luis also lean in. "He can move anything that I bring him."

When Gerardo has finished his pitch, Little Luis and the Monkey are silent. Little Luis gazes with deference at the Monkey, who seems to be reflecting on something while drinking his beer.

"Gerardo," says the Monkey, "I like that you have ambition. We have to start slow. If you want to work for us we have to know that you're for real."

"Okay," says Gerardo.

"You have to pass a little initiation," says the Monkey. Little Luis is nodding in affirmation. "A rite of passage."

"Sure," says Gerardo. He is prepared to fight, to steal—if necessary, to kill.

"You have to get up there and sing."

A thin man in glasses is doing his best to intone "¿De Qué Manera Te Olvido?" but he can barely carry the tune. Gerardo says, "I'm a terrible singer."

"So what?" says the Monkey. "It's a karaoke bar. No one here knows how to sing."

"Come on," says Little Luis. "You can't be any worse than that faggot up there."

"Do they have any hip-hop? I used to be pretty good at rapping."

"No," says the Monkey, and looks Gerardo in the eye. "No hip-hop. You have to sing 'A Mi Manera.'"

"Okay," says Gerardo, and shrugs. "Everyone knows that one." He is taken aback. When the Monkey spoke of a rite of passage he thought they were going to put him through a much harsher trial, something that required balls of steel. All they want him to do is get up and sing a stupid song that his mother used to like. Piece of cake.

LET'S MAKE A DEAL

The corridor that leads to the contact room reeks of syrupy disinfectant. The floors may be clean, but Burt notices the walls are scuffed, as if people had rubbed the soles of their shoes against them. As a guard takes him and Catherine down the hall, a line of three men in black and white stripes passes. Burt avoids eye contact. While he knows the uniform means they are trustees, the fact that they are unsupervised frightens him. What if one of them snaps and attacks while he walks by?

Burt hates visiting clients in jail. After he leaves, he feels like he needs to walk naked through a car wash. What's more, he is conscience-stricken because so much time has elapsed since he last came to see Esperanza. What has it been, six months? More like eight or nine. He met her only once, when Catherine brought him to the jail to introduce them. He wonders if she will even remember who he is.

He has not been as attentive to his tasks as Catherine's co-counsel as he would have liked. Burt also has a private practice, and he's been overwhelmed defending a policeman accused of shooting some black guys in the days after the hurricane hit New Orleans. But he knows she is a superlawyer, so he feels less guilty about laying back.

Once inside the little room with the cinder block walls and the musty carpeting, the meeting proceeds smoothly. Liliana, the official from the Mexican consulate, a slender middle-aged woman in a beige pantsuit, translates when Catherine speaks to Esperanza at a snail's pace, so she can interpret accurately. "The way the law works," Catherine purrs, "is that whenever the prosecution offers a deal to the defense, it is the defense's obligation to relate that offer to the client." She looks at the middle-aged woman. "Is she following me?" Liliana and Esperanza nod. "Even if it isn't the best deal in the world. Even if in all conscience I wouldn't advise the client to accept the offer. You understand?"

After Liliana translates, Esperanza nods at Catherine's watery blue eyes, glancing at the man with the orange hair, bulging eyes, and skin so unremittingly pink that she wonders whether he glows in the dark.

"The prosecution will take the death penalty off the table if you're willing to accept a sentence of ninety-nine years," says Catherine. "Basically it's the same as a sentence of life in prison."

The two women exchange some words in Spanish. Burt is surprised at Esperanza's equanimity. He thought she would get angry or burst into tears. While the two women speak, Esperanza nods her head at Liliana and then returns her attentive gaze back to Catherine. Does she have any questions so far?

"No," she says.

"Obviously, it isn't a fantastic deal," says Catherine. "The greatest advantage to accepting it, of course, is that you wouldn't get the death penalty. The other advantage is that we wouldn't have to go to trial. I would advise that we want to avoid a trial at all costs. Juries in Plaquegoula Parish can be pretty closed-minded."

Especially, thinks Burt, to an illegal alien who murdered a baby. After taking a look at the photos of the corpse, they would listen to a medical examiner testify more or less what the police had speculated—that Yesenia's scars were from having been pricked with something sharp, after which she had been shaken, burned, and beaten. They'd blacken Esperanza like a catfish fillet.

"According to the rules of the plea agreement, you would have to serve a mandatory eighty-five percent of the sentence. That would keep you in jail for about eighty-four years," says Catherine.

Burt is amazed that, even in the face of these numbers, she's still cool as a cucumber. Liliana and Esperanza chatter away in Spanish. Although he would like to have a vague idea of what they are saying, in this instance he figures it doesn't matter. There's no way in hell she'll accept the offer.

Burt takes the opportunity to chime in. "Now that isn't necessarily the way it would play out. Especially if the Louisiana economy continues to do as poorly as it's doing now. At some point down the road, the state could decide that it doesn't want to continue to feed and shelter and clothe someone from another country. It could then be negotiated to send you back home, and it would be at Mexico's discretion how you served out the rest of your sentence." *When you wish upon a star....*

Looking at Liliana, Esperanza says something. The consular official tells Catherine, "She says that Richard mentioned something about the economy." Esperanza talks to Liliana, who adds, "She wants to know when he will be coming back here. He hasn't visited in a long time."

Catherine looks at her client gravely. "I haven't had a word from Richard since he went to Ciudad Juárez," she says.

After Liliana repeats the message, Esperanza purses her lips and nods her head. More words are exchanged in Spanish.

Esperanza imagines some of the permutations of Richard in Juárez: his body picked over by buzzards in the desert, or buried under the rubble of a demolished building downtown, or among multiple corpses shot up by cops or criminals. She is certain he is dead. She looks toward a corner of the ceiling, as if it were the horizon. A distant horizon of a valley a thousand shades of green, sun-dappled after a summer rain. Or maybe just a corner of a crumbling tiled ceiling.

She considers telling Catherine what she told Richard the last time he visited her, about what happened after she came home that afternoon and found Yesenia dead next to the kitchen sink. At first she was paralyzed with shock. Then she held the baby's body, already cold, to her chest and wept for what felt like hours. She searched the apartment and remembered that Gerardo had run away with a bag. He had packed his few clothes and taken off.

She went outside to look for him, but, once on the street, had no idea where to go. She walked in circles in the rain for a half an hour, the image of her baby's lifeless body haunting her mind. She didn't have a clue as to where to find Gerardo, and understood only that he was gone for good, probably already far away. Drenched, disoriented, disconsolate, she considered her options. Could she run, as he had? To where? She considered what it would feel like to know for the rest of her life that she had left her dead daughter's corpse in an empty apartment in Louisiana. No. She waited on a street corner until she flagged down the police car.

Of course the cops didn't speak any Spanish, but she registered the shock and the horror on their faces when she showed them Yesenia. When they took her downtown, she was all set to say that Gerardo was responsible, but once she was with the two detectives and the translator, she couldn't bring herself to tell them the truth. She was sure they wouldn't believe her. It sounded like an outlandish story even to her own ears. Who was Gerardo to them? Or to anyone, except his relatives? There was no longer any evidence of him; it was as if he never existed. Most likely he was on his way to Mexico.

And what if the police found him? Gerardo would never confess to killing Yesenia. Even if he did, in her heart, Esperanza knew she was responsible for the baby's death. She hadn't given Yesenia the care she needed and deserved—either the medical treatment or the quotidian safekeeping and custody it would have taken for her to survive. No matter how many people went to jail and for how long as a consequence, the most devastating truth was that nothing, no one, would bring the baby back to life.

Catherine says, "In any case, as I said, it's my obligation to report the state's offer. Does she have any questions?"

Esperanza and Liliana confer for what seems to Catherine like an uncomfortably long time. Again, Esperanza appears unruffled. In a halting voice, Liliana finally says, "She wants to accept the offer."

At first the lawyers are stunned. Stuttering, Catherine says, "Please tell her she doesn't have to take it. Make sure she understands that."

The two women chatter away in Spanish. Catherine interrupts the two women. "Liliana," she says, "tell Esperanza that when he was in Juárez, Richard left a message that said he had new information from her. Please tell her it's very important that she let me know what he was talking about."

Catherine had planned to talk to Sarah Pendleton, the assistant district attorney, and try to talk her down to fifty years, with parole. This would have required some backbone, as Sarah said that ninety-nine was her one and only offer, take it or leave it. While she might have been blowing smoke, Sarah was one tough little pit bull. But no tougher than Catherine. Maybe they could have met in the middle, somewhere around sixty or seventy.

Liliana says, "She doesn't know what you are talking about."

Catherine says, "Ask her what she told Richard when he was last here."

The two Mexicans confer, and Liliana says, "Nothing that she hadn't told him from the beginning."

While Esperanza keeps talking, Catherine says, "She must have said something!"

Shaking her head in disbelief, Liliana says, "She wants to get this over with. She says the offer is better than going on forever without knowing what might happen." Esperanza nods her head, an expression of relief on her face.

Liliana begins to address Esperanza in Spanish. Catherine says, "Please repeat that she doesn't have to accept this offer. Tell her that when the DA makes an offer, most of the time it's just the beginning of a negotiation. I can try to get her something better."

Burt watches the client shake her head no. Catherine keeps insisting, but as he looks at Esperanza's lovely face, now impassioned with conviction, he realizes that, dollars for doughnuts, the case is settled. It is all he can do to contain himself from breaking out in an enormous goofy grin. There will be nothing left to do but a little paperwork. If only they were all this easy. Once he leaves the stifling claustrophobia of the jail, he will get in the car, loosen his necktie, and drive to the Pig Pen to treat himself to some pulled pork. The holiday weekend is coming up next month. He will call Margaret and tell her to book for Disney World.

HABEAS
CORPUS
PETITION

I f you walk down the streets of Rancho Amargo, the only thing that distinguishes his place from any other is the high walls. They are bare brick with broken glass embedded on top, to discourage anyone who might attempt to scale them. Neighbors may have noticed that a few times a month, and sometimes more frequently, pickup trucks appear, and after he has opened the solid metal doors, they back up inside. He closes the doors behind them. The people who have arrived lift the plastic tarps that have covered the cargo in the beds of their trucks, unload the merchandise, and leave. If the neighbors have observed anything, they immediately avert their eyes and pretend they didn't. It is better not to see in Ciudad Juárez, and if you do, you try to erase the pictures from your mind as soon as possible.

Pozole is a kind of soup that was first eaten hundreds of years ago, long before the Spaniards came to Mexico. The principal ingredient is dried kernels of hominy that have softened after being soaked in water. The hominy cooks in broth, and then the *pozole* is served garnished with shredded meat—usually pork but sometimes chicken—as well as slices of avocado and radishes. Most people add chile, oregano, and a squeeze of lime. Legend has it that back in the old days, *pozole* was served to the entire community in a ritual act of spiritual union. Ancient Mexicans believed that humans were made from the dough formed with cornmeal. So the kernels of hominy represented all of humanity, each kernel symbolizing one of us. The meat in the soup was not pork. The Aztecs would adorn the *pozole* with strips of human flesh, from people who had been sacrificed for the ceremony.

He doesn't know how to make *pozole*. His wife does the cooking in the house. But as a joke his employers call him El Pozolero. They trust him to take the cadavers of people they have killed—those are the commodities they leave in his backyard—and make a kind of soup out of them. If there is only a small number, he puts each body in a barrel with water. If there are many, they are dumped in an underground concrete pit in the yard, also filled with water. Then he adds lye so they will quickly decompose into a kind of brownish gelatinous goop, which he pours down the drain in an industrial sink. It takes a lot of lye. He buys a couple of hundred kilos at a time. Once, the salesman in a hardware store asked him why he needed so much. He looked him in the eye and said he had a business cleaning office buildings and used the lye to make liquid soap. Then he found another hardware store where they didn't ask questions.

He has never killed anyone. Whether or not he makes *pozole* out of them afterward, his employers' victims will be murdered. He certainly could not stop them from killing a single person. That is why he feels there isn't anything strictly wrong with what he does. He is solving a practical problem for people who do wicked things.

All he wants is to provide a better life for his wife and four children. He earns good money—about thirty thousand pesos a month. Even so, they live humbly. Thanks to the little virgin, they eat every day, have clothes on their backs and a roof over their heads, but there are no luxuries in his house.

He has no education. He barely made it through the third grade of primary school. His family needed him to work so they could eat, and when he was eight or nine he began sweeping up the sawdust at a factory where they made furniture. He wants his own children to have a different destiny, to be able to go to school and have other choices. He realizes that sooner or later he will be killed, or arrested and then killed in jail. Every day he prays to the little virgin that she will protect him until he has saved enough money to ensure a better future for his kids.

When he began to do this work, the victims gnawed at his conscience. During the day, and especially at night, he would see their faces in his mind. But after a while he stopped noticing them. They started to gel into a solid human mass. Like the kernels of hominy in a bowl of *pozole*, they all looked alike. Some months are slower than others, but he has been insanely busy in the last year. Once he had to deal with several dozen bodies over a weekend. He has a feeling that he cannot explain. It is as if he is the caretaker of the remains of one continuous person, or else of all of humanity.

Once in a while there is a distinguishing characteristic. Last week, there was a guy who stuck out because he was probably a gringo. It was obvious. He could tell because of his white skin. Even though he had been shot in the face.

THE
DEFENSE
RESTS

So that's how it went down: wrong place, wrong time, caught in the crossfire in a shootout in a karaoke bar in Ciudad Juárez. I took three bullets, one to the face and two to the chest, one of which pierced my heart.

There's something tawdry about bleeding to death on a barroom floor. It's not a dignified way to go. The connotations are embarrassing. Is it the alcohol element? Not exactly. I can't imagine anyone would have felt sorry for me if I had died sipping a Negroni overlooking a sunset on the Amalfi Coast. Is it the fact that I was in a bar? Maybe. Let's just say I didn't buy the farm in the King Cole Bar at the St. Regis. The violence? Most of the time, you feel sorry for someone who gets killed accidentally in a brutal incident. Think of the innocents torn apart by the grenades in Morelia on Independence Day, or the urban infants hit by stray bullets when gangbangers take their addled aim at each other. The indignity comes from the stupidity and arrogance of leaving my hotel to go for cocktails in Ciudad Juárez, as if I'd been on a holiday weekend in Puerto Vallarta.

If I'd had a looser definition of war, I could have claimed to be the victim of one, or even say I died in battle. But it would be disingenuous to define a collection of slap-happy drug peddlers, kidnappers, and extortionists—and the soldiers, cops, and politicians who wanted a piece of their action—as warriors. And while it would also be a stretch to say I died while in the line of duty, I am glad that when it happened—the reason I was in Juárez in the first place—I was trying to help out another person. Still, it's quite possible Esperanza would have had a different fate had I lived any longer. I cannot rest because I didn't send that e-mail.

A woman I used to go out with told me about a friend of hers who died of heart disease while in his early fifties. He had never married, and at his funeral a couple of dozen weeping women mourned his loss. I always liked that image and could picture them dressed in black, dabbing at their eyes with balled Kleenex, the mascara leaking in lines and blotches. I wished to be the kind of guy that would have aroused such a ceremony.

What makes you that kind of a man? There is a character in Roberto Bolaño's *2666*—a French academic, no less—who can have sex for six hours straight without ejaculating. His rival, a professor from Spain, can do it for three hours, meanwhile coming two or three times.

I was good for an hour. And that was the whole show, from the first kiss to the afterglow. I'd picked up a couple of tricks along the route, and didn't live long enough to be such an old dog that I couldn't learn new ones. Still, at the end of the day I wonder how much women remember men for sex at all. There are those unexpected moments: the tickle of the unshaven face brushing across an area of skin most often ignored, a sudden eruption of laughter during orgasm. But there are other things that are probably more important.

It was only just before dying that I realized that, instead of a platoon, it might have been preferable to be remembered by one person to whom I had truly made a difference. A person I could have visited from time to time and tried to console when it mattered. Someone into whose account I could have fed money, via a machine in a fluorescent-lit cubicle off the lobby of a prison, so she could buy herself a Coke when she felt like one. Someone who could count on me to send her a letter from time to time, or a package, that would improve her mood. Who would know that I couldn't fulfill every need or wish, but that I was out there somewhere thinking of her. Someone for whom I could have been waiting outside the gates of that prison, no matter how old we would have both been on the day of her release.

Even though my professor in Maryland stressed that all love stories were about bad timing, Chekhov's "The Lady with the Dog" has an ambiguous ending. You don't really know whether the protagonists—a jaded Muscovite and a much younger provincial woman, who fall madly in love, but are married to others—will triumph over their predicament, or be ruined by it: "And it seemed as though in a little while the solution would be found, and then a new and splendid life would begin; and it was clear to both of them that they had still a long, long road before them, and that the most complicated and difficult part was only just beginning."

It was a nice thought, but it didn't happen for me or Esperanza.

It's pitiful of me to scavenge for anyone who might remember me at all. If you are that person, think of my escape to Mexico—even (or especially) if you're Mexican. For the deliverance that the journey across the border bestowed on me, no matter how much of prison your country is to you.

Maybe you think that my face on a book jacket is sexy. Or maybe you think there was something juicy about my day job—showing up in the middle of nowhere, knocking on a stranger's door looking for two things: a compelling story and justice.

When I was in high school in New York, it was still possible to open the emergency doors of the subway cars and ride between them as they hurtled down the tracks. I often did this on the way to school, and it felt as if the commute were an amusement park ride. I sort of tried to continue to do that as I proceeded through life, riding the tracks not taken, on an adventure that some might have been afraid to embark on.

I want you to think of me during the orgasmic explosion of flavor that is biting into a cherry tomato. When you have the sensation of being bathed in lavender while walking under blooming jacarandas in spring. Waking up at a cloudy dawn when the first thing you see is that curve between the neck and shoulder of your lover. When your child tells you that she loves you. When you smell some Nescafé freshly degranulated in a Styrofoam cup.

These moments will pass. They all do. When you notice a moment like that, remember to steal it. Luxuriate in it. Acknowledge it, cradle it in your arms. You don't know how many more you have left. Life is precious. Don't waste it.

MAY IT
PLEASE THE
COURT

The way Esperanza sees it, there are a few things to look forward to in the state prison. For over a year she's lived in a maximum-security cell block with women reputed to be the most dangerous in Louisiana. Of the six in the cell she shares, three others have been convicted of murder. One stabbed her lover to death to prevent him from further abusing her, while another shot her companion to stop him from beating her children. A third had been a passenger in a United Cab, along with a man who put a bullet through the driver's head to rob him of twenty-seven dollars and a cell phone. Her affiliation as his companion spelled complicity clearly enough for a jury to convict her of second-degree murder and a mandatory sentence of life without parole.

Despite the reputation of her coterie, Esperanza does not suffer any aggression during that stretch of time. Mostly by keeping to herself, by locking her mouth and eyes in a tight, mean squeeze, and by dint of her poor (although improving) English skills, she manages to avoid altercations with the other prisoners and the uniformed personnel who keep vigil over them.

From time to time during that year someone mentions other areas of the prison, where some women live in spaces like college dormitories. Esperanza has only the vaguest idea of what a dormitory might look like; in her mind's eye she pictures a huge hall with dozens of beds, like an old photograph of a hospital she saw somewhere.

To her surprise, after fifteen months she is transferred to a room with white-painted walls, two single cots, some shelving, a table and chairs, and a TV. A window looks onto another of the prison buildings, as well as a patch of lawn and another of sky. The room has a separate bathroom with a toilet and a stand-up shower. Nominally Esperanza is placed there because of her exemplary behavior, but in truth there is overcrowding in the cell blocks and some movement is necessary. Most women who are transferred have been incarcerated far longer than she, but prison authorities notice with approval her unfaltering obedience, her hard work at the jobs she's been assigned, and her strict attendance at chapel services.

She feels lucky because the woman with whom she shares the dormitory room is even more easygoing than the ones in her cell block had been. Esperanza and Janice make a communal effort to keep their room spotless. Though the door is kept locked every night, and the presence of the guards is unceasing, Esperanza has to admit that it is a nicer room than most of the places where she lived in the free world.

There is a relative tranquillity to the prison that she never felt in the parish jail. Some of it has to do with the landscaped lawns where she and the others are allowed to relax a couple of hours a day, and the fountain near the entrance to the institution, inside the chain-link fence topped with razor wire surrounding the property. However, the architecture is the least important element to her inner harmony. Esperanza believes that much of the difference between the parish jail and the state prison has to do with resolution. Here, the cases of the incarcerated have been settled. They are no longer waiting to find out their destinies.

Esperanza mostly works in the fields within the grounds, planting and harvesting strawberries, oranges, and sweet potatoes, for which activity she earns two cents an hour. In the fallow months she works in the prison's factory, where she stitches children's garments, and her salary is more than doubled to five cents an hour. It's exhausting and monotonous work, but it's a lot better than staring at the walls like she did in the parish jail. Her supervisor is so impressed with Esperanza's diligence that she has applied to higher-ups so her rate of pay will be raised. However, she has warned Esperanza that there simply isn't a lot of money in the system, and sometimes it takes years for a raise to be approved. In any case, Esperanza earns enough to buy some personal items such as soap and deodorant, as well as, once in a blue moon, a Coca-Cola.

The food is more edible than in Plaquegoula Parish, and Esperanza even looks forward to a few of the items served, among them fried fish sticks with black-eyed peas and soggy spaghetti in a sweet-ish red sauce.

Janice, her cellmate, has long white hair, slack and wrinkled skin, and a voice both deep and raspy. Prison has been her home since she was Esperanza's age. A priest from the New Orleans Baptist Faith Seminary tapped Janice to be an elder inside the institution, and she spends much of her free time proselytizing. The atheist inmates avoid her, but her faith is reassuring to Esperanza. They pray together. From listening to the older woman, as well as from a Bible that Janice gave her as a gift, her English is slowly but surely progressing.

Classes are currently overcrowded, but Esperanza is on a list for "Literacy and Basic Adult Education," an idea that thrills her. There are also vocational classes in IT, custom sewing, upholstery, and culinary arts. It has been explained to Esperanza that it might take years before she actually enters a classroom, but she sanguine: she has nothing but time. Occasionally she receives a letter from María Concepción. Her sister explained that a gringo had visited a couple of times, asking all manner of questions about the family, but then disappeared. María called the telephone number on his business card several times without getting any answer, until ultimately someone else picked up the phone and said they had never heard of him. María pestered a bureaucrat at the office of the foreign relations ministry in Morelia until he got sick of seeing her, and he found out where Esperanza was interned.

When she read in María's first letter that the family still loves her, notwithstanding the crime for which she has been convicted, it came as an immeasurable relief. She has read this letter so many times, and shed so many tears over it, that it is practically illegible and has a texture close to tissue paper.

Tears also come to her eyes when she imagines what happened to Richard in Ciudad Juárez. At first she figured he stopped visiting because he lost interest in her case or had something better to do, but that explanation didn't make sense. He came to see her every two or three months for a year and a half. It was his job, no matter how taciturn and uncooperative she was to him. She wishes she had been friendlier. She will never forget that the last time they saw each other, he told her he loved her. Sometimes she wonders what would have happened if she'd had the opportunity to share that love.

She despairs when considering what it would be like to spend as many years locked up as Janice has. It is unfathomable to her that she may live another thirty, forty, even fifty years in the prison's confines, that as a lady with white hair and a raspy voice she will still be eating prison food and picking strawberries for two cents an hour. But in truth, the decision to plead guilty and spend the rest of her life in jail also came as something of a relief. Every decision Esperanza had ever made—to go to Morelia and then to Juárez, to take up with Leonardo and then with Gerardo, to leave her country, to have a child—ended tragically and disastrously. She could not recall a single day of her life before sentencing that had not been an ordeal. When she told Catherine that she would accept the state's plea offer, she was utterly exhausted. It is an exquisite consolation to know that she will never have to make a decision or exercise free will again.

For Esperanza's second Christmas in prison, in an idle hour in the afternoon she watches from a corner of the yard the party that is thrown for the children and grandchildren of the incarcerated. A year earlier she stayed as far as possible from this annual ritual, afraid it would only make her think of the loss of Yesenia. Somehow her feelings changed. As she watches the toddlers run around the yard, climb on the inflatable "bounce house" that had been rented for the day, and wrap themselves in the arms of their mothers, clad in prison denims, the event seems miraculous. If God is not ready for Esperanza's redemption, she feels His benevolence because He bestows it onto others among the incarcerated.

When someone has served the entire term of her sentence or is granted an early release, the "freedom bell" at the entrance to the prison is rung. For the moments that the bell vibrates, Esperanza is sometimes crestfallen. Why that woman, and not her? Yet she is also able to feel vicariously the thrilling joy of liberty. How she wishes she could be one of them. She keeps telling herself that God is great, so magnificent that she believes that sooner or later a wish of hers will be granted. Esperanza wants a picture of the Virgin of Guadalupe.

She'd like a large one, but even a wallet-size *estampita* would do. The idea is to tape it to the wall beside her bed so the image would be the first thing she sees in the morning and the last thing before she goes to sleep. That during slumber the little virgin would watch over her, and that she would be subject to her constant protection. She's there in her mind's eye often, and Esperanza hopes it's only a matter of time until she manifests herself in more tangible form.

ACKNOWLEDGMENTS

I am grateful to many people who, consciously or unknowingly, helped me to write this novel. Eric Martin, Yehudit Mam, Juvenal Acosta, and Janet Steen read earlier drafts, and their comments were crucial in helping me finish. Myriam Blundell gave me a place to write unencumbered for a month in a farmhouse in southern France, thanks to the Signy and Olaf Willums Art Foundation. Doris Wollers took care of that house with kindness and efficiency while I worked. Damian Fraser and Paloma Porraz allowed me to spend a few weeks in their *casita* in Malinalco, Mexico. These episodes of isolation with no responsibilities except writing were extremely valuable.

Daniel Pastor gave me useful information about the life of a Mexican banker in New York. Mara Muñoz offered a precise list of songs from which I could choose the most perfect. Sergio González Rodríguez, as always, helped me to understand how Mexico works (the chapter title "Bones in the Desert" is of course an homage to his great book with the same name on the subject of femicide in Ciudad Juárez). When I have felt adrift as a writer, Francisco Goldman has insistently validated my work. At a crucial moment, Timothy Young at the Beinecke Library at Yale gave me a valuable opportunity to read from the unfinished manuscript to a sympathetic audience.

Readers of the *New York Times* with long memories may recall a story by Norimitsu Onishi that ran on February 6, 2010, with the headline "Sinatra Song Often Strikes Deadly Chord," about a series of killings in karaoke bars in the Philippines, in which the victims were men with the temerity to sing "My Way" out loud. Mr. Onishi's story is, of course, the inspiration for my Mexican version.

I couldn't possibly put into words how indebted I am to my agent, Jennifer Carlson. I am also enormously grateful to Chris Heiser, my editor, and his unflagging enthusiasm for the book, and to Olivia Smith, Madison Clapp, the astonishingly astute copy editor Nancy Tan, and the rest of the team at Unnamed Press.

All the clients and their families, who shared their stories with me, and all the lawyers and investigators with whom I've worked or studied as a mitigation specialist, have given me invaluable opportunities to learn about justice and life. Sadly, I don't have space to list all of them here. But among the most significant have been Debbie Nathan, Joseph Flood, Danalynn Recer, Steve Malone, Naomi Terr, Brian Stull, Tami Goodlette, Kathryn Kase, Gregory Kuykendall, Teresa Norris, Dhyana Fernandez, Laura Ferry, Alma Lagarda, David Lewis, Cessie Alfonso, Greg Kanan, Pheobe Smith, Lyndon Bittle, Neil Burger, Todd Doss, Alvin Aponte, Randi Ray, Richard Bourke, Christine Lehmann, Ethan Brown, Claude Kelly, Kerry Cuccia, and the mother of us all, Scharlette Holdman.

PHOTO BY CHRISTOPHE VON HOHENBERG

DAVID LIDA is the author of several books, including *First Stop in the New World: Mexico City, Capital of the 21st Century*, a collection of short stories called *Travel Advisory*, and *Las llaves de la ciudad*. *One Life* is his first novel. His journalism has been published in magazines and newspapers in the U.S., Mexico, England, Canada, Australia, Peru and India. Based in Mexico City, when he is not writing, he works as a mitigation specialist, assisting lawyers in the U.S. who defend Latin Americans who are charged with capital murder and are facing the death penalty. His website address is www.davidlida.com.

@unnamedpress

facebook.com/theunnamedpress

unnamedpress.tumblr.com

www.unnamedpress.com

@unnamedpress